SHE'S TOXIC

SHE'S TOXIC

MATT ABRAMS

Riverfront Publishing

RPSTL
Published by Riverfront Publishing

Publisher's Note:
This is a work of fiction. Names, characters, places, and incidents are either the product of the author's imagination or are used fictitiously, and any resemblance to actual persons, living or dead, business establishments, events, or locales is entirely coincidental.

First Printing, September 2016

Copyright © 2016 by Matt Abrams
All Rights Reserved. Printed in the United States of America.
No part of this book may be used or reproduced in any manner whatsoever without written permission except in the case of brief quotations embodied in critical articles and reviews. For information address: Riverfront Publishing, PO Box 775367, St. Louis, MO 63177.

Library of Congress Control Number: 2016949819

ISBN 978-0-9977489-0-1

10 9 8 7 6 5 4 3 2 1

RPSTL

SHE'S TOXIC

For all the women who have shaped my life

"I pray you, in your letters,
When you shall these unlucky deeds relate,
Speak of me as I am; nothing extenuate,
Nor set down aught in malice. Then must you speak
Of one that loved not wisely but too well;
Of one not easily jealous, but being wrought,
Perplexed in the extreme…"

- William Shakespeare, *Othello*

SHE'S TOXIC

One

I turned my Jeep onto Interstate 155 to drive the remaining five miles north to Gentry. Thanks to the stifling June heat, my gray "Bulldogs Football" T-shirt was sticking to my back. Corn and soybean fields dominated the surrounding landscape, along with the occasional farmhouse.

AC/DC's "Back in Black" was pulsating through my speakers when I arrived at The Barnyard, a bar and grill squeezed between a consignment shop and a beauty salon in downtown Gentry. The Barnyard had long been the local watering hole of choice, dishing out the delicacies of central Illinois: fried fish, hamburgers, and cheap beer.

I parked behind Mike's Chevy Silverado, on the opposite side of the street; I stepped outside into an eerie calmness suffocating downtown. I took a couple steps toward the restaurant, but stopped in the middle of the street, entranced by the graphite and charcoal thunderheads towering overhead. It was calm now, but the serenity wasn't going to last. After a moment's hesitation, I continued walking—toward the heart of the storm.

Once inside, the familiar smell of fried walleye and the music of Eric Church overwhelmed my senses. *Springsteen*. The Barnyard was a decent place for a small town; a long bar stretched to my right, and a dozen high-tops stood between me and the jukebox. An adjoining room to the left housed a larger dining area, which also contained pool tables, dart boards, and a shuffleboard table.

I waved to a group of former classmates sitting at one of the high-tops before spotting my friend at the bar. I saw only the back of his head, but his sandy mop gave him away.

I pulled up a barstool next to him; we exchanged greetings, but his face showed no emotion.

"We need to talk," Mike said. His voice came out soft, but his words were jagged.

"And what do we need to talk about?" I asked with a smirk.

"I'm not sure how to say this. You're my best friend. Always have been, always will be." Mike placed his hand on my shoulder, softening me up for a death blow.

"Yeah, same here. Please just say what you need to. I've been dreading this since I got your text this afternoon." My right leg bounced against the barstool in anticipation.

Mike was silent for several seconds, his eyes seemingly trained on the litany of kitschy bumper stickers lining the back wall. He clicked his glass of lager against the bar before turning back to me. He opened his mouth to speak but hesitated.

"Well?" I asked.

"I didn't want to bring it up tonight, or at all, but it's getting worse." He took a long drink and furrowed his brow. "I'm not sure how much you actually know."

SHE'S TOXIC

"How much I know about what? About how much better the Cardinals are than the Cubs?" I laughed as I gave my friend a hearty slap on the back, trying to lighten the mood.

"No, it's *definitely* not that." He flashed a smile before regaining his focus. "You've been dating Britney for a while, right?"

"Yeah, I'd say so. Almost five years."

Mike sighed and shook his head. "I don't think you should keep seeing her."

"You don't think I should keep seeing Britney?"

"No, I don't." His voice never wavered, and the punch line never came.

As I dug out the shrapnel from his attack, a red-haired waitress approached with a smile and food. She handed us two appetizers that Mike must have ordered—spinach artichoke dip and fried pickles. But I wasn't hungry; I was sweating—it had suddenly become more humid inside than outside.

"This is unbelievable!" I raised my voice, prompting several people in the bar to cast curious glances our way. "You call me up here, just to drop this on me? Wait, are you already drunk? You must be because you're not making any sense. Britney is the best thing in my life."

"Are you sure about that? I might be wrong. I hope I am." Mike was proceeding with caution, pausing between every couple of words, gauging my reaction. "I don't want anything bad to happen, but I'm afraid it will."

"Unbelievable." I took a long, final drink of my beer and slid the glass away. I nearly misjudged my strength as the glass came inches from toppling over the other side of the bar.

A flicker of lightning appeared through the back door; it was followed by a crash of thunder in the distance.

"Can I get another Bud Light?" I asked.

Both of us fell silent as our bartender, Carly Campbell, grabbed another frosty glass and began pouring. I had always despised confrontation, and I knew Mike wasn't used to a blowout like this either. We never argued, other than during baseball and football games.

Mike, perhaps at a loss for words, plunged into the food. He spooned a hearty portion of the cheesy, spinach artichoke dip onto a blue tortilla chip. I was falling into a daze until I heard the crunch of his teeth shattering the chip to pieces.

Carly placed the beer in front of me while I took a deep breath in a failed attempt to compose myself.

"Two-fifty," she said, flipping her hand through her bountiful blonde curls.

I floated back a five-dollar bill. She gave me a concerned look before sauntering away to tend to four presumed golfers who had just arrived—probably chased off the links by the approaching thunderstorm.

I launched back in. "You're doing a wonderful job of making yourself look like an idiot. It's like you want me to suffer more than I already have."

"I definitely don't want you to suffer, but it's not that simple. I want you to have a great life." He rubbed his hand along the bar, his stubby fingers trailing the smooth edge of the wood-grained top. "Your relationship isn't healthy; you don't know her as well as you think you do."

SHE'S TOXIC

"This is absurd." I laughed. "I know damn well who Britney is, and I love everything about her. If it meets with your approval, I might even ask her to marry me someday—someday soon."

Mike placed his hand against his forehead and let out a long sigh. I took another pull from my already half-empty beer. More lightning, another crash of thunder. I tried a few fried pickles, but my stomach turned.

Mike's hand traveled from his forehead, down his face, and settled across his mouth and chin. His steel gray eyes were cold and distant, yet he seemed poised to launch another attack on my relationship. I watched as he made a fist, and I panicked for a second, believing he was going to punch me. Instead, he brought it down to the bar in a crash. The percussion of his fist against the bar corresponded with a loud clap of thunder.

Carly looked like she wanted to ask us about our food, but she must have thought better of intervening. Her bulging blue eyes looked like they might pop out of their sockets.

"You need to get ahold of yourself. You need to cut this girl loose before it's too late!" he yelled. Mike never yelled. "This relationship isn't healthy for you. It's not good for anyone, and I'm trying to tell you this as your friend. We've been through a lot together, and I'm trying to look out for you."

He took a drink and said, "I can see this relationship destroying you. She's toxic for you."

"She's toxic? I'm not hearing this," I said, still stunned by Mike's outburst. I threw both hands in the air, surrendering. "If you have such a problem with Brit, then maybe we shouldn't be friends anymore."

I looked past Mike, diverting my eyes to two middle-aged women who had just entered the bar. They hollered to Carly for a round of shots as they made their way to the jukebox. Tonight would be their attempt at reliving their wilder years, hanging onto a past that threatened to slip away, into the abyss.

I finished my beer and directed my attention back to Mike. I stared into his eyes, trying to manipulate his thoughts or read his mind—not sure which.

He stared back. I tempted him to destroy me, knowing it wouldn't take much of a finishing blow at this point.

Mike calmed to an extent. "I hope you don't mean that. I understand you're upset with me, but I'm just trying to help you."

"I don't understand why you decided to drop all this on me tonight. You never said anything about her before."

"I've been thinking about speaking up for the last week or two. I'd hoped I was wrong about Britney. It's getting worse, and I think it would be best if you moved on."

"I need to move on? Move on from what? I'm sorry, but I need to leave." I prepared to step down from my barstool.

Mike grabbed my arm, impeding my progress.

I wriggled free from his grasp. "Let go of me—I can take care of myself. I've made it this far."

"Ty, you don't understand what I'm trying to say. She's not the same girl you used to know." He paused. "You must be blind not to see that."

"Okay, now I'm blind? I'm out of here." I stood and turned toward the exit. "You can go fuck yourself."

He took off behind me, sending his barstool crashing to the

ground. The metal of the barstool hit the cold concrete, sending a high-pitched, reverberating shriek throughout the bar.

Everyone looked, including the two middle-aged women—now sitting at the bar. Concern overtook their previous laughter. One whispered to the other, and they both forced sympathetic smiles. They tried to make small talk as I rushed outside; I replied with a simple nod. I tried to smile, but it probably came out looking more like a scowl.

Now outside, I spun on my heels as Mike burst through the door behind me. We were now face-to-face, or at least as close as possible considering our disparate heights; I had him beat by several inches.

"Okay, I'm sorry about what I said, but I don't know what's possessed you. I'm in love with a great girl, but for whatever reason, you're suddenly not impressed with her." My heart pounded through my shirt. "You live in your perfect, fantasy world. I have *one* positive remaining in my life, and now you're trying to take her away from me. You're trying to convince me that she's not good enough ... or am I not good enough for her?"

"That's ridiculous. You can't even say that with a straight face." He leaned forward, taking one of my arms in each hand. "Ty, buddy, you've had an amazing life."

I broke away from his grasp. "Yeah, I had an amazing life. It's like you're trying to kick me while I'm down, keep me under you for some reason."

"I don't want to kick you while you're down, believe me."

The thunderstorm made its final approach. The leading edge of the dark shelf cloud overtook the town.

"Look, I don't want to talk about this ever again. If you can promise me that, maybe we can still be friends," I said. We were no more than two steps apart. Spinach and Bud Light dominated Mike's breath.

"I'm not sure I can make that promise, but if you won't listen to me, I might not have a choice. Who knows what's going to happen to you, but it won't be good."

Increasing winds rustled the leaves on the trees across the street; the scent of a purifying rain hung thick in the air. A couple raced from their parked car, seeking refuge in the shelter of The Barnyard. Lightning lit up the sky once more.

"Well, I'm tired of listening to your bullshit. I'm going back inside before all hell breaks loose out here." I gave him a dismissive, backhanded wave as I turned away.

"Whatever, I tried to help, but I have nothing left to say. Good luck with her."

I looked back at Mike, walking down the sidewalk with his head down—shaking it from side to side. Another powerful clap of thunder added pep to his step.

I watched as the leaves and branches intensified their frantic dance. Sporadic large drops of rain came down for a few seconds before the storm unloaded on Gentry. The rain came down in sheets, guided by the accompanying wind gusts—punishing the side of my face.

Two

You need to get ahold of yourself! Cut this girl loose! The words repeated in my mind as I stepped back inside The Barnyard, which was now full of life, ironically. I saw only one couple enter while I was outside, but more patrons must have arrived through the back entrance.

I made my way back to my barstool and slammed my hands down. "Give me another one," I yelled, louder than I intended. I added, "Please." I needed to calm down before I said or did something I would regret. My heart and mind raced each other in a dead sprint.

"Are ya okay, hun?" Carly asked. She was a couple years older than me, but she had been a cheerleader, so we knew each other well. She remained single and childless, which was somewhat uncommon for a beautiful woman of twenty-three living in a small town.

"Ah, I'm okay. Well, I'll be okay after a few more beers." I managed a smile.

"That's what I'm here for." She grinned and placed a fresh

Bud Light in front of me. "I'll keep ya setup all night as long as ya don't give me any trouble."

Before responding, I caught my reflection in the mirror behind the bar. On the outside, all looked well enough—yet I was dissatisfied. I brushed my thick brown hair into place and stared into my eyes for several seconds, attempting to penetrate the window of my soul. My eyes looked darker than usual—almost black instead of brown, thanks to the alcohol dilating my pupils.

I snapped out of my trance. "Thanks, Carly." I wanted to salvage the night. I wanted nothing more than to drink a few beers and to enjoy a civil conversation without someone criticizing my relationship.

"You got it. It's nice to see you back here; it's been a while," she said while mixing three "Dirty Barnyards." Efficient.

"I'm sure I stopped by last weekend." I laughed. A tall, lanky meth head with three (or four) teeth weaseled in next to me and flashed a five before ordering two Stags.

"Probably, ya lush. I haven't worked much lately, but I didn't see you in here most of last year," she yelled over the music as she handed the beers to the man with impeccable taste.

"Yeah, I've been down in Reedville quite a bit. I was back in school this spring after taking the fall semester off. I'm still at Central Illinois though."

"I thought I heard something about that. Is everything okay now?" She didn't miss a beat behind the bar. It was impressive to watch.

"Yeah, I needed some time off. A guy needs a good break once in a while." I took a drink and thought back to last fall. I

SHE'S TOXIC

couldn't believe I'd lost my football scholarship. I had put in countless hours of training and practice to reach the pinnacle, only to see my future disappear in an instant. Gone. I tried to remind myself that life could be much worse.

We talked for fifteen minutes about everything other than my fight with Mike. I downed two beers and took a couple shots—courtesy of the two women at the end of the bar. Equipped with more alcohol in my system, I couldn't resist shifting the conversation to Mike. I was sure Carly didn't want to deal with my problems, but I concluded it was in her job description.

"I hate to bring this up, but I know you saw what happened earlier with Mike." I hoped I wasn't slurring my words yet, but I couldn't be sure.

She scrunched her nose, but managed to remain attractive. "That was ugly. I'm sorry. What were you two fighting about?"

"Britney. He told me to cut her loose." I leaned back in my stool as far as possible (without falling backward).

"Why would he say that?" She leaned over to the other bartender and asked if he would man the ship for a minute. The dinner crowd had died down, but the bar was still busy.

"No idea. It's like he relishes that I'm somehow below him now. Mike with his perfect life."

"I'm sure Mike wants what's best for ya. It's crazy for you to think differently. You two have been friends for as long as I can remember." Carly brushed her curls away from her eyes. "We all want what's best for you, Ty."

I downed the last of my beer. "Tonight should have been a good time. I just finished my finals and Mike was promoted at his dad's restaurant. I swear he gets everything handed to him. Damn, what can a guy do?"

"Well if it makes you feel any better, Alexa Paulson is coming back to town this summer."

"Alexa?" I hadn't thought about her in a while. She could complicate things.

I turned down Carly's offer for another beer and emerged back outside, where the downpour had slowed to a drizzle. My feet were a little unsteady—maybe the additional drinks weren't the best idea. I looked around for Mike's truck, but he must have already left. I stumbled into the bar around the corner, Carter's, and sure enough, he wasn't among the five or six lone souls at the town's most notable dive bar. Probably for the best, I wasn't sure what I might have said or done.

I slipped back outside, thinking about what Mike had said, shaking my head in bewilderment. I had always valued his input when it came to my relationships and life in general. Mike had always been there whenever I needed to vent over a couple beers. He was usually reliable, and I knew he wouldn't bash my relationship unless he had a damn good reason.

We had attended kindergarten, junior high, and high school together, only separating when we went off to college. I went to Central Illinois University, but he took classes at the community college as a formality. Everything was lined up for him; he didn't have to work for anything. He was a lucky son of a bitch and I was stranded in Gentry—too drunk to drive myself.

I had limited options. Britney was out with her friends, and I wasn't sure if she would be sober enough to pick me up. She was

SHE'S TOXIC

under twenty-one and relegated to the hit-or-miss house party. I considered joining her, but figured I'd run into Mike, and I wasn't ready to dive back into that mess.

I called Brit anyway. I'd saved her number under "BB" for "Britney Boyer," but it was also shorthand for "BaBy" and even an acronym for "Beloved Britney." She had insisted I save her as "My one and only," even changing it herself on occasion, but my friends had given me too much shit. I figured "BB," however defined, was endearing and simple enough to recall.

"Hi! You have reached Britney. Please leave a message!"

Damn. I wondered why she wasn't answering her phone. She had probably turned it to vibrate or silent. I trusted Brit, but I had a fleeting tinge of concern, wondering what she might be doing that would keep her from answering. Maybe Mike wanted me away from her so he could be with her. Maybe they were together right now. *No, that would be ridiculous.*

The rain had now come to a complete halt, and the streets were clear except for a few vehicles in front of the two bars. I happened to run into Jason Kell, a former teammate who was picking up a young lady leaving The Barnyard. She lived in Reedville, so he offered to give me a lift back to my apartment. *Anything for Mr. All-State, championship-winning quarterback!* Jason assured me he was sober enough to make the drive, so I hitched a ride in his truck.

Reedville was a slightly smaller town located twenty miles southeast of Gentry. Reedville had five thousand residents to Gentry's six thousand, so they were about the same in every way. I had found a steal of a deal on an apartment, which was nice because Reedville was midway between Gentry and Decatur (the home of CIU). It was also convenient for Brit to stay with me, as her parents had moved to Reedville following her high school graduation.

My apartment was nice for a small town. It was on the second floor of a downtown law office, an open concept with a spacious living room adjoining the kitchen. The kitchen housed new stainless steel appliances and large granite countertops. The lone bedroom was enclosed behind the kitchen; the bedroom came complete with a private bathroom.

Once back upstairs in my apartment, I microwaved leftover spaghetti and downed a large glass of water. The combination of being drunk and exhausted should have knocked me out, but I tossed and turned for an hour or two before dozing off. I wasn't consciously thinking about what happened at The Barnyard, but I sensed its presence—clawing at my insides.

I awoke earlier than desired due to chickadees singing outside my window. The yellow sun peaked above the horizon, projecting its radiance against the pale blue wall opposite my headboard.

I'd planned to drive to my parents' house for Sunday lunch, but I didn't have a vehicle and my head throbbed, likely thanks to the shots I'd taken. I was reminded of the two women, hanging onto to their past. I wasn't much different in a sense; I wanted to believe I was still the hometown hero.

My phone rang and my hand instinctively reached for my nightstand, but my phone must have still been in my jeans. I rolled out of bed, shot my hand in the front right pocket, and answered just before the voicemail picked up.

SHE'S TOXIC

"Hey baby, I want to see you." It was Britney.

"Hey, how was the party? I tried to call you last night," I said. I took a drink from the cup on my nightstand.

"Didn't go. I passed out before nine while watching *Beauty and the Beast*. Don't laugh!"

"That's cool." I laid my head down to ease the pounding. "I love how you can relate, being such a beast and all."

"Uh, don't make me come over there and hurt you, because you know I can. And I will."

I knew she was joking, but for some reason, her voice gave me the chills, like her words were tapping into a forever damaged realm of my being.

Three

It was difficult to recall a time before I knew Britney Boyer. She had not always been in my life, but life before her seemed like a charade. I remembered every detail of the night we met.

It was the opening game of my junior year of high school. I'd played wide receiver during my freshman and sophomore seasons, but my coach had moved me to quarterback once he realized that I had a much better throwing arm than the senior incumbent.

Small towns rally around their high school football team, generally regardless of success. Bleachers and grandstands were packed for the season opener. The track surrounding the field was lined with lifetime mega-fans, high school girls wearing their boyfriends' away jerseys, and younger kids throwing Nerf footballs around. The aroma of fresh-cut grass infused the unseasonably cool air.

I joined the team in a large circle for a rousing pregame speech. We stood just outside our locker room, cleats scratching against the sidewalk. Coach Summers gave a short speech before handing over the reins, asking me to add a few words.

SHE'S TOXIC

"Let's get it, men! This is the moment we've been waiting all summer for. All of those two-a-days in the hundred-degree heat mean nothing if we don't go out there and win this! Let's trust each other out there, play hard on both sides of the ball, and we *will* win this game! Bulldogs on three, baby! One! Two! Three! Bulldogs!"

The crowd heard our break and erupted into a chorus of cheers. The PA announcer gave the cue, and we began our triumphant march into battle. I lead *my team* through the paper banner, held taut by a dozen crimson-clad Bulldog cheerleaders. Some of the guys stole glances at the girls, but I was too focused. The game was all that mattered. It consumed me.

We went back and forth with the Vandalia Vandals for four quarters. I had thrown one interception that led to a quick touchdown in the first quarter, but then I settled in. (I chalked up my slow start to butterflies.) Our offense began to click, even against one of the most revered defenses in the state.

The seesaw affair was approaching its climax. Vandalia had just scored a touchdown to take a 48-45 lead.

It was my chance to be the hero.

After an offensive holding penalty, we began the drive on our own 10-yard line, which meant we needed to cover 90 yards in the final 54 seconds.

I took the snap and looked for my target receiver. *Covered.* I maneuvered to avoid the rush and looked for my second option. *Covered.* I finally connected with an open receiver in the middle of the field; he was tackled on our own 36-yard line. I spiked the ball to stop the clock. Twenty seconds remaining, 64 yards to go.

I looked over to the sideline for the next play, and that's when I first saw her. There wasn't much that could distract me in a moment like this, but if she had been on the sidelines all along, I couldn't believe I hadn't noticed her.

It was a crisp night, so she was dressed in warmups with gloves and a headband. I couldn't see much from my position in the middle of the field, but I was intrigued. I could see her smile, I could hear her laugh, and I could see a sparkle in her doe brown eyes. An angel had appeared to give me the inspiration to finish the game.

I struggled to focus on the next play—likely the deciding play of the game, but all I could hear was her laugh. It rang through my ears, drowning my thoughts, draining my focus. It was the sweetest sound I had ever heard.

My coach relayed the play and I called my offense to a huddle. I glanced at the sideline; her silhouette danced along the track.

I was captivated.

"Ty! Ty! Ty!" Our running back, Jason Kell, brought me back to reality. "Hey, bro, what's the play?" Jason asked. A few guys laughed nervously at my mental lapse. "Let's get this thing, bro! Come on!"

I cleared my mind, called the play, and stepped up to the line of scrimmage. I surveyed the defense, their eyes hungry in anticipation. I heard Britney cheer. I tried to focus. I called out, "Red seven! Hut! Hut!" I took a three-step drop, avoided the rush, and launched the ball downfield over my slot receiver's right shoulder. He caught the ball in stride; it would be a footrace to the goal line.

30, 25, 15...

If he didn't score, the game would be over.

10, 5…

Touchdown!

The crowd exploded. We had clipped Vandalia, 52-48. After running to the end zone to celebrate with my team, I looked over to the sideline. I caught Britney gazing right at me.

"Good job, Ty!" she yelled.

"Yeah, baby!" I smiled and threw my arms into the air. I wasn't sure how life could get any better.

It was a crucial, early season win against the defending class 3A state champions. I was thrilled about winning our first game, but I could not get that girl out of my mind.

As I listened to the coach's post-game speech, high-fived my teammates, and changed into my street clothes, I hoped she would be among the revelers waiting outside the locker room.

I knew my family would be eager to congratulate me and that I'd also have to answer a few questions from the local media. It was my first game as the hero and I should have been nervous about the interviews, but they were far from a concern.

"You better be coming out to the pond tonight." Jason gave me a powerful slap on the back, knocking me forward. By pond, he meant lake. I had already spent several Friday nights hanging out at Clearwater Lake after football games.

I laughed and told him I might be able to make it, but I was going to eat dinner with my family first.

Upon finishing my sentence, I turned the corner and came face-to-face with Britney Boyer, nearly running her into the red and white checkered floor. I threw both arms out to brace myself.

"Woah!" I said. I tried to keep from falling and also tried to keep my momentum from plowing her over. She took a couple quick, small steps backward as she steadied herself. Her cheeks turned pink.

She was beautiful from a distance, but breathtaking up close. She was short-to-average height, with an athletic figure—maybe a bit of an hourglass. Her straight, dark brown hair fell just below her shoulders, long bangs down near her eyes. Her skin resembled the softest beige cashmere.

Her aura absorbed me, pulled me in, refused to let go.

"Hey, um," she said. I waited for her to say more, but she stumbled on her words.

"Hey, you snuck up on me. Great job tonight," I said.

"Me?" She giggled. "No, I didn't do anything. But you—you were amazing. You won the game!"

"Thank you, but don't sell yourself short. Those cheers were sick." I raised my eyebrows and grinned.

"Oh, come on. You didn't even notice us!" I watched as she fidgeted with her gym bag, transferring it from her right to left hand, then back to her right.

"I swear I did, and I've already memorized most of your cheers," I said.

She cocked her head back and laughed. "Oh my gosh."

"I'm Ty."

"I'm Britney."

She held out her hand for me to shake, but I wanted to pull her close for a kiss. Her lips looked so soft, full, and inviting. I settled for a handshake—my hand might have trembled.

SHE'S TOXIC

"It's a pleasure to meet you, Britney. How did you get in here anyway?"

"I forgot something in the locker room," she motioned to her bag, "so your coach let me in. Well, I think he was your coach, but I'm not sure. He was wearing a hat like your coach, so I figured it was him."

I had to remember she was probably just a freshman—so cute and innocent. "You're lying to me," I said. "I think you broke in to kidnap me and hold me hostage. You're a spy from another team, aren't you? I don't recall ever seeing you around here." I gave her the inquisitive side-eye.

She laughed. "Oh my, you're hilarious. Yep, that's exactly what I'm doing. I'm a freshman, so maybe that's why you haven't seen me."

"I knew it. Well, I guess I better get out of here before you throw me in the back of a van. But maybe I'll see you around." I tried to hide my goofy smile as I walked away.

I mentally prepared for the crowd of family, friends, fans, and media. *Damn, I forgot to ask if she would be at the party. Damn, I didn't get her phone number.* Oh well. If I didn't run into her at school, I'd see her at the football game next Friday night. At least I'd left on a high note.

Once outside, reporters from the local newspaper and radio station greeted me. There were even reporters from both the St. Louis Post-Dispatch and the Chicago Tribune—likely thanks to the Vandals' past success. I gave the obligatory, clichéd responses: *It was a team effort, my offensive line gave me time to throw all night,* and *we're looking forward to building off this success.*

I broke away from the media and joined some of my teammates and classmates. We exchanged a few more high-fives before I found my family.

"Great game, Tyler!" my mom said as she hugged me.

"Easy, a little sore." I cringed. "But thanks."

My dad shook my hand. "Boy, that was some game. Good job out there." His brown eyes blazed with pride. "I think I saw a few scouts in the crowd." My dad had played defensive end in high school and received scholarship offers from several Big Ten schools, but he stayed home to farm instead.

"Scouts?" My eyes widened. My dad beamed and nodded. Whew, scouts. It was getting serious. I'm sure they weren't there to watch me considering it was my first game at quarterback, but I may have given them a reason to come back.

As we walked to the parking lot, my younger sister Kourtney pulled me aside. Kourt was only a few inches shorter than me. Whenever we had family pictures, she would wear heels to be my height or even a little taller.

"So who was that?" she said with a wide smile. "Was that Britney Boyer? She's just a year older than me." Kourt's long brown hair bounced around her freckle-dusted face.

"I have no idea what you're talking about. Who?"

"Who? The girl who followed you outside. You know who I'm talking about! She couldn't stop looking at you."

I hadn't even realized that Britney followed me outside. *Wait, she couldn't stop looking at me? Nice.* "Oh, some freshman forgot her bag in the locker room." I tried to play it off, but I knew Kourt saw right through me.

SHE'S TOXIC

"Ah, a freshman. It had to be Britney Boyer. Are you two madly in love?" She raised her eyebrows, then checked me hard with her hip, almost knocking me to the ground.

"Geesh, that's the hardest hit I've taken all night. You're such a big bully."

"Well? You didn't answer my question," she said, smiling.

"What question?" I asked.

Kourt rolled her eyes. "Are you going to get married? Can I be a bridesmaid?" She turned her head to the side and gave me her puppy dog eyes before bursting into laughter.

"Wow, marriage? That happened fast." I laughed. "Do you want to babysit for us too?"

"You're already thinking about having babies with her? Wow, you *are* in love!" she yelled, prompting half the parking lot to turn and look.

I returned her prior hip-check, nearly knocking her to the ground. I thought I'd hit her too hard, but her initial shriek was followed by uncontrollable laughter.

"You're in love, just admit it!"

I hadn't given my sister many opportunities to intrude upon my love life. I had never taken a girl home to meet the family. I had taken a couple girls *home*, but only when my family was nowhere to be seen (except for a certain ice cream sandwich incident).

"She's cute. I'll leave it at that." I rolled my eyes, but a telling smile crossed my lips. My cheeks flushed. I wasn't prepared to give my sister the satisfaction, but her persistence wore me down, and hell, maybe I wanted to tell someone.

"I knew it, I knew it!" She ran ahead to tell my parents all about her recent discovery. "Mom, Dad, Ty is in love!" I had to hand it to her, she was quite the detective.

I hung my head, but continued to smile. I'd always considered *love* to be such an ambiguous term, often both overused and underused, but I knew I was feeling something I'd never felt before. I wanted to see Britney again. I wanted to hear her voice, to hear her laugh, and to feel her skin against mine, if only for another simple handshake. With other girls, sex was the first (and often only) thing on my mind. Britney was different. She triggered something new inside me.

My adrenaline wore off during dinner, and I felt every hit from the game. I tore through my roast beef sandwich and ate some of my dad's leftover curly fries before ordering another sandwich. My parents asked a few questions about Britney, but I avoided giving any straight answers. *Thanks, Kourt.*

It was close to eleven when my parents dropped me off at my Jeep, but there were still numerous vehicles in the lot. Most of the vehicles belonged to cheerleaders or football players who had carpooled to the party. The football players all had the same red-colored football emblems with their respective numbers in the middle. Cheerleaders had red-colored pom-poms with their first names scrawled underneath in cursive.

Sydney and Amanda were parked on either side of my Jeep. I'd gone to school with them since junior high, but they had never paid much attention to me, always opting to date older. It seemed to be the natural order for the guys to be two-to-three years older than the girls in high school relationships. I had two years on

SHE'S TOXIC

Britney, so I suppose I was following some unspoken biological, evolutionary mandate.

Once in my Jeep, I checked my phone. I had eight new voicemails and twenty-eight text messages. *Wow.* Friends and family members had texted to congratulate me on the game. I had a few messages from girls, such as *u were soooo amazing! We should hang tonight (;,* and *heyyy u (:.* A junior cheerleader named Alexa had sent a message telling me to get my "fine ass" to the party. I also had messages from some of my teammates, which were all nearly identical to Jason's text: *where ya at u sunuvabitch???*

It felt good to be in such high demand.

I listened to the voicemails—much of the same, but the last message caught my attention:

"Hey, um, what's up? I hope you don't mind I'm— (Don't say that!). I mean, what's up? They told me to call you. We're going to kidnap you! (Hysterical laughter from at least three girls). Oh, this is Britney Boyer. Text me! Bye!"

I felt a huge grin spread across my face. *Awwww.* This girl was so adorable. I didn't want to text her back right away, had to make her wait a while. *Right? Oh well...* I began my text game: The language of love.

Me: *You will never find me...*

Brit FR (freshman): *I'm sorry, who is this?*

Me: *Ty Reynolds. You said you were going to kidnap me, but you have to find me first.*

Brit FR: *Ohhhh Tyyyy!!! (: Lol Yes I am! You better watch yourself Mister!*

Me: *I'm not scared... What ya up to tonight tiger?*

Brit FR: *Grrrrrr! Lol I'm out at the lake, but I have to leave soon): Stupid curfew! Wahhhh!*

Me: *Well I might see you there, if you're lucky.*

My phone rang as I sent the final text.

"Ty! Where are you?" A female voice came through the line. She sounded like she might have already had a few drinks.

"Sorry, who is this?"

"Aww, you don't recognize my voice? It's Alexa. Why didn't you text me back, punk?"

"Oh, hey! I just opened my messages. What's up?" I asked.

"Suuuure you did." She laughed. "Come to the party so we can hang out. I miss you."

Four

Remembering the night I met Britney made me want to see her, but first I needed to retrieve my Jeep. I called Jason and was able to hitch another ride with him. We're both "glory days" kind of guys, so we spent the entirety of the drive reminiscing about our state championship and all the parties at the lake. He dropped me off outside The Barnyard, and I called Brit to make the drive back to Reedville more palatable.

"I can't find anything to wear tonight. Ugh, I swear I have no clothes. What should I wear?" I pictured her running circles around her room, trying on clothes before dismissing them into a jumbled heap.

"I wouldn't argue if you wore nothing." She laughed, but then told me to be serious. "How about your red dress?" I asked.

I was lying down on the chocolate suede couch in my living room, watching the Cardinals game; the Phillies were up, 6-1.

"Eh, no dress tonight. I'm not even sure I have a red dress. Hey, I'm turning on speaker phone." A pause and a click. "Wait, this looks kind of cute."

"It might be too old anyway—the one you had back in high school. I can never hear you when you're on speaker phone."

"How about now?" she yelled, followed by laughter. "What might be too old? Oh, the dress. You said I had it back in high school? Hmm. Anyway, this looks good."

She might have forgotten about the red dress, but there was no way I would ever forget. She wore it the first night we had sex. I remembered peeling her out of it, watching it hit the floor, my hands caressing her body.

Britney had completed her first year at West-Central Illinois Community College a month ago, but I wasn't sure what she was currently majoring in She had changed her major at least three times within her first year. Back in high school, she had wanted to be a dental hygienist. She'd planned to finish her program in eighteen months, find a job in a Chicago suburb, get married, have a white picket fence, *ride off into the sunset*, and live happily ever after. I had inserted the joke about riding off into the sunset, which always elicited a smile and an eye roll.

Her first semester of college went by in a flash. I couldn't even remember when she first switched her major. The next thing I knew, she told me she wanted to be a nurse. All of her friends were going into nursing, and she thought it would be a great fit for her as well. She had also liked the prospect of making more money. But early in the spring semester, she had switched to teaching. I couldn't remember which classes she'd taken in the spring, but I knew she'd had a full schedule.

During the remaining drive to Reedville, I thought back to my crazy suspicion that I'd loved Britney in all of my past lives, but

SHE'S TOXIC

this was the first time we'd ended up together. Our impediment may have been a Romeo and Juliet scenario, or she might have been lost at sea while attempting to meet me in the American Colonies. Or we could have simply passed each other like ships in the night, with sweet serendipity eluding us.

There are infinite possibilities as to why two people don't end up together, even though they might be kindred spirits. Feelings can be no match to the whores of timing and chance. But I didn't need to be concerned with that, at least not in this lifetime.

Brit's parents lived on Walnut Street, across town from my apartment. I was ecstatic upon discovering her parents had moved last fall. A sudden move, but they did it for Brit. They were willing to do anything for their only child.

Their house was a two-story craftsman with a large maple in the front yard. It was a modest home while their place in Gentry had been extravagant. Her dad's early financial success as an accountant and investor allowed him to retire once they moved to Reedville. Her mom had abandoned her day job and was trying her hand at writing a romance novel.

The door opened and two figures emerged into view. Britney kissed her mom's cheek before stepping off the front porch and down the sidewalk. Her mom gave me a cordial wave before closing the large crimson door. I returned the gesture with a halfway genuine smile. I liked Britney's mother, but her demeanor toward me was unsettling, though it hadn't always been. If I had to pinpoint an exact time, she seemed to change when they moved to Reedville.

But maybe her mom knew something I didn't regarding Brit's

toxicity. I wanted to forget about what Mike had said, but a gut feeling continued to prod me.

Brit was wearing white crochet shorts with a black halter top. She had curled her hair, which was always a welcome change. Her hypnotizing brown eyes were already reeling me in.

I greeted her with a kiss, and we took off for our favorite place to eat. It wasn't Mike's restaurant, so I felt a little guilty. Instead, it was a wood-fired pizza joint named Gentry Peel. It made me feel like I was cheating on Mike, but I couldn't care less following our little brouhaha.

I looked over at Brit at one point during the drive and was overcome with affection, though the feeling was mixed with lingering confusion about what Mike had said at the bar. I wavered in deciding whether to share the fight with Brit. After some inner debate, I decided to tell her. If I didn't speak now, I would only delay the inevitable.

"I'm fortunate to have you in my life," I said.

"Aww, you're adorable. I feel the same way. I just wish I wasn't taking this summer class."

An abrupt change of subject, but I rolled with it. "And why would you want to take summer classes? That's not my idea of a vacation."

"I'm behind because I switched my major so many times. And I might try to get back into nursing. Yep, that's what I want to do." She flipped down the sun visor so she could use the mirror to apply some finishing touches.

"Sounds good. You have to do what makes you happy." I had to spill it, enough stalling. "I don't know what Mike's problem is."

SHE'S TOXIC

"Well, okay, that came out of nowhere." She pushed the visor back and turned her full attention to me. "What about Mike?"

I hesitated. "He doesn't think we're good for each other. We had a big fight last night at The Barnyard. It was stupid."

If my revelation bothered her, she hid it well—for now. "What do *you* think about me? Isn't that what matters?"

"You know I love you. I've always loved you. But I wish he accepted you. Hell, I thought he did." I looked over at her every few seconds while trying to keep my eyes on the road.

"I don't want him to hate me. Does he hate me? I don't know what I ever did to him." Her smile faded with each word, as if the weight of my revelation was finally taking effect. She generally had a positive disposition, but the news had to be concerning.

"Yeah, I don't know either. It's frustrating." I widened my eyes as I turned left off of the frontage road and onto Rountree Avenue, heading out to the restaurant.

"What did he say?" she asked, while sitting on the edge of her seat, like a puma ready to pounce on an unsuspecting vole.

"He said quite a bit. He said I need to cut you loose and that you're toxic for me."

"What?" she yelled—infuriated. "How am I toxic?"

My stomach muscles tensed. I regretted relaying the exact words Mike had used. I should have conveyed his general message; she wouldn't have known the difference. Too late now. I'd need to be more careful about disclosing my other secrets.

"No idea. I swear I don't agree with him."

"You better not." Fire and smoke raged in her eyes. "What else did he say?"

31

"Not much. I didn't want to talk to him after he insulted you. I told him to go to hell," I said. I needed allay her concern, to keep her from going ballistic.

She closed her eyes and remained quiet for a moment before a sinister smile crossed her face. "I probably would have done worse than that." The brief, evil look quickly subsided to concern. "You should have kept talking to him though."

"No way; he pushed me to my limit. He needs to apologize if he wants to talk again."

"This doesn't make any sense. I can't believe he would say that. You know what? I don't even feel like eating right now." She looked through the window at the restaurant. "Why do we always have to eat here?" she asked.

"I thought you loved it."

She shrugged.

"We should still eat," I said. "Let's try to forget about Mike and have a good time tonight."

Tension drained from her face, but she remained silent.

"I'm sorry, but I felt like you deserved to know."

"Thank you so much," she said while rolling her eyes.

I brought my right temple to my fist as I parked. "GENTRY PEEL" glowed above us in large orange lettering, with a blue-stenciled pizza peel underneath the two words. It was nearly eight, but on the longest day of the year, the sun was winning its struggle to remain above the horizon. Reds, oranges, purples, and blues shot out across the sky.

"Maybe we should all hang out sometime."

"Yeah, you could find him a girl to hang with."

SHE'S TOXIC

"That's a good idea," she agreed. "It shouldn't be too hard to find someone for him." Her fingernails trailed along her chest, just above the hem of her top. I followed the trail of her fingers and felt a surge below my belt before I realized what she said.

"'It shouldn't be too hard to find someone for him.' What's that supposed to mean?"

She smiled. "Well he's a nice guy and isn't bad looking, right? Don't worry Ty, I *love* you."

It wasn't something I'd really thought about. But I had almost made something out of nothing by misinterpreting her gestures. I was on edge. *Calm down.* I needed to disregard Mike's warning as much as possible.

We went inside, and after a brief wait, the hostess called my name and led us to our table. It wasn't the most romantic dinner we ever had, as I found myself analyzing Brit throughout the evening. Mike's comments continued to prod me.

After dinner, I drove toward my parents' house northwest of Gentry. Any vestiges of sunlight had been vanquished by a thick blanket of darkness.

"Where are we going, baby?" Brit asked but should have known based on our trajectory.

"Oh, I have a little surprise for you." I shook Brit's left knee and smiled.

Brit was still the same girl I'd loved since high school, and it would take more than a few words from Mike to change my feelings for her.

"Awww, that's sweet. You're not taking me out to the country to kill me, are you? My mom knows I'm with you, so you won't get away with it." She stared into my eyes before erupting with sweet laughter, like the sound of a folk string band.

"Damn. I didn't think of your mom." I slapped the steering wheel in feigned disgust. "I'll have to save that for another time."

"What, another time to kill me? I'd appreciate that; there are still many things I need to cross off my bucket list. Like, I must eat huevos rancheros before I die."

"Huevos rancheros?" I laughed. "Isn't that eggs, salsa, and beans? On a tortilla maybe? I might have made that once without even knowing what it was."

I was remembering a night when Mike's parents went out of town. We had a few people over and got drunk and hungry, so we had cooked anything that sounded appetizing. We had put together the unhealthiest combinations imaginable, but Mike had exclaimed, "It's good for ya!"

"You've eaten huevos rancheros? Lucky! And yes, that's exactly what it is, and I need to experience that greatness before I die. Please, Ty, grant me my one request."

"Oh, I suppose. I'll make you huevos rancheros tomorrow morning, and then I can do whatever I want with you."

"Whatever you want." She looked at me and raised her eyebrows, running her hand up my arm before kissing my cheek. "So where are we going?"

"Right here." I beamed as I pulled my Jeep to a stop along a field road running perpendicular to a dirt road. Most people would call them both field roads—not knowing any better.

The unimposing spot was my sanctuary. The stars were always visible, the air always fresh, and my mind always clear.

SHE'S TOXIC

I exited the vehicle and pulled a blanket, a bottle of red wine, and two Dixie cups from the back. It was just like an old Kenny Chesney song.

"Let's have a little dessert." I grinned.

"We already had tiramisu, but I love it," Brit said before sitting down on the blanket next to me. She cuddled into my body for warmth, as the temperature had dropped since we began our night. Her shorts weren't quite doing it anymore.

"I went all out for this wine, it was like fifteen bucks." I poured wine into a cup and handed it to her.

"Woah, look at you." She took the cup and held it toward the star-filled sky.

"Yeah, yeah. It's not much, but this stuff is tasty." I finished pouring my cup and brought it next to hers. "A toast to us—to our past and future. I love you, baby."

We laid there together for over an hour enjoying each other—counting the stars, drinking wine, and laughing like the joyous couple we were. I had all but forgotten about my fight with Mike. My goal was to show Brit a good time, as always, but I also wanted to get out into the country, ensconced from the concerns that had developed the previous night.

After packing the blanket back into my Jeep, my phone beeped. I had a new text message from Britney's friend Madison (Maddie) Ross:

I need to talk to you about Britney. It's been bad lately.

Five

I suffered through another sleepless night, the second in as many days. I spent hours turning over Maddie's message. Maddie never texts me, so she must have had a good reason. Her message, coupled with Mike's comments … I feared a sinister presence lying in wait, beneath the surface, just like a gator near the shore of an opaque bayou.

There aren't any gators in Illinois, but I had recently taken a trip to Louisiana with Brit. We went to New Orleans, Baton Rouge, and took six plantation tours. The highlight for me was an airboat tour, piloted by a guy straight out of *Duck Dynasty*. He explained the gators' predatory patterns, how they lurk—waiting for the perfect moment to attack. They can go up to three years without eating, but when the time comes, they explode from the murky bayou, like a bullet through a still night.

Not a comforting thought; I needed to reply to Maddie. I'd wanted to respond right away, but couldn't find the opportunity to call because Brit had stayed over. I'd considered texting, but Brit always looked at my phone. She didn't look because she was suspicious, but because she liked to use some of my apps. It was never a big deal because I'd never had anything to hide, and after deleting Maddie's message, I still didn't.

"Good morning." Brit rolled over and smiled before nuzzling her head into the nook of my shoulder.

"Morning." I brushed her hair back from her eyes and kissed her forehead. This was what I needed to be doing. I couldn't let others dictate my emotions or my relationship's trajectory. For all I knew, Maddie and Mike had made a bet to see who could break us up first. People have harbored crueler intentions. It was amazing how one message had amplified my developing paranoia.

"You talked in your sleep again. It sounded like you were having a horrible nightmare. Do you remember it?" Brit rubbed her hand across my hairless chest as she spoke.

I was getting antsy.

"Nope. I don't remember dreaming about anything." I may have slept two or three hours. I didn't want to tell her I'd had trouble sleeping because she would pry, and then I'd feel compelled to tell her about Maddie's message.

I hated to keep secrets from her, but I needed to protect our relationship. And although Brit and Maddie weren't hanging out as much, I also wanted to protect their friendship. Brit might not respond well if she knew Maddie was sending messages to me behind her back.

"Your nightmares are getting worse. What's wrong?" she asked, sitting up.

"You always say I have nightmares, but I never remember having any. Maybe you're having nightmares that I'm having nightmares." I snickered as I sat up with her.

She laughed. "I guess it's possible."

I seldom remembered my dreams. If I remembered one, it was always about Britney. I had a recurring dream where I was driving my Jeep to pick her up at her old house in Gentry. She would call to say she was ready and waiting on me, but I'd never arrive. She'd call back, and I'd find myself trapped—navigating through a twisting labyrinth, experiencing sharp pain and regret. It was probably symbolic of her waiting for a proposal, coupled with her forlorn feeling after I'd lost my football scholarship.

I was finally able to get Brit out of my apartment. She had to go eat lunch with an older cousin who was visiting from North Carolina. I felt bad for wanting her to leave, but it wasn't that I necessarily didn't want to see her, I simply needed to find out what Maddie's message was about.

I had my phone in my hand before Brit closed the front door. I felt guilty for calling another girl, but at least they were friends. Actually, I wasn't sure if that made it better or worse. Probably worse. I should have come clean and told her about the message; there may have been a simple explanation. Once I started down this path, there would be no turning back.

It took six rings for Maddie to answer; she sounded like she just woke up. I checked my watch: 11:02. She must have had a late night, not surprising though—she was probably drunk when she sent the message. Her reliability was suspect, yet Mike had always been trustworthy.

Maddie and Brit had been friends for years. Maddie had moved to Gentry from Shelbyville, Illinois, during grade school. Brit, Maddie, and Kayla Morrison were inseparable through junior high and high school. Maddie and Kayla played volleyball and softball together, but Brit had been a football and basketball cheerleader. Kayla and Maddie might have been a little closer because of their athletic preferences, but they all considered themselves the three best friends that anyone could have.

"Hey, I got your random message. What's going on?"

"Oh, hey!" She perked up, but her tone quickly shifted back to somber. "Sorry, rough night. I was a little drunk. I wish things could be like they were back in high school. Sorry. I'm sure I'm stating the obvious. You're much closer to her."

Oh boy. This is what I was afraid of. Maddie also sensed something was wrong with Britney, even though I wasn't sure how much Maddie and Brit were still hanging out.

"I'm not sure what to think. Mike was also talking about her the other day. We got into a fight about it. He made me feel like I've lost my mind."

"I think we've all lost our minds a bit." It sounded like she was fighting back tears.

"Yeah, you're right." I humored her even though I hadn't yet experienced the gravity of her concern—I hoped I never would. Britney seemed the same to me.

"I hope you'll be okay. If you ever need to talk, I'm here for you," she said.

"I'm here for you too, Maddie." It was a predictable, instinctive response, but it came out too quickly.

"Thanks, Ty. You're sweet." She smiled through the phone and through her tears. "Remember that one time we all went to Six Flags? It was me, you, Brit, and Kayla. Do you remember?"

I'd never forget that day. It was during the summer after my junior year. I'd been dating Brit for eleven months. The three girls had all planned to spend the day at Six Flags after Maddie picked up her license (she had an early birthday). A hell of a plan, but Maddie's birthday fell on a Monday, and our DMV was closed on Mondays. Brit had called me crying, wondering what they would do, so I finagled my way out of a 7-on-7 summer football tournament by convincing Coach Summers that I was knocking on death's door.

"Oh yeah, I had to put up with you crazy girls all day."

Maddie laughed, this time a hearty laugh, no longer muffled by her tears. "It was a blast. I'm surprised you ever wanted to see me and Kayla after that."

"I've had worse experiences. Let's see, I broke my nose once during a football game. I had an allergic reaction to mangos."

"Oh, shut up! You loved it! Remember how me and Kayla kept hitting on guys?"

"Yes, I definitely remember. You told them I thought they were hot." I rolled my eyes though I realized she couldn't see me through the phone. "By the way, I rolled my eyes while I said that," I said.

"Hey, that's not nice!" she shrieked. "But you thought they were hot; don't deny it." Maddie was back to acting like herself. "We should go again. You could see your old boyfriends."

"Ha ha, funny. You know I'm straight."

"I don't know for sure," she said, and then gulped. "I didn't mean anything by that, sorry. That would be weird, right? Damn, I'm sorry."

SHE'S TOXIC

"Hey, no problem. I guess you're right though. You can't be sure." I laughed to keep the mood light.

"Sorry. I guess I'll let you go. Bye, Ty." She hung up before I could respond.

Our conversation was all over the place. Maddie was crying, then laughing, and then embarrassed—all within three minutes. She had been out of sorts for some time now. I hadn't talked to her much since Brit graduated high school, but even when I did, she wasn't the same girl.

My thoughts were interrupted by my ringing phone.

"Hey brother, can you meet me at Panera in thirty?" It was Kourt.

"Eh, better make it thirty-two minutes. I have a couple things I need to do first. I'm in Reedville, but I'll head up there."

"Funny. See you soon."

My sister and I were close growing up. She's my only sibling, with only three years between us. Kourt and Brit were friends to some extent, especially after I graduated. Kourt had acted as our intermediary during the school day, transferring notes between us. It was an old-school tactic, but Brit enjoyed the romance.

My sister and I hadn't talked much in the last year. I'd lost touch with quite a few people after moving to Reedville, which seemed to intensify each year removed from high school. I knew I needed to make more time for her, so we had planned monthly lunches—or at least we tried. They were probably closer to bi-monthly.

We usually met at Panera Bread, my sister's favorite restaurant. Having a Panera in Gentry was a benefit of living along the interstate. Otherwise, there's no way a town of our size would have had one. People were flocking to the cities and suburbs to eat higher quality, fresh food, whereas small towns depended on fast food and generic bar and grills.

I waited for my sister at a table for two near a wall of windows; the sun poured in. My phone rang again. I expected a call from Kourt—probably running late as usual, but the call came from an unknown number. I recognized the Springfield area code, but I let it go to voicemail. I reasoned that the caller would leave a message if it was important enough. Kourt would arrive soon, and I didn't want to be in the middle of a conversation.

I caught sight of Kourt's black Chevy Camaro just before she turned into the parking lot. The car reflected her personality well. She was always a rebel, at least after her sophomore or junior year of high school. I was away at school, so I wasn't sure when she changed. One day she was my kid sister; the next, she was the quintessential wild child. We grew further apart. I didn't hear many sexual stories about her, but every now and then, I'd get wind of a guy hooking up with her—often guys who had already graduated. She never claimed she was misunderstood or had daddy issues, yet I knew something was eroding her spirit.

Kourt was a cheerleader, popular (among certain groups), but she'd occasionally ditch school for several days. I suppose the primary reason she got away with it was because she was an American sweetheart—and it probably didn't hurt that her older brother had won a state championship for the town. It gave her some leeway in her actions, but I realized I had also given her a high standard to match. It may have been enough to crack her.

SHE'S TOXIC

She stumbled out of her car and pulled her sunglasses down over her eyes. She walked into the restaurant and turned to look for me. I acted like I was hiding by putting my hand in front of my face. She spotted me, flashed a weak smile, then proceeded to the cash register to order her food.

She sat down after ordering. "Hey brother, miss me?"

Kourt looked haggard, yet exceptional. She still had the same dark brown hair, and her piercing green eyes complemented the dark tan she kept regardless of season or latitude.

"Of course I miss you." I leaned forward and gave her an awkward hug. "Where have you been hiding?"

"I tried calling you a couple times last week, maybe the week before. You never answer your phone." She gave me a frustrated look. Her breath carried a trace of alcohol, but I wasn't touching that one.

And she was lying. I hadn't missed any calls from her—or maybe I'd let them go to voicemail.

"Really? Shit, I must have missed them."

She raised her eyebrows and murmured *mhmm*. I didn't want to fight with her so I dropped it there. We needed to revitalize our relationship. Some siblings are best friends and we used to be, but now we're closer to strangers.

We retrieved our food and grabbed a couple coffees.

Hazelnut. *Such an amazing creation.*

"How's life? Still trucking?" she asked, sounding like a shade of her former self.

"Yeah, for the most part. I can't complain." I didn't want to talk about what Mike and Maddie had said.

"What do you mean?" Her eyes darted around the restaurant, occasionally landing in my general vicinity.

Yup, I'd already said too much. My sister had a gift for reading me, for reading anyone. I'd always told her she should be a detective or psychologist, primarily because she knew each girl I hooked up with in high school. It wasn't like there were *too many* before I met Brit, but I had put up numbers as a sophomore, especially during the summer before my junior year. I was an athlete who matured early and liked to party, so my success with girls was only natural.

There was the one time I made the mistake of thinking Kourt had gone to Lake Michigan with my parents. I'd come home with a girl named Sarah Allison after spending the afternoon out at Jason's. We came into the house sucking each other's face, racing to undress, when I looked over and saw Kourt, wide-eyed at the kitchen table, eating an ice cream sandwich and listening to Selena Gomez. I'd made that one easy on her.

Kourt would find out about the fight sooner or later, so I decided to save us both the headache of beating around the bush all afternoon.

"Mike and I had a ridiculous fight at The Barnyard."

Her eyes continued to dart before lingering on three college-aged guys who had just sat down. She made eye contact with one of them and blushed before turning back to me. "Were you guys drunk?" She put down her steaming coffee and blew. "Did you actually fight?"

"Not really. We weren't hammered, but we were both feeling good—buzzed. It wasn't physical, just yelling back and forth. We each said some nasty things to each other. He said that I needed to ditch Brit, and then we argued. He's acted weird about her before, but he's never been so blunt. We haven't talked since."

For the first time, Kourt made direct eye contact with me. "Well, what did he say about her?" She attempted another run at her coffee. *Just right.* "She's always seemed *nice...*" she trailed off as she took another quick drink. Her eyes fell from mine as she dropped her head. I wasn't sure if she was praying or fighting back tears.

"Where should I begin?" I took a hearty bite out of my grilled chicken salad—a healthy choice. I'd always taken care of myself while playing sports, but that had gone by the wayside, along with my football career. "He said it wasn't right, that the relationship would ruin both of us, or something along those lines. He said I needed to cut her loose."

"Interesting." She blinked hard and pursed the corners of her lips. "What else did he say?"

"He made it sound like she's psychotic." I threw my hands in the air, recoiling at the memory.

"Hmm." She paused. "Maybe he's trying to look out for you. Are you and Britney good?"

"I guess. I'm not sure why we wouldn't be. Are you worried?"

Her tone was catching, suggesting that she was holding back. I'd had the same sensation during my conversation with Mike and my phone call with Maddie. I felt like I was on the outside of my own life, fighting for a glimpse inside. It had been two short days, less than forty-eight hours, since Mike had confronted me. I hadn't yet caught my breath.

"No, I'm not worried. As long as you're happy and everything's good, then you shouldn't be worried either."

"Exactly. That's what I tried to tell him. I think I would know if she was a psycho unless she's living a secret life behind my back." It was ludicrous to even consider. Britney wouldn't do that to me, and I wasn't sure how that tied into what Mike said anyway. My mind was wandering down a dark road, hitching to any post that seemed halfway plausible.

"Yeah, you two have been together for a while now. I'm just glad you're doing okay. I hate not talking to you as much anymore. We only see each other every month—or try to, anyway. That's not enough for a brother and sister. We used to be closer, you know?"

"Yeah, I know." I tried to smile.

"You should try to forget about what Mike said and live a normal life."

"I had a normal life, until last fall," I said. She drew a sharp breath. "Maddie also sent me a message the other day." I figured I might as well spill that too.

"Maddie?" she said with a tear in her voice. "How is she?"

"She's a wreck. She sent me a text message last night about Britney, and I was on the phone with her before you called."

"Poor girl. I hope life works out for her. I remember the first time Maddie and," she paused and looked hard into my eyes, "Britney asked me to hang out in high school."

"Yeah, I wish life could go back to how it was. It still seems okay for the most part, until Mike had to run his mouth."

"Like I said, Ty, if you believe your relationship is great, you can't be worried about what Mike said." She hesitated. "But I don't want to see you to get hurt."

I chose to ignore her hesitation and cryptic warning.

It would be difficult to forget Mike's words that were repeating in my mind. My lifelong best friend had criticized the rock and foundation of my life. I couldn't simply disregard his warning and move on. And then Maddie's concern only enhanced Mike's usual credibility.

We finished our lunch, and I successfully steered the conversation to baseball. Although it was early in the season, the Cardinals were looking good. I promised Kourt I would take her to a game later in the season. She replied that *we would see*. Such was the unfortunate state of our relationship.

"Thanks for calling today," I said.

"Sure thing." Kourt smiled, for once. If she was hungover when she arrived, maybe the coffee and food had helped. If she had just started drinking, maybe the alcohol had taken its effect.

Kourt said, "I'm sorry we haven't been as close as we used to be. It sucks. Let's change that, okay?"

I nodded and hugged her.

As she rolled away, I caught her taking a long drink out of a brown bag special. It was a Monday, but my sister had just graduated high school. I'm sure I did the same thing a few times back when I was her age. I didn't want to judge her, but Kourt had spiraled downhill.

I missed her.

Six

Britney and I were sprawled out on the couch at my apartment, one uneventful week after my lunch with Kourt. School kept Brit busy, and I'd spent most of the week trying to get into a new workout and nutrition plan. I still had hopes of getting back into shape and rejoining the football team, but it would take a determined effort. I'd also had plenty of time to consider my conversations with Mike, Maddie, and Kourt. Nothing out of the ordinary had happened with Brit, but that was about to change.

We were watching a reality show about a *famous* family—not my choice. I was wearing my red basketball shorts with a white "Bulldogs Basketball" T-shirt. I was a football legend in Gentry, but I had also been a good basketball player. Brit looked radiant in baby blue sweatpants and a small yellow T-shirt from a 5k she had recently completed.

My apartment's air conditioner was working overtime, as the outside temperature had reached triple digits. Despite the oppressive heat, it was almost a normal afternoon.

"So Mike still has a problem with me? Why did he tell his

mom? That's weird." She took a long drink from her glass of orange juice and placed it back on the coffee table.

"I guess so. He tells his mom about everything, and then she tells my mom."

My mom had called an hour earlier; she'd asked me to come out to the homestead because she needed a favor. Before hanging-up, she asked about my relationship with Brit. I had a good idea why. It had been more than a week since Mike and I had our fight. We hadn't spoken, but he was still trying to bury me. His persistence was both agitating and alarming.

Brit shook her head. "Not cool. I don't want anyone coming between us. Are you still thinking about what he said?"

"Nope." I lied. "He was spouting bullshit." I forced a laugh. "You're not crazy and we have a great relationship." I tried to sound convincing, but pessimistic thoughts continued to swirl inside my head. It would be impossible to outright dismiss such direct comments from my best friend of two decades. I was in a heightened state of awareness, and every little anomaly fueled my paranoia—like oxygen to a dying campfire.

She remained quiet.

I brought her hand to my lips, giving it a slight peck. "Love you, Brit." She melted into my arms. I could fabricate the truth when necessary to protect someone, even myself.

"I love you, too. But you need to talk to Mike again. You're still thinking about what he said, and that might be why you had a nightmare the other night."

"I'll see what I can do, but I don't want to talk to him," I said, stroking her hair.

"Then maybe I should." She smiled. "Would that be okay? Maybe I could set him straight."

My skin prickled. Her intent may have been innocent, but her words caught me off-guard. *Set him straight?* I imagined her with a gun to his temple, making him an offer he couldn't refuse.

"What do you mean? What are you going to do?"

"Oh, I can be convincing. You should know that by now." She climbed into my lap. "Hold me, Ty. I love being in your strong arms. You make me feel safe and secure." Nice of her to say, but I felt like I was back in the bayou—wading into the dark waters, needing to escape to the shore, but anchored by an unseen force. Just waiting for the inevitable strike—rendered defenseless by my reluctance to accept the truth.

The drive out to my parents' house brimmed with nostalgia. They lived in rural Nash County, ten miles northwest of Gentry, which made it about thirty miles from Reedville. I'd made the same trip—from my parents' house to Gentry—every day after I'd earned the privilege to drive during my sophomore year.

The majority of the drive to their house was along an unlined—and often unpatrolled—blacktop, which often resulted in high speeds. I remembered drag racing a certain section with Mike—back in the days when I had a Ford Mustang and he had a Mitsubishi Eclipse. I would hang my head out the window and yell, "It's the Autobahn, bitch!"

As I got older, I drove slower to enjoy the trip. I used to speed through the countryside, seldom giving a second glance to the passing scenery. Most people wouldn't consider the prairie of

SHE'S TOXIC

central Illinois as a beacon of breathtaking vistas, but I enjoyed the dramatic expanse, the panoramic sunsets, and watching an approaching thunderstorm.

The sun was already well into its daily plunge. Vibrant pinks and purples filled the western sky. I drove by fields of corn and soybeans shooting toward the clouds thanks to the rain we'd received throughout the early growing season. It was like the plants were being pulled skyward by millions of strings. The crops looked healthy—I thought so anyway. But looks can be deceiving.

This trip was indeed a slow one. My speedometer reflected forty miles per hour, but I figured forty was more than adequate in rural America. I was still driving much faster than the farm machinery that often snagged backroad traffic.

My mind was transported back to my high school days. If I didn't know any better, it could have been just another day during my senior year. I might have been driving home from football practice, going home to get ready to hang out with Britney or to drink a few beers with Mike. Things had changed though, as much as I wanted to avoid the truth. While living in Reedville, it was easy to lose sight of the past, but whenever I came back to Gentry, it seemed like I'd never left.

Cross Canadian Ragweed said it best: "You're always seventeen in your hometown." I just hoped that I wouldn't be clinging to the past in another twenty years. Maybe it's a symptom of a small town—and Gentry certainly was that—that for some, even after graduation, high school never really ends.

I approached the turn to my childhood home. There were two houses on the corner, one on the northeast, another on the southwest. A widowed woman, Mrs. Stine, owned the northeastern home. I used to stop by about once a month to chat with her about a variety of subjects ranging from the good old days to Cardinals baseball.

I remembered when I'd first discovered that she was an avid baseball fan. I'd stopped by one afternoon while the Cardinals were playing a day game. When I walked in the front door, she was cussing about the shortstop making an error. It was quite the spectacle, an 81-year-old woman cussing about one run, which had cut the St. Louis lead from 8-0 to 8-1. It was impossible not to laugh. But one small mistake can lead to a chain reaction, resulting in losing a perceived stranglehold on an opponent—or on life itself.

My childhood home came into clear focus as I made the turn onto *our* road. The house sat to the north, nestled between two sheds. An imposing shed sat on the west side of the homestead, full of my dad's farm machinery. An older, smaller shed sat to the east, housing everyday items and toys such as their lawnmower and four-wheelers. The larger shed dwarfed the house, but the house was far from diminutive. It was a classic two-story farmhouse; an exquisite porch wrapped around each level. My dad owned 160 acres spreading northward from the house—mostly fields, some timber.

I pulled down their long gravel driveway and spied my mom through a large bay window. She threw her basket of clothes to the ground, spilling most of its contents. She jogged to the door and stepped outside. My mom was young—in her forties—so she still got around well.

SHE'S TOXIC

Kourt got her green eyes from Mom but must have gotten her height from Dad. My mom was several inches shorter than Kourt, but otherwise they looked similar. They had the same emerald eyes, dark complexion, and brown hair—though my mom styled hers shorter.

"Tyler, I'm so glad you made it. It's been too long since you've been out to see us."

I wasn't sure how long it had been. I thought I remembered coming out just a couple weeks before, but it may have been a month or two. Or maybe it had only been a couple weeks; maybe that's all it took for my mom to miss me. Not the worst thing in the world.

"Hey, Mom." I hugged her before going back to my Jeep to retrieve a small bouquet of blue and yellow wildflowers I had picked from along the blacktop. One of my favorite parts of summer has always been the wildflowers (though I was careful who I admitted that to).

"Ty, you're so sweet." She smiled as she took the flowers into the house. "I need to get these in water. They are so beautiful!"

I wasn't always convinced when my mother showered me with adoration. I'd disappointed them by losing my scholarship, but they also loved me and were grateful that I didn't give them too much grief. They had their hands full now with Kourt—from the marathon school absences to her many trips to the doctor in Springfield.

"You're welcome." I followed her into the house.

She lingered in the kitchen while I made a quick jog up to my bedroom to retrieve my prom picture with Brit. I'd taken it with me to my apartment in Reedville, but I must have brought it back out to the house at some point.

My mother was fond of rustic décor, so the house was more like a barn. She even hung a refurbished barn door between the kitchen and dining room. When my mom would ask us if we were raised in a barn, Kourt and I would howl and respond in the affirmative.

Hardwood floors filled the entire home, except for the finished basement. The first floor of the house included all the classics: the kitchen, dining room, living room, bathroom, and my parents' master bedroom. My childhood bedroom was upstairs, across the hallway from my sister's. We each had a bathroom in our room, which came in handy during the school-year. I never endured the torment of waiting hours for my sister to get ready.

My parents had left my room untouched after I moved to Reedville. An eclectic, curious mix of books and sports memorabilia decorated my room. Posters of Mark Twain and William James hung next to those of Matt Holliday and Dan Marino. Dad had made a shelf into the wall for all of my football and basketball trophies. There weren't any participation ribbons.

After the abrupt halt to my football career, I was grateful that I'd remained somewhat of an intellectual through high school—I had options if I didn't make it back to the gridiron. I hadn't yet declared a major, but I had plenty of interests ranging from law (like my cousin, Sam) to weather.

I found the picture sitting on my desk, grabbed it, and took off back down the steps. I made a quick right at the bottom of the stairs and rejoined my mom in the kitchen-dining room area.

SHE'S TOXIC

"How's the family?" I asked as I scavenged through the fridge for leftovers. *Ah, ham and cheese turnovers.* I shot mustard onto a plate along with my treats; they'd always tasted better cold. I had flashbacks of raiding the fridge after a night of drinking when the microwave was out of play for fear of waking my parents.

"Well, we're all healthy and in one piece, but I can't say the same about your uncle."

"Uncle Patrick? Didn't they get a divorce?"

My Uncle Patrick—my dad's brother—lived south of Decatur in Shelby County. My cousins lived in Edwardsville, just east of St. Louis. Josh was my age; Sam was a few years older. Uncle Patrick and Aunt Christine were the last couple I'd ever expected to divorce; nobody had any idea what had driven them apart.

"They did. And now Christine has vanished. She disappeared without a trace. Patrick isn't doing well and the boys are struggling, especially Sam. I don't know what it is about this family." She sighed. "We seem to get hit with one calamity after another."

"Wow, she disappeared? That's crazy. Is she dead or what?"

"Nobody knows. I feel awful for your cousins."

"Yeah, life can be cruel." I wasn't sure what else to say. I wasn't apathetic—I felt bad for my cousins, but I was mired in my own predicament.

"We've all learned that unfortunate truth by now. But enough negative talk. How are you?" she asked.

"I can't complain. I talked to Kourt the other day at Panera." In light of what my cousins were going through, maybe my problems weren't so bad.

She filled a glass of sweet tea to the brim and took a seat at the dining room table. "Kourtney mentioned something about that. She said you had a fight with Mike."

Great. Kourt had told Mom what I said. Kourt and I might not have been as close anymore, but I wanted to believe I could still confide in her. I guess that had also changed.

"Yeah, we just had a stupid fight." I rolled my eyes, hoping she would let it go. I didn't have the energy to dissect it again.

"Sorry if I worry too much, but I'm your mom and I want to make sure you're okay."

"Yup, life is great. I can't complain."

"I hope so. How is Britney?" I guess I knew where Kourt got her detective prowess.

She took another drink from her tea as I dipped a forkful of turnover in mustard.

"Britney is as sweet as ever. We went out for a little picnic the other night."

"You're such the romantic, just like your father, or how he *used* to be anyway." She laughed. She looked like she wanted to say more, but instead, she just walked over and hugged me.

"What was that for?" I tried not to complain.

"I love you, and I want you to be safe." She gave me a sympathetic smile, patting me on the shoulder.

She wants me to be safe? Yup, I was almost certain that Mike had told his mom, and she called my mom. I was still debating what Mike told me at The Barnyard, but I didn't need everyone examining my relationship. It was too much. I sure didn't need the sympathy at a time like this. It served no purpose aside from making me analyze the minutiae of my life.

SHE'S TOXIC

And she had to rehash last fall. They'll never let me live down losing my football scholarship.

I remembered my dad's excitement when the recruiters were beating down the door. "Central Illinois!" he had exclaimed. Central Illinois had come from nowhere to become a national powerhouse in the last decade. I'd turned down offers from other schools—where I was sure to start as a freshman—because I wanted to be part of a championship-winning team. I had redshirted my freshman year, played backup during my first year of eligibility, and I was projected to start during my junior year. I was even named to the preseason all-conference team, but then I lost my scholarship.

All I had to do was show up, but I didn't.

"Life is great. I'm happier than I've ever been." I gave her a cheesy, fake smile, like I was posing for a family picture. All we needed was Kourt standing next to me in her stilettos. It was enough to prompt a restrained laugh from my mom.

"I hope so. Please remember that you can talk to me about anything. I know it's hard to talk to your old mom about things, but I'll always be here to help you in whatever way I can. I'm serious. You used to fit right here in my arms."

"Yeah, yeah. Thanks, Mom." I fought back the emotion building inside me. I didn't want her to see a tear forming because that would make her cry—without a doubt.

"I know you hate when I ask this, but did you grab your prescription the other day? If not, I can get it for you."

"Yeah, I did. It's been helping."

Allergies had always been my Achilles heel. They were far

worse when I stayed in the country. My severe allergies must have been God's way of saying that the farming life wasn't for me.

"That's good since you might be stuck out here for a while, which is a perfect segue to why I called. Will you be able to house-sit while we're in Hawaii?" She smiled as she asked.

My parents were heading to Hawaii for their anniversary; it had somehow slipped my mind. I might have been pre-occupied. They planned to be gone for a month and had an itinerary for six weeks *if they liked it*. Hawaii wasn't a bad anniversary gift. I wouldn't say that my parents were wealthy, but we were among the most affluent families in Nash County. Mom was a pharmacist, and Dad owned a large grain farm. They had planned their vacation so that Dad could return home before the fall harvest.

It would be nice to spend time at the homestead by myself. It would give me additional time to think. I could head off into the woods behind our house and meditate. I'd always wanted to do that.

"Yeah, I suppose I can be a sweetheart and do that for you guys. Do I need to be out here every night?"

"You *are* a sweetheart, Tyler. No, not every night, but at least a few nights per week. Kourt *should* be here, but we can't count on her. She'll be in and out as usual. She said she'd try to give you a heads-up when she won't be here." My mom paused, and I already knew what was coming. "Are you sure you don't want to talk?" She must have been apprehensive about asking, hoping that I wouldn't lash out.

I wanted to snap back, but I restrained myself. "Yeah, I'm sure. No worries. I'm not sure what Kourt or Marcy told you; I'm sure Mike probably told his mom all about what happened." I narrowed my eyes, which she met with a guilty look. "But don't worry. Like I said, I'm fabulous."

My mom's concern was pure instinct, a mother's love. She knew I was keeping something from her, but I kept shooting down her valid concerns. She used to annoy me when she'd ask when Brit and I would have kids, but she'd eased off the gas lately. Maybe there was a reason why.

"Okay, okay, I get it. If you say everything is fine, then I believe you." She relented and switched gears back to house-sitting. "So we'll be leaving on July seventeenth. You need to stay out here for at least the first few nights. Enough people know we're gone, and you never who might try to do something."

"No problem. I hope you guys have a great time. You better bring me back a pineapple."

She laughed. "Oh, I almost forgot. Give GG a call; he misses talking to you." By "GG," she meant her father-in-law—my Grandpa Gene. All the cousins had always called him GG.

"Will do. I'm going to take a nap downstairs—haven't been sleeping well."

I bounded down the staircase before she could pounce on my last comment. The basement was the only carpeted area of the house. Its crown jewel was a large entertainment area with a 60" TV, Playstation 4, and a Bose surround system.

A dark gray L-sectional and a red Bulldogs bean bag chair hovered around the TV. Two guest bedrooms and a stocked bar also graced the basement. The bar was great for entertaining friends back in high school—when my parents left town.

I kicked back on the sectional and checked to see if there was anything good recorded on the DVR. There were several corny sitcoms, but nothing caught my eye until I found an old episode of *Seinfeld*. I'd watched the episode numerous times before: Jerry was dating an amazing woman, but his friends kept telling him that she was flawed. Fitting enough. I turned it on, but I was out within minutes.

I awoke to the sound of my mom and dad speaking in hushed tones upstairs. I walked over to the staircase and sidled up a few steps in an attempt to hear their conversation.

"What did he say when you asked?" my dad said—just above a whisper.

"He didn't say much; it was so hard to get anything out of him. You know how he can be when we talk about Britney," my mom whispered back.

I advanced a couple more steps, careful not to let the stairs creak beneath my weight. The more I tried to be quiet, the more noise I usually made. It wasn't the first time I'd tried to sneak up the stairs to overhear a conversation. I did the same thing when my mom and dad would talk about Kourt's problems or her boyfriends. It always cracked me up to hear them bash the losers she dated. They were always so concerned she'd run off and they would never see her again.

"I don't understand how he can still be with her. It's not right. Do you think he's living in denial?" my dad said. He added something else, but I couldn't make it out.

I took another step, holding my breath and bracing myself for a loud creak. Nothing.

SHE'S TOXIC

"He told me not to worry, Wade. Maybe we should let it go and have faith."

The onslaught was never ending. Now my dad had joined in, and he wasn't easily swayed. It would have taken much more than a few cautionary words from Marcy Thomas to concern him. Then again, I had become a disappointment. It's easier to find fault with a disappointment. I got away with everything in high school because of my success, but life was different now, as much as I hated to admit the truth.

"I'm not so sure, but if he insists everything is okay, then maybe it is," my dad said. "Who are we to say? We don't know what's going on with them."

"I wonder if he even knows or remembers. It scares me too, considering what he's been through."

"All we can do is step back and let it take its course." My dad's voice became more confident. "He can take care of himself, Jackie. He's a strong boy."

"I sure hope so," my mom said.

My parents joined in an embrace and kissed. Even at twenty-one, I still didn't want to hear that.

"Ty? Are you awake?" My mom yelled.

I crept back down the steps and tiptoed my way to the couch.

"What? Yeah, I am now. What's going on?"

"Dinner will be ready in fifteen minutes if you're hungry. I'm not sure if you'll like what I made, but it's a free meal."

Hell of a plan. A guy needs to eat and a home-cooked meal may have been just what the doctor ordered. I turned off the TV and jogged up the stairs.

"There he is," my dad said as I summited the stairs. "Good morning."

"Ha ha. Funny," I responded. I took a seat at the table across from my dad. Dad would tell us *Good morning* whenever we woke up late or from afternoon naps

My dad's dark eyes were about even with the top of my head (when standing). He would have been muscular enough by virtue of working on the farm, but he also made time to lift. His bench press total crushed mine, even when I was lifting for football.

I scarfed down two plates of sweet potato lasagna and five pieces of garlic bread. It wasn't the typical country meal, but my mom was on a meatless kick. She continued to use copious amounts of high-fat dairy products, so it wasn't much healthier than anything else she could have made.

"So where did you run off to this afternoon?" my mom asked as I opened the door to leave.

"Huh? What do you mean? I was taking a nap."

"I was sure you left, but I was busy trying to finish laundry."

I was confused. I knew I'd slept the entire afternoon.

At least I thought I had.

Seven

After listening to my parents' *riveting* conversation, I made plans to watch a movie back in Reedville with Brit. During the drive back, I remembered our first date, back when life made sense. I needed to recapture those feelings to remind myself that my life was once amazing, and still could be. I wanted to believe that I'd misinterpreted my friends and family in some critical way.

Our first date was the night after we met at the football game. A quick turnaround, but I had to see her again. She didn't have her license and had an eleven o'clock curfew, so dating her would be a little different than what I was used to.

I drove past her house at quarter to six, but decided to make a large circle around town to kill time. Even though she was only a freshman, I'd blow it if I looked too desperate.

I knew a senior who had fallen hard for a freshman the year before. He had suffocated her by coming on too strong, too early, and she didn't want to see him anymore. It crushed him, even though he had plenty of other options. His ego probably got the better of him. I didn't want to repeat his mistakes.

Britney walked out of the house moments after I pulled into the drive. I respected that she wasn't forcing me to walk to the door and meet her parents on the first date.

Her appearance blew me away. Wedge sandals, jean shorts, and a low-cut pink blouse had replaced her cheerleading attire.

The girl was going to get me in trouble.

I opened the passenger-side door like a true gentleman. It might have been the first and last time, but it would make one hell of a first impression, especially if her parents looked out the window. Considering I was a junior dating their freshman daughter, I knew they were probably spying.

"Awww, are you opening the door for me?" she cooed. She was glowing.

I was captivated, amazed, mesmerized: all the above.

"I need to be sweet so you won't kidnap me." She giggled. I smiled and gave her a quick hug before letting her inside and shutting the door. I was careful not to let the hug last too long because of those pesky parents—who I clearly noticed sneaking an obvious peak from behind the "closed" curtains.

I was melting like a lovesick schoolboy. I looked over and smiled, which she returned in spades.

"So are you ready to lose at mini golf?" she asked. Her face was serious, but she fell into laughter after a brief second.

"You have no idea what kind of trouble you're getting yourself into, Miss Boyer. I'm gonna beat your butt." I kept my straight face.

She laughed. "Uh huh, sure. At least you talk a big game."

"I'll back it up, don't you worry." I winked and said, "Okay, I

SHE'S TOXIC

have a serious question for you. If you answer correctly, you might win a gold star from me, and I rarely hand those out."

"A gold star? Me? Tonight keeps getting better and better."

"This is serious." I couldn't help but laugh a little. "Okay, so what kind of music do you like?" The radio was off, but I had several CDs loaded on standby.

"That's your serious question?" She laughed. "Ummm, I like just about everything. I like country and anything that's current. And I love Taylor Swift."

"Ah, how did you know? Taylor Swift is my weakness." I was dead serious. I loved Taylor Swift, always had. Her music was soothing, especially her country music.

She cracked up. "You're joking, right?"

"Nope. My favorite Taylor Swift songs are 'Story of Us,' 'Fearless,' and 'Love Story.'"

"Oh my gosh, you are serious! My favorite is 'Fearless.'"

"Well, Miss Boyer, I've given this some serious consideration; I'm awarding you with your first gold star. This is a high honor. It's not quite a platinum star, but you'll get there someday if you play your cards right."

"Yes!" She pumped her little fist into the air then fell back into her seat laughing. "Don't you worry; I'll earn that platinum star. I know it!"

"*I won't worry my pretty little mind.*" I smiled after referencing the Taylor Swift song, "Ours."

"Awww, you're so cute. But that doesn't mean I'm going to take it easy on you. No sireee. You are going down tonight, Mister Reynolds."

The mini golf course was located in Lincoln, which wasn't much more enticing than Gentry. It had twice the population and two interstates running through, but other than that, the towns were about the same.

I played a Taylor Swift CD, and we continued to joke around with each other during the thirty-minute drive. I'm not sure I stopped smiling once during the trip. I felt like a kid waking up to a fresh blanket of snow on Christmas morning.

"Are you ready to lose?" Britney taunted me as we walked toward the golf course. She skipped ahead but turned back and said, "I am the best miniature golfer you've ever seen!"

"You're not *that* short. It's not fair to call yourself miniature."

"Oh, you're so funny. And I noticed you avoided my question. That's because you know that you're about to lose," she said the last four words in singsong.

"Yeah, you better keep walking away. You wouldn't say that to my face."

She skipped ahead. "You're scared."

"Hush now, BB. Or I won't take it easy on you."

"BB?" She laughed. "What's that mean?"

"You know, Britney Boyer. Both of your initials put together: BB." I curled my lips into a half-smile.

"I kinda like it. It's cute. But now I need a name for you."

I left her deep in thought as I ordered our games. After I ordered, she said, "I got it! I know what I can call you. Are you ready to be blown away with this amazing name?"

I collected our putters and balls; I had to pause for a moment to compose myself before turning around. I must have had the goofiest smile on my face while listening to her carry on. After a brief delay, I turned back to her.

"Okay, enlighten me, BB."

"Yeah, I do like that name. Okay, I will call you … we need a drumroll. I will call you My-Ty! You know, it's like that drink, but it's also like, *My*-Ty."

"Oh, so you think I'm yours already?" I smiled and raised my eyebrows. She blushed under the weight of my knowing question.

She knew that *I knew*. I knew that *she knew*.

It was shaping up to be the best date of my life. I wasn't quite seventeen at the time—not until October, so I didn't have a considerable frame of reference, but I was head over heels.

Was it possible to fall in love so young? I couldn't even think straight when I was around her. She had an energy that radiated positivity, and I broke into a smile whenever I looked at her. I needed to play it cool though and somehow not let her know just how much I liked her.

"I beat you! I can't believe I won," she said as we walked across the adjoining parking lots to the frozen yogurt stand. The stars twinkled overhead.

"Pshhh. You had an unfair advantage. You're a miniature golfer playing miniature golf; that's not cool. I had to lean down so much farther to hit the ball."

"Whatever!" She inched closer, begging me to take her in my arms. "Tall guys can be good golfers too. That's no excuse. You just suck! Admit it."

"Hey now." My eyes met hers as I pulled her into me, pausing for a moment. We were standing in the middle of the parking lot.

People were walking around us, but I didn't care. We had been in our own little world all night.

"*Hey now*, what? What are you going to do about it, My-Ty?"

I looked in her eyes, then at her lips, then back to her eyes. "This." I leaned down and pressed my lips against hers. I kissed her with my lips closed for several seconds before allowing my tongue to push her lips apart. She returned my advance. Her body went limp in my arms. Her heartbeat intensified. I gave her top lip a parting kiss as I backed away. When I opened my eyes, she grinned back at me with her eyes still closed, skin flushed. I noticed my breath had become short. I blinked, wondering if I should pinch myself. It felt like a dream.

Her eyelids fluttered open, her breathing still short. "Wow. That was incredible."

"Yes, it was. We might have to do that again sometime," I said. Another couple walked by; the guy gave me a thumbs-up.

"If you're lucky." She tried to hold a straight face, but she relented. She bit her lip and giggled.

While we were ordering our frozen yogurt, Britney received a notification on her phone. She let out an exasperated sigh and excused herself. She walked over to the hot pink benches nestled behind the stand. I watched as she brushed her hair out of her eyes and typed away. She suddenly wasn't as cheerful as she had been during our entire date. I didn't know what she was dealing with, but it wasn't any of my business.

I waited a minute before walking over to her. She slipped her phone in her pocket as I handed her a strawberry sundae sprinkled with chopped peanuts.

SHE'S TOXIC

"You left me," I joked.

"I promise I'll never leave you again." She smiled and took a bite. "This is amazing." She was back to her usual self—well, as far as I knew.

Her phone vibrated.

"Ughh, I'm sorry. I feel terrible. I should have turned my phone off earlier." She frowned and powered it down. "There's a guy who is obsessed with me. It's kinda creepy. He keeps texting me and trying to call me." She took another small bite of her sundae.

"No need for you to be sorry. I'm sorry you have a guy who's obsessed with you. I can't say I blame him though." I reached over and rubbed her back. The corners of her lip curled into a grin as she leaned into me.

"Gosh, you're such the sweet talker."

"Well you're kind of awesome." I pulled her close, leaning in for another kiss. When my lips met hers, time stood still. I somehow already knew that I'd love Britney for the rest of my life.

A beautiful memory, but that's all it was—a memory from a time that no longer existed. I was someone else, and so was she. I believed our love was strong and would continue to persevere, but my doubts were increasing by the day.

I wanted to call Mike and chastise him for talking to his mom, but I wasn't ready yet. I was upset with him, but also embarrassed about the rift between us. I regretted what I'd said, but he could have called me. Nothing was stopping him from apologizing. I hated to be stubborn, but I had to take a stand.

I cleared the thoughts from my mind as I pulled into Gentry's two-screen movie theater. I would not let outside influences capsize my relationship.

We watched the movie without incident and shared several laughs together. It was just another normal night out, for a while anyway.

As we were leaving the theater, an unfamiliar voice called out, "Mr. Reynolds?" I turned toward the voice to see a tall man in dark blue jeans and a long-sleeve white oxford. He had blue eyes, a thick crop of blonde hair, and a chiseled jawline. Yes, he was an attractive man. "Are you Mr. Tyler Reynolds?" His expression was somber.

I kissed Brit goodbye. "I need to see what this is about. See you later."

"You need to see what what's about?"

"There's a guy coming over here asking for me. I've never seen him in my life."

She looked back. "Oh, okay. I'm sure it'll be fine. Maybe he's here to offer you a scholarship. Good luck." She smiled and leaned into me. "I'll see you later, baby."

I kissed her before responding to the unknown man. "Yeah, I'm Ty Reynolds. What's this about?"

"Girlfriend?" He asked, nodding toward Britney as she disappeared around the corner. "She's a cutie, Tyler. That's the kind of girl a guy would never want to lose. You'd hang on to a girl like that forever."

The bluntness silenced me for a moment. "Yeah, Britney is great. We've been together since high school," I said.

SHE'S TOXIC

"Since high school? That's hard to believe these days. It's hard to imagine people sticking together like that. But you're not too old, are you? Either way, not bad, son." He gave me a pat on the back; wasn't expecting that either.

I realized that he kind of reminded me of the actor, Matthew McConaughey. I was waiting for an *all right, all right, all right*. But I still didn't know who he was. Who approaches a random stranger and comments on the guy's girlfriend? I wasn't a random stranger to him though; somehow he already knew me. He might have known me from football; everyone else did.

"Thanks, I guess. So what's this about?"

"I apologize, Ty. I am Ronnie Minden. Detective Ronnie Minden. I'm actually from Gentry, a little older than you though." He coughed to clear his throat.

"Nice to meet you," I obliged, shaking his outstretched hand. His handshake was one of the firmest I'd ever experienced. He squeezed my hand hard. I wondered if he would ever let go. "Is there something I can help you with?"

The handshake finally ended; blood flow returned to my right hand.

"I'm not sure if you'll be able to help; we'll have to play that one by ear. But I do have some news for you, Ty. Would you prefer to speak somewhere else?" He reached into his briefcase and pulled out a small thermos. "These are difficult times. I often need a little pick-me-up to get me through the day—snuck a little Jack in here this afternoon. You want some?" I thought he must have been joking, but his face was sober.

"No, I'm good. We can talk here."

"Ah, I suppose we can. It's a quiet parking lot, not too many cars driving around."

"That's fine with me. I just want to know what's going on."

"I hate to be the one to tell you this, son, on such a beautiful night, but there has been an accident involving Michael Thomas."

Eight

My knees gave out. I crashed to the pavement. It must have hurt on some level, but I was impervious to the pain.

"An accident? Is he okay?"

"I'm afraid not, Ty. There's no easy way to say this and I'm sorry to be the one to tell you, but Michael Thomas passed away earlier this afternoon. I realize words don't mean much at a time like this, but I am truly sorry for your loss."

"What? Are you sure it was Mike? What in the hell is going on?" A lump formed in my throat. My stomach sank.

"I'm sorry and you have my condolences. The medics did all they could upon arriving, but it was too late. I'm lucky I found you in this parking lot though. I went out to your parents' house, but they weren't home. I ran into your sister as I was leaving—or at least I assumed she was your sister, Kourtney? She said that you would be at the movies with your girlfriend. Again, Ty, I'm sorry to be the one to break the news."

"No. No, that's bullshit. There's no way that Mike's dead." My heart was beating out of my chest, my head was buzzing, and my world was spinning. My immediate surroundings morphed into an indistinguishable blur.

The detective continued talking, but his words sped past me—something about blunt-force trauma and multiple, deep lacerations to the torso. Two couples walked by, each person gave me a concerned look. My mind went back to the good times Mike and I had shared, from playing sports as little kids, to riding four-wheelers, to splitting a case of beer while fishing. Then back to that damn night. The last night I saw him. I was going to vomit.

"Mr. Reynolds," the detective brought me back to reality as he continued, "I'm afraid there's more. We have reason to suspect foul play, and that's why I'm here. I'm conducting an investigation—well, our office will be investigating his unfortunate and untimely death. I would appreciate if you could let me know of anyone who may have had a grudge against Mr. Thomas."

I had nothing to say.

"I'm sorry for my insensitivity. I realize this isn't the best time. These things aren't easy on anyone. And I'm sorry I had to be the one to tell you about your friend. I truly am. I understand that you're in no position to talk tonight, but please let me know if anything comes to mind."

Most of the detective's words continued to ricochet off me. It wasn't possible. My friend couldn't be dead. I'd just talked to him. *No, I hadn't just talked to him.* I was too stubborn and held onto my foolish pride. Yep, I was going to be sick. I puked right there in the parking lot.

The detective finally left me alone with my thoughts and tears. I reasoned there had to be some kind of mistake. I fumbled for

SHE'S TOXIC

my phone and did something I should have done long before this moment.

Tears rolled as I waited for my friend to answer.

One ring.

Two rings.

Three.

Four. *There's no way he could be gone. Not Mike ...*

Five. *No, not my best friend, no way ... Impossible ...*

Then to voicemail. I was out of thoughts. A vast nothingness surrounded me, crushing and evaporating everything I thought I knew. I couldn't breathe.

I hung up before his greeting; I couldn't bear to hear his voice. I finally gasped for air.

The silence was killing me. I needed to talk to someone, so I tried my sister. She picked up after the second ring.

"Hey, Kourt, I'm sorry it's so late." The prevailing state of shock and numbness allowed me to speak without sobbing, but I wasn't sure if my words were audible.

"Hey brother, it's not that late. What's going on? Is everything okay?"

"It's Mike." I took a deep breath. It hurt bad enough just to think about what had happened, but this would hurt so much more. It was as if verbalizing the event would make it more of an actuality. If it stayed inside my head, maybe it would be easier to move on. Or maybe telling someone would be cathartic.

"Ty? What happened? Are you there?"

"Sorry. A detective came by—" The words didn't come. My entire body burned from the inside—a cauldron of agony. The tears were rushing forward with a vengeance, like rapids around a river bend. I was about to unload.

"Ty?"

"Mike's dead." I lost the tenuous hold on my tears and unleashed them into the phone.

"Oh. My. God. Ty, I'm so sorry. Where are you?"

"I'm in the parking lot at the movie theater—in Gentry. I watched a movie with Brit, then the detective caught me as we were leaving." I tried to get the words out between sobs. I wasn't sure how she could have understood me.

"Oh my God. I'm at a friend's house, but I'll drive over there if you need to talk. Damn, I'm so sorry. This is unbelievable. Total déjà vu. I'm so sorry."

"No, that's okay. I want to be alone tonight."

"If there's anything I can do, please let me know. I'm here for you, brother. I'll always be here for you. I love you so much."

We ended our call.

I wanted to hide out in Reedville by myself, at least until the funeral—allow the dust to settle. Brit had planned to meet me at my apartment, but I told her to stay at her parents' house because I wasn't feeling well. I didn't want to communicate with anyone, but she was one of the last people I wanted to see. Brit was the reason Mike and I had fought and the reason we didn't get to speak to each other again.

I realized that Mike and Brit weren't sneaking around behind my back. Or maybe they were; maybe Mike had decided to come clean and Brit had to keep him quiet. Mike had acted out of the ordinary the last time we spoke, but she couldn't have murdered him. No, that would be insane. My thoughts were all over the place. I needed to pull myself back together.

My mom told me to call my grandpa, so with a trembling hand, I called him. I didn't want to worry him with the news but sought reassurance from his voice. After dialing, I realized it was past ten, but he picked up after the second ring.

"Tyler, it's great to hear from you. Shouldn't you be out with a pretty girl?"

A weak laugh snaked its way through the pain. "I was with one earlier tonight. How are you doing? Sorry it's late."

"No, not at all. I was up watching a replay of the Cardinals beating Cubs yesterday. Carlos Martinez is 9-3 now." My grandpa liked nothing more than to watch the Cardinals win and the Cubs lose. "Tyler, I'm great. Every day I wake up above ground is a beautiful day."

"Yep. We should get pizza soon." If I said any more, I was going to burst into tears.

"Just say when. I don't mean to pry, and you don't have to say a word, but you don't sound like yourself." I bit my lip to keep the waterworks at bay. "You're a strong boy. You've already suffered through more than most young men your age. But sadly, the peaks and valleys are a part of life. You are resilient and you will come out of this stronger than you ever thought possible. Trust me; I know. It's crucial to remain positive and optimistic."

"Thanks, GG. I'll try, but sometimes it's hard." I choked on the last few words.

"Yes, life can be tough. It's important to stay the course—circumstances will improve. You'll be all right."

"Thank you." I told him I needed to go. He made sure I understood that I could call whenever I needed to talk, even in the middle of the night.

I found my Jeep under the pale glow of the parking lot lights. Incessant tears made the drive to Reedville next to impossible.

I endured yet another restless night of sleep. It was becoming a theme. I alternated between wishing I'd called Mike and blaming him for our fight. But then I would consider the comments made by Maddie and my parents regarding Britney—combined with what the detective said about foul play. It was too much.

Minden said that Mike died in the afternoon, so I assumed his accident must have occurred while I was out at my parents'—before the movie.

I had no idea where Brit was or what she was doing earlier in the day. I didn't want to ask her because it seemed so asinine. She couldn't have done anything so drastic.

I'd dreamt of a large pile-up—cars crashing into each other, one after another. Mike, pinned beneath the carnage, kept calling out for help. I couldn't reach him. But I soon realized that the crashing noises weren't coming from my dream, but from someone knocking on my front door.

"Ty! Let me in!" Brit yelled as she pounded away.

Thump. Thump. Thump.

My room was bright, illuminated by a sun that was already high in the sky; it must have been close to noon. My original intention had been to avoid human contact, but I needed to be comforted. I needed someone to tell me it would be okay.

SHE'S TOXIC

"Just a minute," I yelled as I walked from the bedroom to the living room. It was a good thing I'd left my bedroom door open or else I might not have heard her knocking (or screaming). I wondered how long she had been beating down my door.

I opened the door, she hurtled past me.

"Jesus Christ, Ty. What on earth have you been doing all day? It's almost one! You haven't responded to my texts, you haven't answered my calls, and it took you thirty minutes to come to the door. Are you sick?"

"Sorry. I didn't sleep at all last night. I haven't even checked my phone this morning. Thirty minutes, seriously?"

"It felt like thirty minutes. Why didn't you get any sleep last night? Did you have someone over?" She still had no knowledge of Mike's death—at least I hoped she didn't.

"No, I didn't have anyone over; I swear. I wouldn't do that to you," I said as I took her in my arms.

"I didn't think you would, but I wasn't sure. Why didn't you get any sleep? Are you okay?"

"No." I shook my head and released her. I was about to make his death a reality once more. I wanted to put on a strong front, but it was impossible.

"What happened, baby? You can tell me."

"Something bad happened yesterday," I started. I made my way to the couch and took a seat. My head fell into my hands. I wasn't crying yet, but I was close.

She joined me on the couch and put her arm around my shoulders. "It's okay, baby. It's okay."

"Mike died yesterday." I tried to keep myself from breaking

down. "That's why I couldn't sleep. I kept thinking about our fight. I feel so guilty."

"Mike died? No way." She removed her arm and leaned back into the couch. "Do they have any idea what happened to him?"

"Just that he died sometime yesterday. The detective told me they have reason to suspect foul play, but they're not sure what happened." I punched the couch behind me and collapsed upon myself. "God, I'd give anything to have him back."

"I'm so sorry, Ty." She paused. "Do they have any suspects?"

"What? Why would you ask me that?" I looked up from my prone position and burned a hole through her with my eyes.

"You mentioned foul play, so I was wondering if they had any suspects, or if they had made an arrest. Sorry, I didn't mean it like that. I don't know what else to say. It's terrible." She hugged me hard. "I can't begin to tell you how sorry I am."

Reasonable response, but I had been up all night wondering who could have been responsible. It wasn't fair to suspect that Brit had anything to do with Mike's death. Despite Mike's warnings, Maddie's phone call, and my parents' discreet conversation, Brit hadn't done anything violent. Not yet.

"I'm sorry, BB." I returned her hug, caressing her back through her red tank.

"You have no reason to be sorry, baby. I'm sorry. Damn, I feel so bad. It's my fault you two haven't talked since then—you two fought about me."

The fight had indeed been about Brit, but I couldn't blame her—at least I didn't want to. Her professed remorse was unconvincing; her response to the news of his death was unsettling. I thought about how the detective stressed that I wouldn't want to let go of a girl like her. I wondered if he already knew about her involvement at that point or had a healthy degree of suspicion.

She had always been there for me, so I wanted to give her the benefit of the doubt. She consoled me and brought me out of my rut after I'd lost my football scholarship. She had continued to be there for me even after my fall from grace. It was easy to love me when I was a star, but she had stayed with me, and that's what made her so special.

"No, baby, it's not your fault." I kissed her forehead, pulled back, and looked into her eyes while sliding my fingertips down her cheek, to her neck. She closed her eyes and moved closer. I ran both hands through her hair, to the back of her head, and pulled her into me—my lips collided with hers.

She responded to my advance, "Oh, Ty."

"I love you, baby." I whispered, continuing to kiss her lips, and then her neck. Sex hadn't been on the agenda, but maybe it would help clear my mind, ease my concerns—my pain, my guilt. Maybe it was just what I needed.

"Right here?" She asked. We were still on the couch.

In that moment, I blamed her. I blamed her for everything. She was the reason I'd fought with Mike. She was the reason I would never talk to my friend again.

I pulled her hair back and rasped into her ear, "Yes."

Nine

Friday morning was miserable. It was cold, it was raining, and I was attending the funeral of my best friend. It was early July, but the thermometer was stuck in the fifties. A cold front had blasted through the area, leaving a light drizzle and blustery winds in its wake. Dark gray clouds hung overhead. It had been three days since Mike's death and too long since we had last spoken.

His funeral was held at Holy Cross Lutheran Church, located along one of the straight country roads between Gentry and my parents' house. The church was first constructed in 1916 but was decimated by a lightning strike in 1934. As a result, it had been rebuilt. They had tried to keep the new design true to the original, but with more effective lightning rods of course.

They had learned from their mistake.

The church was a small brick building complete with a bell tower. The bell rang every Sunday morning at nine and at weddings and funerals. One was a celebration, the other a calamitous time of mourning. I'd previously attended funerals for my great-grandparents, but nothing had prepared me for this.

"Hey babe, are you okay?" Brit asked as we walked toward the imposing front doors of the church.

Mike was inside, lifeless atop a bed of satin. How in the hell could I be okay?

"Yeah, I'm okay." I lied. "I love you." I tried to maintain a strong front, but I was inconsolable on the inside. The northwest wind kicked up, forcing me away from the front of the church. But I pushed through.

"I love you, too," she whispered into my ear, then nibbled on my earlobe—taking advantage of her proximity. Inappropriate considering the circumstance, but I smiled.

I brushed my hand across her lower back and let it come to rest around her hip. I pulled her into me and kissed her cheek. Brit was there for me, and she was all I needed.

I had talked to Brit and Kourt about Mike's death, and my mom had also called to say she was "so sorry" and to remind me of house-sitting in two weeks. But otherwise, I'd stayed in Reedville and tried to ignore human contact. It was all going to be the same thing: *I'm sorry, Ty. Please let me know if there's anything I can do, Ty.* I didn't want to deal with that shit.

My smile faded upon seeing Mike's parents. They were standing outside the church, under the stone awning jutting outward from the brick facade.

I wasn't ready to face them. Robert Thomas donned a well-fitted black suit with a dark green tie. Marcy was wearing a mid-length black dress with matching heels. She was young, lower forties, about the same as my mom. I had known Mike's parents just as long as I'd known Mike.

As I approached, Marcy tried her best to smile. "Tyler, thank you so much for coming."

"I'm so sorry, Marcy." I hugged her, not knowing what else to say or do. I tried to maintain my composure, tried to avoid breaking down.

"There, there. He's in a better place now. It just happened a little sooner than we would have liked." A tear rolled down her face. Robert draped his arm around his wife's shoulders.

I shook Robert's hand before walking away. We approached the mahogany casket at the head of the church. I saw some of Mike's other family members lined around the casket. A few guys from high school sat in the pews, including Jason, who gave me an ever-so-slight head nod. There weren't as many classmates as I expected, but that was probably the product of being a few years removed from high school—bonds of friendship had already diminished between many. Such is growing up and moving on.

"Can I have a minute with him?" I said to Brit, kissing her forehead before turning back to face the casket. I finally had my chance to apologize.

I wanted to shake him and tell him that he couldn't be dead. He had a long life ahead of him; we had more experiences to enjoy. No words escaped my lips as I stared at the casket. My expression was surely blank, but my outward placidness merely masked the tumult inside.

I thought of how sorry I was for what I'd said to him. I'd told him to go fuck himself, I'd refused to hear him out, and I didn't apologize until it was too late. Foolish pride ruined a lifelong friendship. I was launched into a viper pit of regret.

SHE'S TOXIC

"I'm sorry," I choked out, wiping the tears from my face. I wasn't sure if I was saying sorry to him or myself—maybe both. I'd saddled myself with an unshakable depth of guilt.

I pulled myself away before I broke down. Brit nudged me in the back—a little too eager to move on. Then again, I wasn't sure how long I had been standing there. It may have been a minute, but it may have been fifteen—I couldn't be certain.

I was immersed in a fog of memories and pain. I thought of what my grandpa had said during our phone call, but I wasn't sure how to remain optimistic at a time like this.

"Ready?" Brit asked.

We made our way around the pews and found seats in the balcony. I wanted to be closer during the service, but we had arrived too late, thanks to Brit.

My attention was everywhere except on the priest. I thought about Mike, thought about our conversation, and wondered how I was ever going to move past his death. I felt guilty for multiple reasons. I should have talked to him after our fight. I also wished that I could have been there when it happened. Maybe I could have somehow prevented his death.

The funeral concluded, and we traversed the quarter-mile hike to the cemetery for the burial. Rain continued to fall during the supplementary proceeding. Some of the attendees let the rain soak through their clothes, but others came prepared with umbrellas—most were black, but there was a spattering of color among the gloom. I could have seen the colored umbrellas as a beacon of hope, but they registered as painful reminders of a bright past and of a lost future.

I let the rain soak through my suit. Brit coaxed me to stand under her umbrella, but I kept gliding away, preferring to let the water run off the lip of the umbrella and onto my face. I just wanted to get the afternoon behind me.

The lowering of his body into the ground was the most painful aspect of the proceeding. I tried to stay composed, but tears streamed down my face. My tears were in a frenzied competition with the rain. At first, I tried to brush the tears away, but in time, I let them take their course, unabated.

After Mike was in the ground, we walked through the muddy mess, back to Brit's car. The rain had slowed to a drizzle, but the wind was unrelenting.

I was ready to make my escape, but Jason caught up with me before I could sneak away.

"Ty, wait up," Jason said just as I opened the door.

"I'm getting in the car. It's too cold out here," Brit said.

I ignored her. "Hey," I said to Jason.

"I hate these things. I never know what to say. How are you holding up? Is she okay?" he asked as he motioned toward Brit.

"Yeah, why do you ask?" I sounded sharper than intended.

"I'm sorry, it's just because of what you said on the drive back to your apartment—after you and Mike had that fight."

"All is well, other than the obvious. I wish I could talk to him again. It doesn't seem real." I rubbed my face with both hands, wiping the moisture onto my already saturated pants.

"Yeah, these things are never easy. Well, I'm sure you'll get another chance someday," Jason replied with a tinge of optimism.

"Yeah, I guess you're right."

SHE'S TOXIC

"Amen, brother. Amen. Hey, I need to get going though. Great talking to you and I hope you and Britney work out. You deserve to be happy, Ty." He walked away, but after an extended pause, he turned back to face me. "It's crazy how much our lives have changed, but I don't have to tell you that. Man, I'd give anything to have everyone back at the pond, but that's impossible now. Life changes, doesn't it?"

I let the conversation die there. I needed to get back to Reedville.

I hopped into the passenger side of Brit's Toyota Corolla. I feared an inquisition regarding the conversation. Instead, she smiled. If she was masking her guilt, she was doing it well.

Jason's statements lingered with me throughout the ride back to my apartment. I continued to turn over the last words I'd shared with Mike. It wasn't fair that we didn't get the chance to reconcile. My stomach was in knots, so many questions remained unanswered. My foremost concern was what happened the afternoon he died. It was a mystery to everyone. I needed to speak with Detective Minden to see if they had made any progress on the case.

For some reason, I remembered the car Brit drove in high school, her silver Toyota Celica. "I miss your old car."

"My old car? What made you think of that?"

"I don't know. I've been thinking about high school lately."

Brit looked at me with sad eyes. "I'm sorry, Ty." She placed her hand on my arm. "I can't even begin to imagine what you're going through, but we'll get through this. I'm here for you no matter what happens."

We arrived back in Reedville. Brit walked up the narrow stairway to my apartment, several steps ahead of me.

I lingered behind her. I had an impulse to get in my Jeep and take off. If I drove through the night, I'd be in Florida by sunrise. I wasn't sure what I would do when I got there, but at least I'd be able to distance myself from this nightmare. But I couldn't leave Brit. I would never leave Brit.

At least that's what I'd believed until that afternoon.

"I can see why you're sad baby, but it will be okay. It wasn't like he was your family or anything," Brit said as she entered the bedroom.

Her comment floored me. I took a deep breath and tried not to lash out. Mike's funeral had worn me down and it wouldn't have taken much to set me off. Silence prevailed as I considered the best way to respond. I followed her into the bedroom and watched her change clothes in the mirror. She slipped into a pair of my basketball shorts and a hoodie.

"He wasn't my family, but he was my best friend. I don't know how you can sit there and make it sound like everything is okay." Despite my best intention, I lashed out, "I mean, seriously, what is wrong with you? How can you be so insensitive? My best friend is dead!" I kicked the wall before collapsing onto my bed. I threw a pillow across the room, missing her by inches.

Brit smiled, somehow unfazed by my response. "I know you miss him. You two have been friends for a long time. I shouldn't say anything, but…" She stood next to me, put her hands on my shoulders, and looked into my eyes. "I'm not sure if I should tell you this. I swore I wouldn't say anything."

SHE'S TOXIC

"Tell me what?" I put my hands on hers. My pulse increased.

"I'm not supposed to tell you this, but ... I talked to Mike yesterday. He said he would be back soon." She grinned from ear-to-ear. She kissed each of my cheeks before kissing my forehead.

The hair stood up on my neck. Goosebumps formed on my limbs. "What did you say?"

Her grin was unwavering. She looked me in the eyes. "He spoke to me because he wasn't sure you were ready. He made me *swear* not to tell you, but I wanted you to feel better."

I looked at her in disbelief; she looked back at me smiling, like some kind of lunatic. "You want me to feel better? It seems like you're trying to piss me off!"

"He thought you might react that way. He said he understood if you weren't ready to see him." She gave my shoulder a shake and walked away. I saw her look into the mirror, still smiling.

"Not ready to see him? That would be impossible."

"Ty, baby, you need to have an open mind like me. Anything is possible. I'll let him know that you said hi."

Ten

The next week crawled by without incident; the Fourth of July came and went without celebration—it always feels so cheap when the Fourth falls on a Sunday. Brit had her summer class throughout the week, so I had plenty of time to spend alone with my thoughts. Considering what she had told me following Mike's funeral, I needed time to myself.

I'd also had to deal with Kourt. We got into a fray after the funeral until I gave in to avoid further conflict. I often had to humor Kourt by agreeing with her—I didn't want her to regress. Talking to her was like trying to poke a sleeping grizzly with a stick. It was often advisable to just keep walking. We would be tag-teaming the house-sitting in a week, and we needed to be on good terms to coordinate the effort.

My attempts at getting back into shape had fallen flat. I went to the Reedville YMCA on the Tuesday following Mike's funeral, but I just sat on a bench and stared at the wall. I sat there in a daze until someone wanted to use it. I muttered an apology and moved to a weight machine—not sure which. All I needed was a place to sit down and break down. By the time I'd left, I'd spent an hour in the weight room and hadn't lifted one weight.

I spent most of the week thinking about Mike and how he had vanished from my life. It didn't even seem real. I remembered the detective telling me his death could have been the result of foul play. I considered what Brit had told me, but I also thought about what my mom had said—that I'd left the house during the afternoon of his accident. Brit could have parked down the road from my parents' house, driven my Jeep, and she might have been working on framing me. It wasn't a thought I wanted to entertain, but it was possible. I guess. By now, I'd realized that anything was possible.

I wasn't answering my phone much. I had several missed calls from the same number, probably Detective Minden. If he needed me, he'd find me.

I was sitting on the couch at my apartment—trying to hatch a plan for my life—when Brit arrived with a cheese pizza from Domino's.

"I brought you a pizza." She placed it on the coffee table. Pizza was the last thing I wanted.

"I've been doing a lot of thinking," I said.

"Sorry, I need to get going. We can talk when I get back later, okay?" She took off for the bathroom.

"Where are you going tonight?" I rose from the couch.

She stopped short and turned to face me. "I told you earlier today, I'm going out with my friends." She seemed annoyed. "Maybe I told you yesterday. I don't remember, but I told you."

I couldn't remember her telling me, but my mind had been all over the place. It shouldn't have mattered—I wanted to be alone, but she annoyed me nonetheless.

I tried to hide my inner conflict.

"Okay. That's cool, I guess," I said. "How should I entertain myself while you go out partying?"

"We're not partying. We'll probably split a bottle of wine and watch a movie. Okay, I lied, we might split two bottles." She laughed. "You should go to The Barnyard and try to unwind. You haven't been sleeping well." She walked toward me and stopped just a few inches away.

Her perfume was strong.

I took her in my arms, taking in her essence. I exhaled. Relaxing was a good idea though I wasn't fond of the way she said it. She was floating along, ignorant to the turmoil surrounding us.

She had acted so strange following Mike's funeral. The comment she made about Mike speaking to her was haunting, not to mention the look in her eyes. I didn't want to broach the subject again, but I had to see if she still believed what she said. Maybe I'd heard her wrong or misinterpreted her—that's what I'd tried to tell myself during the past week.

I'd tried to let it go, but it kept prodding me.

"Have you talked to Mike this week?" I ran one hand through my hair and grimaced, bracing for her answer.

Her eyes twinkled, not quite a glazed-over look, but something was off. "I *told* you, I'm not supposed to say anything. But hold that thought, I need to go to the bathroom real quick."

I'm not supposed to say anything? Yup, she still believed it.

Brit took off for the bathroom. I walked into the kitchen.

SHE'S TOXIC

Mike's warning might have been valid—she wasn't acting right. But I needed more proof of her insanity, especially if I ever needed to convince someone else. She was normal most of the time and had been mentally sound for the better part of five years, but there were these brief moments of instability developing.

I needed a drink for this. I took a deep breath and reached in the fridge for a Bud Light. I popped a top, took a long drink, and walked back to the living room. Brit exited the bathroom and rejoined me.

"Why can't you tell me about Mike?" I asked, setting my beer down next to the pizza.

"Huh? Oh yeah, well there isn't too much to say." Her eyes suddenly seemed more distant. "Mike's appeared to me. He's not ready to show himself to you yet. He doesn't think you'd be able to handle it because of how things ended between you two."

I placed my hand against my forehead. We both collapsed onto the couch. My head ached. I was sweating. I leaned back, away from her. I wasn't sure if she actually believed that Mike had appeared to her or if she was trying to push me.

"He has appeared to you? How?"

She furrowed her brow for about eight seconds, then she looked in my eyes and smiled. "It happens when I'm getting ready for bed, but sometimes it's earlier in the afternoon." Her smile vanished. It looked like she'd seen a ghost.

"When you're getting ready for bed?" I asked.

She was somber, looking somewhere beyond me. "Yes. He's always nice, but he's worried about you. He wants you to move on and be happy." She smiled and nodded.

"Does this happen at your house or here?" I wanted to test her delusion. I was restraining the impulse to erupt on her—like Mt. St. Helens on the Washington countryside.

"He spoke to me last night." She continued to smile. "You were in the shower." She showed a flash of concern. "He said that he needed to hurry because he didn't want to upset you."

"Why did he say that?" I was losing my patience.

"Well he didn't want you to see him, and..." Her look of concern had morphed to a terrified shock. Her mouth dropped open and she shook her head violently. "He doesn't want me to say anything else. No, I can't say anything else." The shaking intensified. "Ty, I'm sorry! I've said too much. Please, no!"

I sprung off the couch at the onset of her head shaking. I took a step back and stood against the wall until she stopped. She was unstable. I needed to be careful. I inched back to the couch, knelt down beside her, and placed my hand on her thigh.

She locked eyes with mine and she smiled.

"It's okay. It's okay." I rubbed her leg. "You don't have to say anything else."

"Thank you, baby. You should go have fun tonight; I know I will." She raised her eyebrows twice while biting her lower lip. "I should get going."

I hesitated before kissing her. I took off for the bathroom to shower and change. Distance would be good. I needed to get my head straight.

As I showered, I couldn't help but wonder what I'd witnessed. I caught myself looking around the shower curtain more than once to see if she had followed me.

SHE'S TOXIC

She was deteriorating, but I had to stand by her. I had to help her. I wondered if Mike's death had triggered her decline. She might have felt responsible for his death, or maybe she was trying to cover her tracks. I also wondered if she was trying to build an insanity defense. There were too many possible explanations to entertain.

After my shower, I drove north to Gentry. I needed to have a good time—I deserved it. The stress of the past few weeks had been wearing me thin, both literally and figuratively. I'd dropped at least five pounds, which wasn't helpful when I wanted to get back on the football team.

I pulled my Jeep to a stop in front of The Barnyard; it was the first time I'd been back since my fight with Mike. I wondered if any of our old classmates would be there, wanting to reminisce about the good old days. It might have been helpful, but I sought to distance myself from any of those discussions.

"Back so soon? Guess ya missed me." Carly smiled as I stepped up to the bar. I sat in the same barstool as the night I fought with Mike. I hoped it would be therapeutic.

"Of course. I guess I need to make up for lost time." It was a Friday night, so Carly was slammed with customers. I excused myself so she wouldn't feel compelled to chat.

A tiny finger poked my lower back as I turned away from the bar. "Hey there, stranger." I spun around and couldn't believe who was standing before me.

Alexa Paulson looked the same. She had long, black hair with hazel eyes, and a petite, slender frame. She'd always been sexy. I remembered high school and those post-game parties at the lake. An undeniable sexual tension had always existed between us, but I had remained strong—I think.

She'd made a pass at me the night I met Brit, but I'd spurned her then. The night I'd always wondered about was during our senior year. Alexa had worn her light brown cowboy boots, embossed with little bluebirds around each ankle. She had smelled of cotton candy and couldn't keep her eyes—or hands—off me. Her boyfriend had stood her up and Brit had left early, so Alexa made her move. And I'd been too drunk to remember exactly what happened from there.

After she graduated, she moved out to Boulder to attend the University of Colorado. I wasn't sure if she was drawn by the legalization of marijuana or the proximity to the Rockies, but I hadn't seen her since she left.

Tonight she was wearing tiny denim shorts and a pastel green unbuttoned top over a tight white tank top. Her small but perky cleavage was prominently displayed. Dark strands of hair crashed upon one another in waves. Her contrasting attire complemented her olive, tanned skin—*Damn.*

She stopped just short of throwing her arms around me. I caught her familiar cotton candy scent, resulting in a long, captivated blink.

"Alexa? Wow. You look amazing. It's been a while."

"Yeah, yeah. You were always so sweet, Ty." She went ahead and wrapped her arms around me. "How have you been?"

"I'm good. I'm still dating Britney." Awkward transition, but I didn't know what else to say.

SHE'S TOXIC

She lost a little color, but flashed a weak smile. "The girl I lost out to. Wow, I still remember that night after the football game. Or I should say, 'I don't remember that night.'" She shook her head and blushed. She had never been the shy type. "You've been together for years. It must be going well."

I looked around the bar, long enough for Alexa to sense that my relationship was in trouble.

"You don't have to say anything." She laughed. "We've all been there, but I'm sorry. Do you want to talk about it?"

Where to begin?

"Nah, let's not talk about that." A rare smile overtook my face. "I came here to have a good time tonight, so that's what I plan on doing. What do you say, will you join me?"

"I'm sure I can help you with that." She returned my smile. "How about some shots?"

It was now hours after drinking with Alexa at The Barnyard. She had vanished and I was alone, attempting to track down a ride. I dialed "BB," but her phone went straight to voicemail, once again. I couldn't remember the last time she answered.

Brit had said she was going to be with friends; I assumed that meant Maddie and Kayla, but maybe not. I needed to find out. I wanted to talk to Maddie, so that made my decision easier to dial Kayla. If Maddie came to get me, I wasn't sure what I might try to do—a sad realization.

"Hello? Ty?" Kayla sounded like she had been sleeping. I wouldn't have called so late if I didn't think she was drinking wine with Britney.

"Hey, is Brit with you?" I felt possessive, but I needed information. My reasoning level wasn't at its peak after drinking.

"Britney?" she sounded surprised. So maybe they weren't together tonight. Maybe Britney was out with someone else.

"Yup, Britney." I laughed. "Is she with you?"

"No, Ty. She's not here." She paused. "Ty... Nevermind, I'm sorry. We can talk about this later. Hang in there, okay?"

"Sorry about what?"

"Ty, I'm sorry. Not now. I need to wake up early tomorrow. I'll talk to you later."

If my mind wasn't racing before, it was speeding laps around Talladega now. Where was Britney and why was Kayla sorry? The preceding pause made it sound that much worse, like Kayla was trying to cover for Brit. I needed to see if I could reach Maddie. Maybe it was nothing. Maybe I was overreacting.

I dialed Maddie.

"Hey, this is Maddie. You know what to do! Muah!" These girls with their voicemail recordings...

Once again, I was stranded outside The Barnyard. I tried to get ahold of Alexa, but she must have already passed out. I didn't have anyone else I could call—at least not anyone I wanted to spend time with.

Walking to my parents' house would get me there by sunrise, or I could throw caution to the wind and drive. Somehow, I convinced myself that I was good enough to make it back to Reedville.

I had nothing left to lose.

Eleven

Britney arrived at my apartment early the next day, armed with the beautiful smile that had almost cost me a football game, except now it meant something different. I couldn't take it. Her smile triggered me, made my palms twitch.

I was sitting on the couch with my hands covering my face. I took a deep breath before looking at her.

"So where were you last night?" I asked.

"Huh? I was drinking wine, just like I told you." She sounded like she had a guilty conscience at first, but then played it off.

"I talked to Kayla last night, and she said you weren't with her." I'd caught her in a lie. I could have let her dig herself into a bigger hole, but I wanted to cut to the chase and figure out where the hell she was.

"So you called Kayla to check on me? Psycho alert." Her eyes widened as her tone became aggressive. She walked back to the bedroom; I followed.

"Well I tried to call you first, but you didn't answer, as always. So then I called Kayla. I also tried Maddie, but she didn't answer."

My behavior was far from psychotic. I wouldn't have had to call her friends if she could be honest with me. Now she was attempting to turn things around, classic deflection.

She released a long sigh before hopping onto the bed. "Geez, you called Maddie too? Wow." She paused as if debating whether she should proceed. "Maybe I was choking down cock somewhere. Did you ever think of that? After all, I am such a filthy little slut." She gave me a sly smile as she made an obscene gesture with her hand, mimicking the insertion of a large penis into her mouth. "I wish I could suck a big one for once." Hysterical laughter.

"What in the hell did you just say?" I stood in the doorway, my hands on my hips in clenched fists.

"Yep, you heard me. I'm tired of having nothing but that little thing." She pointed at me and laughed.

My penis wasn't even small. It wasn't *porn star* huge, but it was far from small. I realized facts didn't matter at that point. She would have called me small even if I resembled a Pringles can.

"Are you serious right now? What has gotten into you?" I was back to the familiar battle of maintaining my composure.

"I already told you what's been in me." She licked her lips. "What are you going to do about it, Ty? Nothing, because you're a little bitch. Besides, didn't you rail Alexa last night?"

"This is unbelievable. I will not sit here and listen to this shit." I turned away. I wasn't even going to address the Alexa comment. After what Brit said, it didn't matter. All I did was have a few drinks with an old friend.

"Where do you think you're going?" she said, still lying on my bed, propped up on an elbow. "You have to fuck me before you go anywhere, if you can even get it up after your long night. And I'm sure that nasty slut gave you a disease."

She was carrying on like a woman possessed. Britney never spoke this way, but now the words were flowing out of her like a perverted mental patient.

"I didn't have sex with anyone. Besides, Alexa isn't a slut."

She laughed. "Those are the best jokes I've heard in a while." She swung her legs around so she was sitting on the edge of the bed. "First, you try to tell me you didn't have sex with Alexa. Ha! Then you try to tell me that she isn't a slut. Oh my God, I can't keep myself from laughing. I've said it once and I'll say it again, Tyler, you're such a little bitch. You're a dirty liar. You had sex with Alexa. Everyone at the bar said you two were all over each other, and then you disappeared together."

I assumed she was bluffing, but she somehow knew I'd hung out with Alexa. Maybe she talked to someone at the bar. But I hadn't disappeared anywhere with her. No way. Even though I was upset with Brit, and worried about her, I wouldn't cheat on her with Alexa.

"Okay, I had a drink with Alexa, but I swear that we didn't have sex. I didn't touch her at all. I swear."

"Ty, you're such a horrible liar." She laughed as she hopped off the bed, skipped past me—humming, and made her way back to the living room.

I followed her and watched her lay down on the couch. She scrutinized the ceiling, mesmerized. Her trance finally broke. "Ty, how stupid do you think I am?"

Well, I don't think you're stupid, but I'm beginning to think you're a psychotic whore.

"I don't think you're stupid. Nothing happened between me and Alexa. She's just an old friend I ran into at the bar. I guess I could have told you, but I didn't think I needed to say anything."

"Blah, blah, blah!" She licked her lower lip and rubbed her neck. "Well let's see if that thing works. Come over here and fuck me, Ty."

"Why would I want to have sex with you right now?"

"I don't want to have sex with you. I want you to *fuck* me. Can't you hear? Give it to me hard, just like the other night."

She fumbled with her phone and turned on an old Ludacris song. She began to strip as Luda bragged about his "sex room." Brit gestured for me to join her. The words of the song blared from her phone.

I was confused, upset, angry, sad—and horny. I was all over the place. I didn't want to give in because she was off her rocker, but on some level, I still loved her, and that song always put me in the mood.

Her figure helped as well. She had retained an incredible body. Flat stomach and curves in all the right places—firm and toned everywhere else. I couldn't take it. So yeah, I gave in. We had sex just like the day after Mike died—no romance at all, but a primal ravaging.

Later that night, I sat on the couch while Brit slept in my room. Brit had reached another level of pushing me over the edge, and I hoped she wouldn't get any worse. I needed to talk to someone who wouldn't irritate me and who might understand what I was going through.

I traipsed over to the bedroom door and peered inside. Brit appeared to be sleeping, but I couldn't be sure. My phone was in my hand—I was ready to dial, but then I heard Brit say something. A loud snore followed. Maybe she was talking in her sleep.

I fumbled with the phone. Ripples of sweat coursed down my palm, causing it to slide from my grasp. I was able to secure the phone with both hands, just before it would have fallen to the floor. I scrolled down to Maddie's number.

My feet carried me through the living room.

"You're cheating on me. I'm going to kill you, Ty."

I stopped in my tracks and turned back toward the bedroom door. I slipped the phone back in my pocket and braced myself, listening for another sound. Silence except for the low hum of my air conditioner. A garbage truck drove by on the street below.

I gathered the courage to walk back to my bedroom. My eyes turned the corner to find Brit still in bed—asleep.

Wow. Her words were disturbing, but at least she wasn't awake. My eyes never left her as I backed into the living room. Once I turned the corner, I removed my phone.

As I opened the door to the stairs, I dialed Maddie's number. I felt like a member of the bomb squad—one wrong move and I would be blown all the way to Chicago.

Maddie answered on the first ring. She was always there for me, at least when she wasn't drunk or passed out.

I whispered, "Hey, give me a minute."

I left the door cracked, slipped down the steps, and out the front door. It was a humid summer night; the crickets were belting out a tune. Sometimes I found their songs soothing, but other times I wanted to stomp them into the ground, crushing them to pieces underneath the weight of my boots. Tonight, I wanted to obliterate them. I hoped Maddie would be able to calm me down.

"Okay, I can talk now. I'm sorry to bug you like this." I leaned against the brick wall of the law office, looking across the street at a small insurance office and a bank, illuminated by the glow of the streetlights.

"Ty, I'm here for you whenever you need to talk. I'm the one who should feel bad. Sorry for what I said the other day. I know that I made you feel uncomfortable by talking about how I didn't know if you're straight. So embarrassing. I shouldn't have said that it would be weird if we ever did anything—like that. Damn, and now I'm basically doing the same thing again. I'm such an idiot." She sighed.

"Maddie, please stop," I interrupted her; she was just going to keep rambling. "You shouldn't feel like an idiot. It feels good talking to you; I enjoy hearing your voice."

"Thanks for making me feel better about it, and yeah," she hesitated, "I like talking to you too."

I felt guilty for my brewing thoughts. I wanted to see her. I wanted to hold her and to be comforted by someone who wasn't Brit. It was a disheartening realization. We might have spent too much time together, and maybe we needed to test our relationship. Maybe we were driving each other away.

"We should get together soon," I said. I couldn't help it. "We could talk more about things. What do you say?"

SHE'S TOXIC

"That would be nice. I'd enjoy that."

After saying good night, I crept up the steps to my apartment, finding it sad that I needed to sneak into *my* place. I made my way through the living room, careful not to bump my TV or trip over the couch. I stumbled to the bedroom door and looked in.

I was mortified by what I saw.

Brit sat on the edge of the bed, staring at the wall, shaking. Her shaking became more violent as she turned in my direction. Her eyes were wide and her teeth chattered. I wanted to rush over to make sure she was okay, but I feared her reaction.

"Brit, you good?" I asked. Her blank eyes met mine. I didn't approach her; instead, I prepared to run if she charged.

But as soon as I asked, she broke out of whatever trance she was in. She smiled. "Yeah, I'm swell, why do you ask? Come back to bed, baby." She lay back in bed and patted the spot next to her. "I want you to cuddle with me."

I wondered if she had any recollection of her shaking episode. It was like she went into a trance.

"Okay, babe," I said, positioning myself on the bed next to her, but not too close.

We lay together in silence for several minutes until she said, "I wish people wouldn't get in the way of our relationship. I don't want to do anything bad, but I might have to be bad." She turned to face me, bringing her hand to my face. I recoiled at her touch. "Ty, I'll do bad things so we can be together."

"Okay, baby."

"I have a knife under the bed just in case."

Twelve

Brit spent most the week at her parents' house when she wasn't at school. She'd also told me *she* needed time to reflect on the fight we had. I was no longer even attempting to train for football. I thought I still had a year of eligibility left even if I missed the upcoming season, but I wasn't sure. I was a pathetic disappointment. So instead, I spent too much time on Facebook—looking at old pictures and posts—and on YouTube.

Britney had come over after her morning class on Friday so we could go shopping in Springfield together. After shopping, we had planned to drive out to my parents' for my first night of house-sitting. The day had gone so well that I'd forgotten about her shaking episodes and the great "choking down cock" fiasco.

It may not have seemed possible, but these were still small hiccups in an otherwise great relationship. It was a relationship that approached half a decade. I wouldn't draw the line yet. We had too much positive history between us that outweighed the recent negativity, and I wanted the relationship to work. We had so much invested.

SHE'S TOXIC

I was beginning to put the recent episodes behind me, but she brought them crashing back as we were leaving the mall.

"I looked at your text messages. Someone else is trying to interfere with our relationship and I can't have that." She smiled as she started her Corolla.

"You looked at my phone?" I asked.

"I'm worried. There are so many people who want to destroy us, can't you see?"

"People don't want to destroy us."

"Maddie does. Why are you texting that whore?" She continued to smile, looking straight ahead as she turned north onto the interstate. "And don't call me 'babe,' fucker."

"Oh yeah, she texted me about Mike. She said she was sorry."

"You're lying. Why must you lie to me, Ty? You texted her first, I saw it. Besides, it's been weeks since Mike's been out of the way."

"I swear it's not what you think. I thought she was your friend anyway... What do you mean he's been *out of the way?*"

"That bitch isn't my friend. Do you two have something going on?" She closed her eyes and put her hand across her forehead; the car drifted onto the shoulder. Before I could say anything, she opened her eyes and pulled the car back to the road.

"No, we're just friends. Baby, I swear, nothing is going on between us. Nothing *was* going on between us and nothing *will ever* happen between us. But what do you mean about Mike being out of the way?" She wasn't going to finagle her way out of answering my question.

"Ugh, you know what I mean. Don't call me 'baby' either."

We were both quiet for a minute. I couldn't think of anything else to say.

"Sometimes I want to go fast." She looked in the rearview mirror and smiled, licking her bottom lip. "Want to see how fast this bitch will go?"

A wave of dread overtook me. "Britney, you don't have to do this." I wondered if I could even call her by her name. I also wondered why I'd let her drive.

"Fuck yeah, I do. You won't learn any other way." She shot me yet another smile. She looked so distant—eyes glazed over.

"Let's go back to Springfield and eat. How about *Antonio's*, baby? They have amazing pizza. I go there with my grandpa and cousins." I wanted to remain civil to calm her down and break her out of her trance (or possession).

"But don't you love me? Don't you want to be with me?" She looked back at me with pouty lips, and then she cackled. "I've said it once and I'll say it again: you are such a little bitch. Look at your face." She continued laughing as she launched her foot into the accelerator. "Oh yeah, here we go. Now we're having fun!"

I looked over at our ever-increasing speed. 77. 94. 108. "Baby, do you think we're going fast enough?" She was barreling down the interstate, weaving in and out of traffic, preferring to coast down the middle of the road when there were no cars.

"What did I say about calling me 'baby'?" It looked like a vein might pop out of her forehead. "Don't you ever fucking listen? Do you think anyone would miss us if we died? That is, anyone other than your whores? Yeah, I'm sure Maddie and that little slut Alexa would miss you. What if I drove the car off the road? I bet we could hit that tree right there. Do you think we could hit that tree? Damn, we passed it." She looked back and pouted her lips just as before. "How about this one? Let's do it."

"What are you doing?" I pleaded. "Please, Britney, stop the damn car. This is not a game." I wanted to push her back and grab the steering wheel but assumed any antagonism would only make things worse. She might jerk the wheel if I made any sudden movements.

"That's right, it's not a game. The game is over. We are both going to die. You better call your mom and tell her you're going to die because you cheated on me. You better call Maddie too. And Alexa. God, she is such a little slut! Fuck that girl! Oh, wait, you already did."

"What? Is that what this is about? I told you that nothing happened. Britney, I love you, but you have to stop. I'll do anything, but please. Please, stop the car. I'm begging you. I love you so much."

The car slowed. 96. 88. 82.

"I love you, too." She smiled, but her eyes reflected the same distant gaze.

I was thunderstruck as I looked over at Britney. What was happening to her? She was getting worse, but I needed to help her find herself. She didn't give up on me when I hit bottom, so I wouldn't give up on her.

A weaker man would have run, turning his back against the woman he loved for so long. The highlights of our relationship continued to outweigh the negative. I needed to remain strong and bring her back to reality.

I took her hand in mine and closed my eyes. I wanted to help her, but I also feared she might kill me in the process.

The next morning, I watched as Brit slept in my old bed—it was the first morning after house-sitting at my parents' house. Brit had convinced me to let her stay over so we could talk in the morning. I hadn't slept a wink. Instead, I'd had visions of Brit retrieving a knife from under the mattress, holding it to my throat as I slept—made it difficult to rest easy.

As I continued to watch her, an engine roared from the east. I looked out the window and noticed a black car that resembled Kourt's, but I didn't think it was her Camaro.

I made it outside by the time the car eased into the driveway. It looked like an undercover Dodge Challenger. I had a good idea who it might be. Sure enough, Detective Minden climbed out of the car. He fanned his face with one hand while pulling his white polo away from his chest with the other.

It was a humid Saturday morning. It had rained at daybreak, but the clouds had broken apart, and the sun was now shining through. The cornfield across from the house glistened with the always-welcome July moisture.

"Whew, it's a sauna out here. How are you holding up? These last few weeks must have been hell for you. I heard through the *wine vines* that you'll be back in Nash County for a few weeks." Minden scratched at the accruing stubble under his chin.

"Well, I'm still here, but that's about it."

"That's good to hear Tyler." Minden glanced around, avoiding eye contact. "I'm glad you're still with us, as we need your help. Now again, I hate to be the one to break more bad news to you." He looked me in the eyes. "As I previously stated, I have reason to suspect foul play in Mike's death."

Old news. But I couldn't believe that anyone would want to murder Mike. I tried to think of anyone who might have had a grudge against him, but I came up empty—except for the woman sleeping in my childhood bed, head on my pillow.

"I understand that you and Mike had a fight before his death. Is that correct?"

"Just two guys arguing over a beer. You don't think I had anything to do with this?" I asked.

"What was the fight about, Ty?"

"What does this have to do with anything?"

"Ty, if you want to help Mike, I need you to be forthcoming with me. Do you understand?" he asked.

"I don't understand what our argument has to do with anything. Am I a suspect?" Was this joker suggesting that I had something to do with Mike's death? I was upset with Mike, but I'd never do anything to *seriously* injure him.

"Woah, woah, I haven't said anything like that, Ty. Please let me finish here. I do not consider you a suspect though I'm alarmed at your defensiveness. It isn't helping your case." He widened his eyes. "But in all honesty, I'm not sure which will be worse news for you. We do have a suspect and it is someone close to you."

His eyes narrowed as he took a long drink from his thermos of what looked like coffee. He licked his lips and smiled. "Sorry, I had to spike my coffee with some Bailey's this morning, and it kicked back a little; just a little though, I mean, it is Bailey's after all." *I should have guessed.*

He regained his seriousness and said, "Ty, do you have any idea where Britney Boyer was the night of Mike's death?"

Britney? I wanted to laugh and throat punch this guy. I had my own concerns and considered the possibility, but I didn't believe she was capable of murder. She had been acting strange, and we were arguing more, but none of our fights had been physical.

"There's no way *Britney* did anything." I remembered what my mom had said about me leaving the house during the afternoon of Mike's death, coupled with the thoughts that Britney may have framed me. But those were irrational mind-ramblings.

Minden took another long swig of his coffee-based concoction, smacking his lips together with some exaggeration before capping his thermos.

"Ty, sometimes we view those closest to us through rose-colored glasses. Do you understand the term? What I'm saying is this: sometimes we don't see what's right in front of us simply because we don't want to see it.

"I realize this is difficult, but try to be objective, Ty. Do you think Britney is capable of murder? Sorry for my insensitivity, I know you two are in a relationship and have been for some time, but I'm trying to piece this all together. I'm not saying she did anything, at least not yet. But you and Mike had a fight at The Barnyard, witnesses have stated that your fight was about Britney, and Britney was one of the last people to see Mike alive."

She was one of the last people to see Mike alive? That was news to me. Had she tried to set him straight?

SHE'S TOXIC

"How do you know that she was one of the last people to see him alive?"

"Ty, I have ways of knowing these things. I'm a detective, remember? That's part of my job. My job is to investigate crimes, procure evidence, and then use my intellect and experience to determine what happened. I call it striking gold. I create my own gold rush in these cases. I'm going to strike it rich here; I have that tingling sensation. Woah!" He clapped his hands before taking another drink and looking around at the farm.

I opened my mouth to speak, but he interrupted me.

"Boy, this is some place your family has out here. It's too bad you had to disappoint them by losing your scholarship. You could have been great, the next Drew Brees! Yeah, that's right, I know *all about* your story."

I shook my head. "That's irrelevant. It sucked, but it doesn't matter anymore."

"I'm sorry, Ty. I realize it's still a sore subject. Believe me, it's not personal. It's just what we have to do as detectives to garner information. But let me ask you something: Has Britney been acting a little different?" He knew more than he let on; he was trying to get me to admit something he already knew. He kept his eyes trained on me as he placed an unlit Marlboro Red between his lips.

I wasn't about to disclose what was going on between us. It wasn't relevant, and I didn't want to give him any reason to keep digging around my life. "We're good. I can't think of anything wrong, but I'm more than willing to help in any way I can."

He turned his head to the side and smirked. "Mhmm. Sure."

He closed his eyes and shook his head before retrieving a Zippo from his pocket to light his cigarette. He took a long drag and exhaled. "I'm glad you're willing to help. But I need to get back to the big city of Gentry. There are a few others I need to question. Ty, you know it would be better if I heard it all from you, right? Would you be willing to come down to the station?"

I thought about my fights with Brit and Minden's comment that she was the last person to see him alive. My muscles tensed at the thought of what I was about to do, but I needed to help. Mike deserved justice, but I also wanted to be there for Britney. I wasn't sure if one could be accomplished without sacrificing the other. I needed to obtain more information.

"Could you give me a minute?" I asked.

"Sure thing, I'm not going anywhere."

I raced upstairs to inform Brit that I'd be right back. She was asleep and likely had no idea what I said, so I left a note.

It made me uncomfortable, but I followed Minden into town. The police station was located in downtown Gentry, across the street from the bank—a couple blocks from The Barnyard. It adjoined the fire department and the city hall.

I took a seat in the waiting room in a plastic chair next to a coffee pot. I poured a cup while I waited. It was decent but could have used a shot of liquor.

I waited for five minutes before Detective Minden appeared with whom I presumed to be another detective. She might have been twenty-five but couldn't have been much older. She was curvaceous, mocha skin, dressed in a navy pantsuit. I picked up a hint of coconut radiating from her.

SHE'S TOXIC

"Mr. Reynolds, I'd like you to meet Detective Miller. She has been added to Mr. Thomas's case."

"And you are Tyler Reynolds, correct? It's a pleasure to meet you." She smiled. She flipped her curly brown hair from her face. I could see a file in her hand, but I couldn't quite read the label—probably Mike's file.

"Yes, I'm Tyler Reynolds. It's nice to meet you, detective."

"I understand you have information for us, is this correct?" She caught me looking at the file, so she moved it behind her back. "I'm sorry, that's official police business." She smiled. I thought I recognized my name on a protruding page.

"Sorry, I didn't mean to look," I said.

Minden snorted.

"Don't worry about it. So are you ready to talk?" she asked.

"I want to help, but I can't promise anything."

"Wonderful. Could you follow me to our interview room?"

I followed the two detectives into a small room that resembled a jail cell. Minden wore a smug smile as we entered the room. He whispered into Miller's ear before shaking his head.

I sat on a cold metal chair on one side of the table. Miller and Minden both stood next to the lone chair on the other side. I already regretted putting myself in this situation.

"Now, Tyler, let's make this a productive session. I know you want to get something off your chest; I know it's weighing you down. You need to be brave and let it out," Minden said. He stood next to Miller, who was now sitting. "Detective Miller, do you have any questions for Tyler?"

"Is there anything you would like to tell us?" Miller asked.

I panicked. I'd considered telling Minden about Britney's outbursts and my growing suspicion, but I couldn't throw her under the bus, not yet.

"I can't think of anything offhand," I said. "I was just wondering if you've made any progress with the investigation."

"I apologize, but we can't disclose the findings of an ongoing investigation. I thought you had information for us," Miller said as she thumbed through her carefully guarded file.

"I'm sorry. I wish I knew more." I dropped my head to the floor. It had become fascinating to look at; it was concrete and appeared even colder than my chair.

"Dammit. You're making me look like an ass over here, Ty. I set up this appointment for you and you're not going to help us?" Minden slammed his hand down on the table.

"Sorry, Detective Miller. I didn't mean to waste anyone's time." I peered at the light green cinderblock walls, then at the detectives. My surroundings were closing in on me. I needed to get out of the police station.

"Believe me, it's no problem. And please, call me Veronica. There is no reason to be sorry." Miller looked at me with sad eyes. "We're always here for you if you ever need to speak with someone. Again, please, you have absolutely no reason to be sorry about anything."

"Thank you," I said.

She walked over to me, holding out her hand. I rose to my feet to shake her hand, but she hugged me instead. She whispered into my ear, "Stay strong, Tyler. This must be hard for you."

Thirteen

I drove back to the farm to find Britney sitting at my parents' kitchen table studying a Biology textbook. It looked like she didn't have a care in the world. I wished that I could catch a glimpse of what was going on in her head—all I needed was a brief insight into the cyclone churning inside her dome.

She stirred to her feet, jogged toward me, and jumped into my arms. "Welcome back, baby. Your note was so sweet."

I wasn't sure how she could rebound so quickly from our fights. I knew that manic-depressives could go from the extremes of mania to depression and could block out the manic episodes. I didn't know what Brit was going through, but I'd prefer her jumping into my arms over threatening to drive us into a tree.

She kissed my lips and tugged at my shirt.

I couldn't do this now, no way.

"I need to ask you something," I said, pulling away. I took off for the basement. She followed.

"Well I need to do something," she said as we descended the stairs.

"What's that?" I asked, taking a seat on the sectional.

Brit straddled me, ran her fingers through my hair, and kissed my neck. "I want you so bad. I want to make you happy. We can forget about everything that's happened and be here for each other. That's all I want. I want to help you."

I took hold of her forearms and nudged her away. "Sorry, I can't do this right now." Her pupils were dilated, but I wasn't sure if it was from arousal or insanity. "I talked to the detective again today."

"Ugh, once again, you have to ruin the moment with your pissing and moaning. Okay, what? What did the detective say? Tell me Ty, I'm dying to know! Jesus Christ, all I wanted to do was have sex with my boyfriend, but nope, *can't do that*. So go on, tell me what's *so fucking* important!"

It was like flipping a switch. If she only knew how close I was to helping them build their case against her, maybe she would be a little more grateful.

"The detective said you were the last person to be seen with Mike," I said.

"Oh, okay. Well good for the detective." She clapped her hands and cheered. "Is there something you want to ask me, Ty? Are you sure you want to know what happened to your sexy little friend? Do you think you could handle the truth?"

"Were you with him the night he died?"

"What do you think? Maybe I was, maybe I wasn't. It's not like you can do anything about it now. You couldn't do anything about it before either. You let all of this happen."

"Huh?"

SHE'S TOXIC

"Do you think I'm stupid, Ty? You've cheated on me since I've known you, you've let people get between us, and now you have to pay for what you've done."

I was confused. Nothing she said made any sense. "I've never cheated on you. I tried to tell you that the other day." I took a couple cautionary steps back. I'd thought I could help her, but maybe I'd been too optimistic. She needed professional help.

"You are a piece of shit. You fucked Alexa and probably the entire damn town. Ahhhhh!" Brit pounced into action. She swung her phone at my face. I jumped off the sectional, hit the floor, and tried to roll out of the way, but she had me cornered between the TV stand and the wall.

I looked into her eyes, but *Brit* wasn't there.

She calmed, closed her eyes, and dropped her head. Her head hung in silence for at least ten seconds, but then her breathing increased as she revealed a menacing glare. She was declining by the second. We'd had irrational fights lately but nothing physical.

"Baby, baby, baby, come here, baby, please let me explain. Nothing happened with either of those girls." I lowered my head and inched closer, attempting to console her.

"Lies! Fucking lies! And don't call me 'baby', you sound like Justin Bieber." Brit took advantage of her position, and swung her phone at my face. I fell back on my ass, missing her latest strike by inches, but in my effort, I had become vulnerable. "Cheating bastard. You also fucked Alexa back in high school." She did not miss this time. The phone connected with the top of my head. The blow knocked me back. She jumped on top of me.

Darkness.

Throbbing.

As I attempted to reorient myself to my surroundings, Brit reared back and swung with all her strength; direct contact.

And again.

And again.

"Get off of me! You are psychotic!" I struggled to open my eyes. I threw my arms at her to defend myself. My forearms were the recipients of additional blows. I pushed her away for a second, but I stumbled backward once more.

She led another charge of her one-psycho army, swinging the phone savagely in my direction. She laughed. "You're such a little bitch. I'm going to take you down again." Brit ran toward me, but I needed to ensure that this charge would not be successful.

I scrambled to my feet, lowered my head, and propelled my body through hers—it was a perfect form tackle. It took both of my arms to restrain her and pin her arms behind her back. I wrestled the phone from her right hand, prying her fingers away.

"You're abusing me! This is abuse!" she yelled.

"Crazy, psycho bitch." I was less than enthused and beyond bewildered. "What's your problem?" I had her cradled in both arms—careful not to do anything that could be deemed abuse. I was acting in self-defense, though I wasn't sure an officer would see it that way. Even though I'd lost weight, I was still much larger than her.

"I can't trust you at all. How many other times have you cheated on me? You don't remember because you're a fucking alcoholic!" She tried to wriggle free from my grasp, but I tightened my hold.

SHE'S TOXIC

"None!" I answered. She flailed her arms and legs. "Besides, Alexa is dating someone else." I lied. I needed to calm her down.

"You're lying. Wait, so if she wasn't dating someone else, you'd be interested in her? Is that what you're saying?"

She continued to try to break free from my grasp. She managed to slip away, turning to punch me in the shoulder. It stung worse than expected, but I reeled her back in.

"I didn't do anything," I said. "I didn't have sex with her. Hell, I barely even talked to her."

"But you wanted to, didn't you? Did she blow you?" She calmed to some extent, but her eyes were vacant.

"Nothing happened, nothing at all. We just had a couple of drinks. And no, I didn't want to do anything with her. Jesus. How many times do I have to say the same damn thing?" I shouted, before letting go of my girlfriend.

She slumped to the ground as I turned away. I needed to get her out of my parents' house. I needed to join the rest of reality. I'd endured enough. This was more than I could handle. The fights had become physical, and that crossed the line.

"You need to leave, and maybe we should take a break."

"Why?" She scurried to her knees. "Why are you doing this? I love you, Tyler."

I stopped, stunned by her abrupt change in attitude. I turned around and looked back. My eyes narrowed on Brit—the helpless, despondent young woman slouched over on the floor.

"Why?" she repeated—now sobbing—to the man she had just assaulted. "I love you, Tyler. You don't need to hurt me. You can't leave me like this."

I wasn't sure if I should laugh, console her, or run for my life, never looking back at the train wreck I'd just witnessed.

"Baby, I love you, too." I loved her, so that wasn't a lie. I had loved her since the first night we met.

Maybe it was a misunderstanding. I should have told her about texting Maddie, but I didn't think it was a big deal, just as I didn't think it mattered when I ran into Alexa. But this outburst was the piercing dagger in Brit's veil of sanity. And yet, I felt like I needed to help her. I wanted to leave, but I couldn't let go of our past. There had to be a way to bring her sanity back—perhaps an exorcism. We had been phenomenal together and all of this came out of nowhere.

Or did it?

Maybe the detective was right. Had I been looking at Brit through rose-colored glasses this entire time? There's no way I could have overlooked *this* behavior regardless of how much I loved her. I knew who she really was, and this wasn't her; this was a demon.

When two people get together, the sad reality is that they will either get married or break up. Even when a couple gets married, the marriage will end in divorce or death. I suppose it's the in-between moments that make relationships worthwhile—unless those moments involve physical abuse ... and the murder of your best friend.

Fourteen

The air was cool, aided by a cloudless sky. It was downright chilly for summer. I climbed into my Jeep and attempted to throw my key into the ignition, but two hands clamped down around my wrist—stopping me cold. I attempted to pull back.

A deep voice bellowed, "Where do you think you're going? You're in big trouble, buddy."

I could see only a silhouette, but it appeared diminutive. The figure leaned into me, hands still clamped around my wrist. The person turned on the passenger-side reading lamp, and my mouth dropped open.

"Alexa?"

She slumped back into her seat, grinning back at me, wearing only a red lace bra and matching panties.

"What are you doing in here? And how did you make your voice sound like that?"

"What do you think I'm doing? Oh, with this!" She giggled. I glanced at her phone. An app was open—some kind of voice manipulator. She dropped her phone into the console.

Alexa leaned closer, unhooking her bra with her right hand. She dropped her head against my shoulder as she rubbed her hand down the side of my face, down to my chest. "You're so hot." She bit her lip, closed her eyes, and leaned in to kiss my lips.

I turned my neck and met her advance head-on. My hand fell down to the small of her back, and I pulled her into me, caressing her soft, tanned skin. The kiss became increasingly more passionate, concluding in my nibbling her lower lip. I kissed her lips once more, moved to her chin, then down to her neck. Her body warmed in my arms; a bead of sweat appeared on her forehead. I continued to kiss her neck, moving my left hand to her breasts.

"Bad boy," she whispered between light moaning. Her hand began a journey down my chest, to my stomach, to my waistband. "I want you so bad." She gave me a devilish grin. "I touched myself on the way over here while thinking about you."

I embraced her in another long kiss before I opened the door and pulled her outside. We remained in an embrace—her legs wrapped around my waist; her arms around my neck—as I pulled a blanket out from the backseat and threw it on the ground. I guided her to the blanket, but we rolled right off into the cold, wet grass. I wasn't sure she even noticed.

"You're so sexy," she moaned. She ran her fingers through my hair, grabbing and pulling. Our bodies rubbed against each other. She pulled me into her with her legs. I wanted her, but I knew I shouldn't.

Before I could make the next move, I heard a rustling sound in the darkness behind me. I spun around and attempted to use the blanket to cover us.

SHE'S TOXIC

"What was that?" Alexa whispered.

"Tyyyy, are you out here?" a high-pitched voice asked.

As soon as I heard the words, she came into view. It was Britney. My heart sank. I felt sick to my stomach. A mixture of shock and anger replaced her smile.

"Are you serious? What are you two doing?" She threw her hands over her face and cried.

My face flushed red. This had been a horrible mistake. Alexa laughed. She told the "little kid" that this was "grown-up stuff", and that she needed to go away.

"Ty, how could you do this?" Brit pleaded. "We had something special."

Her words hit me like a train crashing through a small block of ice on a railroad crossing. I shattered into a million pieces. I tried to speak, but my mouth was frozen. My lips parted, but nothing came out.

Britney brandished a tiny pistol from her Michael Kors clutch and shuffled forward.

"I hate to do this, Ty, but you have to learn your lesson. Don't fuck with me. Don't fuck with my emotions. You're a son of a bitch."

She aimed the .22 at my head. Alexa scrambled from beneath me, and I lost my balance. I tumbled to the ground. I couldn't comprehend what was happening.

Britney walked closer, shaking as she took aim.

"Goodbye, Ty." Tears streamed down her face. "I love you."

I took a deep breath and closed my eyes, bracing for the sensation of the scorching bullet ripping through my flesh.

I woke up screaming.

Brit tried to placate me, but it was a wasted effort. It had to take its course. I seldom remembered my nightmares, but when I did, I took a while to calm down.

The dream made me wonder if maybe I had hooked up with Alexa in High School. Even if I had, it was so long ago. But it made me wary of other nights I didn't remember. I thought I'd only had a couple drinks with Alexa at The Barnyard, but I might have done more. And I couldn't remember sneaking out of my parents' basement either, but maybe I had.

Fifteen

Brit drove back to her parents' house in Reedville, leaving me to house-sit for the night. The actual need to stay in rural Nash County had become a convenient excuse to buy time away from her.

In the comfort of my childhood room, I opened my laptop to my Google Chrome browser. Annoying marriage announcements and baby pictures littered my Facebook News Feed, nothing interesting to me—at least not anymore. At one time, I wanted all of that with Britney, but now I wasn't so sure.

Two notifications buzzed through my phone—both were texts from withheld phone numbers.

I opened the first message. I began to sweat immediately, and I sweat a little more after reading each successive word. I finished reading the message, though I wasn't sure how much sank in. After the initial pang of panic, the world around me drifted away.

I exited the message and fumbled to open the other message. It was identical. A new notification startled me—it came in far too loud. I'd received a second message from the first number.

I panicked once more as I reopened the message log. My body trembled as I read both messages together:

Unknown Number: *Stay the fuck away from Britney. She is now property of the Colombian Lords. – ES*

Unknown Number: *I can see you have read my message. We are watching your every move. Stay the fuck away from Britney. She is ours. – ES*

Before I finished reading, I received another message from the second number. The two messages from the second number were identical to the first, except they were signed with "GR" as opposed to "ES." The initials didn't ring a bell and I knew nothing of the Colombian Lords. My only knowledge of Colombia came from Pablo Escobar, which wasn't comforting.

I'd been afraid of what Britney might do to me or to my friends and family, but these threats were on another level, and it was apparent that she was somehow involved.

It was difficult to cope with the reality that my relationship with Britney had reached this point. I'd refused to accept that she was no longer the sweet, innocent girl I'd met in high school. People had tried to warn me, but I was too invested.

Miguel Taveres—a former teammate and the guy she was texting on our first date (which I found out later)—had raised a red flag regarding Britney back in high school, but I'd assumed he was obsessed with her. And I'd ignored the subsequent warnings; Mike, Maddie, and my parents had all made comments alluding to her instability. But I stood stagnant while she deteriorated. Maybe I could have helped her sooner, but it probably wouldn't have mattered.

SHE'S TOXIC

I researched the gang and found no dearth of information. They were a legitimate organization that had a base in Chicago, but they spilled into surrounding rural areas of northern Illinois and southern Wisconsin.

Like most other gangs, they funneled drugs into the United States and discarded anyone who stood in their way. I scrolled through pictures of men with green bandanas and wristbands, sometimes pointing a gun directly at the camera. Brit couldn't be involved with these clowns. No way in hell.

I needed to speak with someone close to Brit—other than Maddie. I'd considered calling Brit's mom, even jumping the hurdle of getting her new number from Brit's phone, but I didn't think she would believe me. I'd struggled to believe Brit's transformation even though I was a victim.

After a quick inner debate, I dialed Maddie. While I waited for her to answer, I heard the floorboard creak near my door. I'd always feared Brit would sneak out to surprise me, and somehow she'd snuck into the house—and up the stairs.

"Who are you talking to?" Brit asked, mere feet behind me. Her voice cut through me like a January squall.

I didn't want to turn around. I didn't want to see her face; I was afraid of what I might do. She grabbed my shoulders from behind and pulled herself up, trying to bring her ear close enough to the phone so she might hear the voice on the other end.

I didn't want to tell Britney that I was on the phone with Maddie. *For some strange reason*, I wasn't sure how well she would respond. I escaped from Brit's grasp and into my bathroom, locking the door behind me.

"Give me a second!" I yelled at Brit, holding the phone away from my mouth. "I'm trying to straighten something out ... I'm talking to Jason."

She banged on the door. At first she used her bare hand, followed by her fist, and then either her head or her shoulder. I couldn't be sure.

"Ty, are you there? What's going on?" Maddie asked.

"She's trying to bust down my bathroom door. I can't do anything to stop her." I looked into the mirror, at the fear in my eyes. My eyes resembled Britney's demonic, glazed-over appearance. I shuddered at the thought.

"Let me in! Let me in!"

"Call me back later," Maddie said.

Thump. Thump. Thump.

I watched the lock move from vertical to horizontal—she must have used the skeleton key. I was too far away from the door to keep it shut. Britney swung open the door; she stood in the doorway with a distant gaze and balled fists.

"Why did you lock me out, Ty? Why do you continue to lock me out? I can't live like this. You've hurt me, so now I need to hurt you." Brit ran, leaped, and jumped on my back as I turned away from her. She struggled to dislodge my phone.

"Get off me!" I tried to shake her off.

"Who were you talking to?" She knocked the phone out of my hands, and it went flying into my room. She jumped off my back and dove for the phone. She secured it before I could react and heaved it at my trophy shelf; two trophies crashed to the ground, their broken pieces scattering across the floor.

SHE'S TOXIC

"You crazy bitch!" I put my arms around Brit and pulled her into my body. Her arms and legs flailed into space. "Who in the hell are the Colombian Lords? Are they a gang? They sent me a message saying you're their property."

"Colombian Lords? A gang? You are delusional! I can't take this anymore. Do you want me to kill myself? Is that what you want? I'll do it right now." She broke free from my grasp and ran back into the bathroom, slamming the door shut behind her. "I'm going to kill myself right now."

A rush of anger come over me. I wanted to take her head and bash it against the bathroom mirror. I wanted to see the shards of glass digging into her skin—blood pooling in the bottom of the sink. *Fleeting loss of sanity.*

I loved Britney, and I'd never harm her. But sometimes, I felt myself losing control, imagining grisly scenes at her expense, which seemed reasonable considering what she was putting me through.

My sanity prevailed. "Baby, please calm down. I love you. I have always loved you and I *will* always love you."

"No, you don't. You think I'm crazy."

No, I know that you're crazy. "I didn't mean it. I'm scared."

"Oh, you're scared of me? I can't live like this. I need to die."

Yes, exactly. You need to die. "No, that's not what I meant. I'm scared of myself—scared of all these deep emotions I have for you, feelings that could never go away." I leaned my forehead and both hands against the door. "I love you, Brit."

It was time to leave, but not right now. It didn't seem healthy to be terrified of my girlfriend. I'd never heard of a long-married couple professing that the secret of their lasting marriage was that at least one person in the relationship was a raging psychopath. I'd watched shows where wives had mental breaks resulting in the murder of their husbands—a more likely outcome at this point.

She made a sound resembling an *aww*, but I couldn't make it out from behind the door. I then heard the click of the door unlocking. I took a step back as the door opened away from me. I was face-to-face with Britney. Although blood trickled from her forearm, she smiled.

"You stopped me just in time. I almost did it."

"Baby, why did you do that? I love you and never want to lose you."

Mike was right, and I should have listened. Britney was a slow-acting poison that was whittling away at my sanity. I kept going back because I knew the real Britney, or at least who I thought she was—who she was when I met her, and who she had been for the better part of five years. But nobody smacks their future significant other on the first date. And by the time there's any hint of abuse, deeper emotions have already set in, making it tough to leave. *That's not who he really is. I love him and I can help him.*

Britney's mental condition made my situation a little different. I'd thought she could snap out of her lapse, but I wasn't so sure anymore. I still loved her—that's what made it so difficult to leave. If I didn't love her, it would be easy to move on and forget that Britney Boyer ever existed.

Sixteen

My patience was wearing thin as my survival was becoming my predominant concern, at least during the time surrounding our fights. In those moments, I wanted out. I wanted out faster than I could drive on the Autobahn. But despite all that had happened, I hoped her condition would improve. I tried to remain optimistic per my grandpa's instructions. I'd been with Britney nearly five years, and I didn't want to let her go. I'd lost too much too soon. I couldn't lose Britney too.

We were sitting in my apartment on Thursday afternoon, as Kourt had relieved me of house-sitting duty. It was a dreary summer day—clouds had obstructed the sun most the afternoon; a few sprinkles pasted my windows.

I looked over at Brit. She was grinning and pounding away on her phone. She giggled—not quite the giggle that had captivated me from the beginning. This giggle had the opposite effect. Somehow, I already knew it was connected to the messages I'd received from *ES* and *GR*.

"You seem to be enjoying yourself over there," I said.

She rolled her eyes, looking at me for a second before going back to her phone. She didn't flat-out ignore me, but her dismissive response was even more agitating.

"Hello?" I stared at her, wide-eyed, wondering what kind of response I would get.

"Hi!" she snapped back and turned away from me. "You are so annoying," she muttered under her breath.

This was a new development. She was upset with me, but wasn't wielding a weapon. Somehow, her current reaction concerned me more.

"Who are you talking to?" I asked.

"Wow, you're possessive. Why don't you call Maddie or Kayla to find out what I'm doing? You've done that before. How can I date someone so crazy?"

"I'm not trying to be possessive, but you're pretty much ignoring me, so it must be important."

She nodded. "Yep, it is important. You can leave me alone now. Bye."

"Who are you texting?"

"Fuck, can you ever shut up? I was trying to protect your feelings, but if you are dying to know, I can tell you. Are you sure you can handle it?"

This was the Brit I had grown accustomed to recently, back in all of her glory. She lowered the phone and glared at me, flashing those evil brown eyes. Her breathing became heavier, her eyes continued to penetrate me.

"Yes. I would like to know who you are texting. I think you owe me that much."

SHE'S TOXIC

"You're such a little bitch. You sneak out of the apartment to talk to your little slut on the phone. Was that who you were talking to the other day, Maddie? Or was it Alexa this time? I'm going to fuck them up, you know that right?"

"You're not doing anything to anyone. And don't turn this around on me; you're texting away over there, trying to hide it."

She laughed. "I'm not trying to hide anything from you. I'm texting the guy who can fuck me right and who won't cheat on me. What are you going to do about it?"

I had a flashback to our first date. She asked the same question just before our first kiss.

"You're not seeing anyone else."

"That's the funniest thing I've heard all day." Her laughter became hysterical. "He's so much better than you are. I didn't know I could be so loud in bed until I started dating him. He touches me in all the right places, with the right pressure. Wow, just thinking about him is getting me hot. It's too bad you can't do anything for me anymore."

"Shut your mouth," I said. I wanted to take her phone from her, but I restrained myself. "You're making this all up."

"Nope, I'm sure not." She smiled as she brought her phone over to me. "Here, look for yourself. Look at that conversation right there. Look at all those messages."

My heart skipped a beat.

I didn't want to look, but curiosity got the best of me. I took her phone and skimmed over the messages with someone named Logan. I registered a few fragments of messages such as *I'm so addicted to you* and *I've been a bad girl.*

"What do you think? I'm sure he could handle both of us. Want me to ask him?" She couldn't stop smiling. She flipped her hair and snatched her phone out of my hands.

"Are you serious? Why are you doing this to me? I've been there for you. I've been trying to help you, even though you're insane. Is this guy part of the Colombian Lords?"

"Wow, this is too good. You should see your face right now." She turned her attention back to her phone.

"I'm not listening to this. Enjoy your lives together."

She gasped and her phone hit the ground. "What do you mean, Ty?" She ran over to me; I cowered like a beaten dog.

"What? You can be with him now because it's clear you don't want to be with me. And I hope you know that a detective is building a case against you for Mike's death. I tried to protect you before, but I'm not sure I can do that anymore."

"No!" She collapsed to the floor. "We're still together. I just needed to get your attention that's all. I promise! I don't love him. I love you!"

I was terrified, but this wasn't really her. Deep down, she was still my girl, despite all the bullshit. There was too much between us. Even if it didn't work out, I knew she didn't need to be involved with a gang member—nobody needed that in their life. I needed to help her. I might have been crazy, but I felt like I owed her that much.

I had talked to someone behind her back, so it wasn't like I could completely blame her for being with someone else. Many couples go through trials, and perhaps this was just a trial—a trial to make us stronger.

The only time there was ever the serious mention of another guy between us was Miguel. I was never sure if Miguel had been obsessed with her or if he'd given me a legitimate warning to stay away. Over time, I'd assumed he was obsessed, but due to recent events, I wasn't so sure.

I didn't know if it was possible to hide a serious mental illness for so long. Or maybe she had it under control with medication, then for whatever reason, she worsened. Her condition may have deteriorated beyond the medication's control, or perhaps she had stopped medicating. I assumed she would have told me about her condition, but most people don't want to advertise a mental illness, regardless of how close they are to someone.

I remembered one day at football practice when Miguel had warned me about Britney. After she had mentioned Miguel bothering her, I felt obligated to say something. I had my chance when we were standing on the sideline. The offensive and defensive subs were scrimmaging for the last several minutes as the starters looked on. As the first team, we were supposed to be "mentally condensing" what we had done, while spotting mistakes made by the second team.

"Miguel, great play on that rollout." I gave him a pat on the shoulder. Miguel was about my height, but more muscular. He was quick and hit hard.

"Uh, thanks." He glanced over at me for a second, giving me a quick half-nod. "So you're dating Britney Boyer, right?" He swallowed hard, looking in my direction, but avoiding eye contact. The sun was setting to our left but was still strong enough to make us squint.

His bluntness surprised me, but it simplified my mission.

"Yeah, I guess you could say that." I wasn't about to tell him that I was madly in love with her and she was all I could think about. He must have felt the same, though I wasn't sure how much they had hung out, if at all.

"Well, she's kind of crazy. I'd be careful if I were you." He looked straight ahead, scratching his left elbow with his right hand. Nervous tick.

"Crazy, huh? She seems cool to me."

Miguel took a deep breath and looked around cautiously. He took a half step in my direction and lowered his voice, "Hey, you didn't hear it from me, but she's bad news." He paused. "There's something that isn't right about her."

"And why would you say that?"

"I've heard things and I know from experience. She won't stop texting me. I feel bad for her. And she's violent. You don't know her well. Just wait. It might not happen today or tomorrow, but at some point, you'll see her true colors. I think she's on medication now, but it can only do so much."

Coach Summers called Miguel away. "I'm just trying to help you, man. We're both Bulldogs, right? Be careful, Ty. Be very careful. I don't want to see anything bad happen to you." He turned away as he strapped on his helmet and ran onto the field.

He was just trying to get in my head, but he succeeded.

Was I was overlooking a manifest defect? Was I blinded by love? Maybe she was lying to make herself look better.

I didn't know Miguel that well, but he was a guy, and guys rarely gossip about bullshit. Then again, maybe he was trying to keep me away from her. It would be difficult to blame him for falling head over heels for that girl.

One night when Brit and I went out for dinner, shortly after speaking with Miguel at practice, he texted me. I wasn't sure it was him at first, but Brit verified his number.

One message said: *She's crazy man. Just trying to warn you. Cray cray.* Another, *Like I said, she might hide it for a while, but it always comes out. She crazy.*

I'd told Brit about the first message and she became hysterical. She claimed that he was obsessed with her and wouldn't leave her alone. She was believable, but she would have answered the same way regardless.

I had let time take its course, and nothing notable happened during our relationship.

Until now.

Seventeen

I removed Brit from my apartment following our most recent blowout. I wondered if she was going to see Logan, but I didn't want to think about the specifics. I longed for what we once had, feared for my safety, and I missed Mike. Too many emotions running together to think clearly. I was becoming a broken man, if I wasn't already.

I dialed a number and placed the phone to my ear.

"Hey, Ty," Maddie said.

"Things aren't good. We need to talk."

She sighed. "Definitely. I was hoping you'd call again."

We planned to meet in the park behind the high school parking lot. It was a park by name, but it wasn't much more than a picnic table with peeling green paint and an old swing set with four rubber swings held up by rusting chains. The alcove was enclosed by a grove of trees leaving one small opening, several feet wide. Students often used the park as a place to drink and smoke cigarettes or weed. Many couples also used the clearing as a place to hook up—the proximity to the high school made the taboo too tempting.

I looked forward to seeing Maddie—someone who could appreciate the dramatic shift in Britney's psychology. Or maybe I just wanted to see her. Through the trees, I watched Maddie pull up in her little red Mazda. She took a long drink out of a can and threw the presumed empty into her backseat before stepping out of her car. She put out her cigarette after taking one last drag, then walked over to me.

"Smoking now?" I asked.

"Shhh, don't tell," Maddie said as a grin formed on her lips. She was wearing a royal blue dress that came halfway down her thighs, or more like one-fourth of the way. She sauntered toward me with a stagger in her approach. She fell into her swing; anyone in front of her would have had quite the view. She had gained a little weight in the past several months, but it looked good on her.

"How was that soda?" I chuckled with a grin.

"Mmmm. I've had five already." She nodded; her ratty blonde hair covered most of her face. "Good soda." She reached into her black, gold-zippered purse and pulled out two beers. "I'll even share. You want one?"

I nodded and smiled; we each popped our tops in unison. It was a Friday, summer afternoon, so drinking a beer was more than acceptable. I'd already downed several beers of my own before meeting with her.

We hadn't spoken since our telephone conversation. Despite my strong desire to see her, I'd exercised self-control. But after the emergence of Logan, I didn't care anymore.

I dove in headfirst. "Things have been crazy. It's been difficult." Maddie's eyes welled as I spoke. She was taking it worse than I was.

"I feel like I've lost a huge part of myself. I've been drinking quite a bit. We shouldn't have to go through this." She took a long drink and lit another cigarette, dragging her sandaled feet beneath her as she swung. "I'm glad you called the other night. I've wanted to talk for a long time, but I haven't known what to say."

I couldn't have said it any better. It was great to hang out with Maddie. I'd spent a lot of time with her in high school, but always when I was with Britney, such as the day at Six Flags.

"It's been rough. I'm at a point where I'm not sure what to do anymore. Mike's gone and Kourt has been hard to talk to. We're in a similar position, so I guess it's only natural we talk, right?" I took a long drink, attempting to match Maddie drink-for-drink. She was throwing hers back.

"Of course." She looked into my eyes and smiled. "Being with you reminds me of being with her, if that makes any sense. That probably sounds stupid." She turned away, taking another drink as she traced the chain links along the swing. "It's so peaceful and beautiful. I haven't been back here for a while."

I wasn't sure which comment to respond to. Her thoughts meandered from one topic to another. I didn't want to make things worse by asking her the specifics of what had happened between her and Britney. I'd heard enough from Britney already. I felt sorry for Maddie; she had done nothing to deserve this, likewise, neither had I. Britney was sick, and she would make all of our lives hell until she improved.

SHE'S TOXIC

"Nah, it doesn't sound stupid. It makes perfect sense. You two are kind of alike. I guess that's why you're friends."

"Yeah, I'm not sure if we were friends or if we are friends. I guess we *are* still friends. If I say it like that, it's almost like nothing has changed. Yeah, we liked a lot of the same things, liked to do the same things." She peered at me with her chin resting atop her left shoulder. She crossed her right foot over her left leg as she swung closer.

Uh oh. We like to do the same things? I might have been reading too deep into the comment, but her body language seemed clear. I saw where this was heading.

A few blackbirds sang in the distance as a light breeze shuffled the leaves on the oak trees within the grove—beckoning me to give into temptation. But for all I knew, maybe she wasn't making a move.

"I know the feeling. I was the same way with Mike." I wasn't sure she even heard me. She brought the can to her lips and finished her beer in one gulp. She tossed it aside without taking her eyes off me.

Total fixation.

She licked her lips and closed her eyes. "Ty, come over here and talk to me. I need to talk to you more, and closer. You're so far away."

My body was now within inches of hers, so it didn't take much intelligence to decipher her intent. I was still dating Brit, but I wasn't sure how much longer it could last. This would still be cheating, but there's usually a reason people cheat—like when a partner has been unfaithful. The dynamics of my relationship with

Brit had shifted. It wasn't my fault, or at least that's what I was trying to convince myself.

Before I could continue weighing the pros and cons of the inevitable, Maddie made the first move. She leaned over and kissed my lips. She pushed her tongue against my lips before I relented and met hers with mine. It was a sloppy, drunk kiss. My tongue continued wrestling with hers, pinning it down for a second before she fought back and twirled her tongue around mine. She was hungry. She sucked my tongue before pulling back.

"Do you think we should do this?" I asked, out of breath. My forehead was pressed against hers. Her skin was flushed; I could feel her heartbeat.

"It's right. Let's just go with it." She kissed and sucked my neck, she thrusted her hand underneath my shirt, rubbing my abs and my chest. "God, take this shirt off. You are so sexy. I've always wanted you, but I couldn't have you," she took a deep breath, "now I can."

She had swung her legs open in my direction and I saw that she wasn't wearing anything underneath her dress. If I had any ounce of self-control remaining before that sight, it had vanished into the brisk Illinois air.

I helped her tear my shirt off and spun her off the swing and onto the ground so that she was lying on top of me.

She tore at my belt.

I tried to enjoy myself, but I kept scanning the area around us for Britney. I was surprised I could even stay aroused. Maddie leaned down to kiss me. After holding back, I finally gave into destiny and stopped searching my surroundings—and my soul.

SHE'S TOXIC

It was wrong, but I couldn't resist. Maddie brought me to life. It was cathartic for us to come together over something that had caused each of us so much pain.

It had been a while since I'd had any real release. She dug her body into mine as I looked overhead at the trees, which nearly canopied over the small park. Part of me felt sick, but somewhere within, I knew that the old Brit was gone and things would never be the same. I looked around to see if she was lying in wait with a gun—like in my dream.

Nope, I wasn't dreaming; this was reality.

Maddie and I hung out several times within the next week. Most of the time we drank, smoked, and had sex, but we also had deep conversations. She also found great satisfaction in being held for hours. It was refreshing to be close to someone without worrying about being beaten. Maddie touched a part of me that had lain dormant for months. We sometimes discussed Britney, how she used to be—how our lives used to be, but how that had come to a crashing halt.

On the next Thursday, Maddie and I were drinking on a blanket out on my dirt road. I had dodged Brit most the week. I was glad she had her summer class—and Logan, apparently. It made me sick, and I could have never envisioned the turn of events, but I guess that's life.

The physical abuse and infidelity had weakened my resolve to stick with Brit through her illness—or whatever it was. I didn't know if I had a future with Brit, but I was at least going to ride this out with Maddie and try to enjoy life for a change.

I had brought along some wine and snacks. It reminded me of the picnics I'd shared with Britney. Hell, it almost felt like I was with Britney. Maddie was filling the void that had developed when Britney lost touch with reality.

I needed Maddie and she needed me.

"Is it true that some of the stars we can see are already dead? How's that even possible?" Maddie asked as she stared into the starlit sky. I couldn't tell if she was mesmerized by the dramatic expanse or in a weed-induced haze.

"Many of the stars are millions of light years away. A star might be dead, but we will continue to see its light for millions of years," I said.

She closed her eyes and smiled. "That's beautiful." I didn't say anything. I wasn't following her train of thought.

She resumed looking at the stars. "Even though a star might be dead, it's still providing light across the universe. It's the same when we die—our light continues to provide comfort for our loved ones." She broke her gaze, turned to me, and asked, "You'd miss me, wouldn't you?"

I'd almost choked up while taking in the gravity of her observation. I didn't know she was capable of such deep insight. Most people aren't.

"Wow, that was deep—and true. And of course I'd miss you. How could I forget an ass like that?" I tried to lighten the mood.

She flashed a brief smile and made herself comfortable on the blanket, laying her head to rest on my thigh. "You might be the only one."

"That's not true. What about Kayla? Your parents?"

SHE'S TOXIC

She pondered my response, but didn't answer. She looked into my eyes and said, "I love you, Ty." She leaned up to kiss my lips before reclaiming her spot. Her eyes closed and she was out within minutes.

I felt the rise and fall of her chest against my leg. It was no mystery that Maddie was struggling. It would be obvious to anyone. Likewise, I was beyond struggling. I wasn't sure if our sexual forays were helping or hurting. I wasn't hurting her; she wasn't hurting me. We were there for each other in a hellacious time and had the same expectations. We offered each other words of comfort, but we craved more. We found more. It made me think of Keith Urban's song, "Break on Me."

In some ways, I was closer to Maddie than Britney. I'd never had to worry about what Maddie thought of me so I was open around her. I was falling in love with Maddie. In my vulnerable state, I might have fallen in love with anyone, especially someone who reminded me so much of Britney, or at least who Brit used to be. I wasn't sure I even knew Brit anymore.

I received a new text from an unknown number:
I'm watching you.

Eighteen

It was two nights after my picnic with Maddie, and I was devising an elaborate plan. I was trapped and needed to break out. I needed to find a weak spot in the surveillance or an oblivious guard—there had to be a path to freedom.

But I was caught shortly after putting my plan into action.

I failed to escape my apartment.

"Where are you going?" Brit stepped out from behind the short wall separating the kitchen from the living room. She had been snoring loudly in bed when I left the bedroom, but she must have feigned sleep—lying in wait. She was wearing a "CIU Football" shirt and black cheekies—disheveled hair.

"I need to go out to my parents' place tonight. It's fine if you stay over here." I flashed a reassuring smile. Brit had come over the previous night saying she wanted to get our relationship back on track. I'd told myself that I wouldn't have sex with her, and despite her persistence, I had stayed true to my word.

She seemed content with my response. She walked into the kitchen and began rummaging through the silverware.

SHE'S TOXIC

"Are you fixing food?" I asked.

"Something like that," she muttered. She added a line I couldn't decipher. It sounded like *I guess I'll go fuck Logan.*

Disbelief clubbed me once more. She had never pulled these kinds of shenanigans in the past. Even when I was at college parties while she was still in high school, she had kept a level head. There were never instances where she felt slighted when I stayed on campus. She wouldn't respond by saying, *"If you're staying in Decatur, then I'm going to a party with Shane Samuels."*

She had never bit back like that.

Perhaps two people can only hang onto that kind of love and trust for so long. Our strong base was dissolving, threatening to snap, just as she was now snapping with regularity.

I didn't want to resent her, and I felt guilty for sneaking around with Maddie, but Brit was also with Logan. *Unless it was an act...* I still didn't have any proof she was with him—other than the messages, but she could have fabricated those. Either way, it wasn't the mark of a healthy relationship. Maybe we could eventually rebound from this setback; recovery wouldn't happen overnight, but I wasn't prepared to burn the bridge between us. Too much history, too many feelings.

"Well if you make extra, I'll clean it up tomorrow. You know how I love your cooking." Her cooking wasn't bad.

I turned to leave, hoping the conversation was over.

"Ty, I have something for you." My skin crawled into gooseflesh. I turned around to see that Brit had emerged from the kitchen. A devious smile crossed her lips. It looked like she was holding an object behind her back, but I couldn't make it out.

"Sorry, babe. I need to go." I turned to the door. A part of me felt guilty for wanting to get away, but I was becoming numb—desensitized.

"No, you need this. I'd be helping you, Ty. Let me help you." Her voice sounded much closer. I recoiled upon hearing her say my name. I turned around to see that she was now standing next to the couch, midway through the living room, her hands still tucked behind her back.

I reached the door; I tried to get outside, but I struggled with the lock.

"Let me help you," she repeated.

I turned around and gasped. Britney was no less than six feet away from me. I didn't even hear her move. It was like she had glided across the room. She stood there smiling, holding a large steak knife in her right hand with the tip of the blade pointed to the sky. Her calm voice struck me as more ominous than her psychotic rages.

"I could help you, Ty. I could make this all end. It wouldn't hurt long. Let me help you."

Her eyes were glazed over.

Panic pulsed through me. I wasn't sure whether I should make a run for it or try to wrestle the knife away from her. She was within striking distance. She could lunge at me and plunge the knife deep inside my chest in an instant. If I lunged at her, I'd make myself an easier target. Damned if I did and damned if I didn't.

"Okay, baby, I appreciate it, but I need to get going." I reflected her calmness with calmness. I hoped it would be enough to disarm her, at least for a second. It had worked during our previous arguments so I hoped it would work once more. All I needed was a second to slide out the door.

I fumbled with the lock as I spoke. She continued to stare at me, knife drawn. The knob wouldn't budge. She stepped closer, waving the knife from side-to-side.

"You should stay here. Let's have fun." She smiled.

Sweat ran down my fingers, complicating the process. I finally found my grip and turned the lock. Freedom.

"I love you, Brit." I said.

It took her several seconds to absorb my message.

"Aww, I love you, too." But she intensified her grip on the knife.

I opened the door and shot down the steps, never looking back to see if she was following me. I looked back only after closing the door of my Jeep.

She had descended the steps and was standing in the doorway waving with one hand, holding the knife in the other. As I pulled away, she used the knife to make a slicing motion at her neck while pointing at me with her other hand.

She smiled the entire time.

"Shit," I yelled to myself while barreling down the highway toward Gentry—to Maddie's apartment. I wasn't going to my parents' tonight, at least not without Maddie. I needed to see her—now. Maddie needed to calm me down before I went back to the apartment and did something I would regret.

I debated calling Kourt; it had been some time since we last spoke, but I didn't want to bring her down. She was struggling enough. Maddie seemed like the only person I could confide in, and it didn't hurt that we could also have sex.

I thrashed through the sheets to reach and silence my ringing phone. I tossed the preliminary obstructions to the side only to be thwarted by a pair of tanned legs. I attempted to maneuver over the legs without disturbing the sleeping beauty.

I was unsuccessful.

"Baby, what are you doing?"

"I'm trying to find my phone. Can't you hear it ringing?"

Maddie laughed. "Yeah, now I can. I *was* sound asleep. You wore me out last night," she said. Her hair covered her face like golden curtains. Before continuing my mission, I gave her ass a hearty slap. She yelped in appreciation.

I reached my phone on the fifth ring, surprised it had not yet gone to voicemail.

I didn't have time to look at the caller ID. Answering was probably a mistake to begin with. I was a little more than preoccupied, and I hadn't slept much the night before, preferring to trade hours of sleep for hours of pleasure.

"What are you doing?" Britney's voice gave me the chills.

"Um, nothing. I was sleeping until you woke me up."

"I texted you all night and you haven't responded. It's already eleven. Why are you sleeping so late?"

Judging by the angle of the sunlight coming through the window, Brit might have been right, but it was too early to deal with an inquisition. I shouldn't have to defend myself. Britney had lost it, not me. She was insane, psychotic, and possessive.

SHE'S TOXIC

"I was vacuuming and must have missed your messages."

I'd given Brit a horrible excuse, but I couldn't think straight; my blood was in my other head. The naked body lying next to me stirred once more. I put my index finger up to my lips to motion for her to be quiet.

"Who is it?" she whispered back. I mouthed, *It's her.*

"Do you honestly expect me to believe that, Ty? Why are you lying to me again? Do I need to go over to Logan's?" Brit asked.

"I don't want to, but I will, for us."

"It's who?" Maddie whispered.

"I swear I'm telling the truth," I said to Brit. "Why can't you ever believe me? Please don't do that."

Britney broke into hysterical laughter. "I'm not stupid. I know exactly what you're doing right now."

Maddie's brow furrowed, sensing the tension in my conversation. She kissed my chest. Her hand continued moving down my body. She pulled on the waistband of my boxer briefs.

"Stop," I was audible this time.

"I'll never stop," Britney said, thinking I was talking to her. Maddie continued on her quest without hesitating. Brit continued, "Mike came between us and now Maddie is coming between us. I'm not going to sit back and let that happen."

"Mike didn't come between us, and Maddie isn't either."

"Hang up the phone. Let's play," Maddie whispered.

I couldn't keep Britney on the line while Maddie was flooring the accelerator. Something had to give, and the choice was obvious. Britney and her antics had to go.

"Enough of this bullshit, you're wearing me out. I gotta go."

"Have fun fucking your whore. Logan will help me, you both will pay for this, you—"

I hung up before I had to endure any more torment.

"Who was that?" Maddie smiled at me from her renewed position between my legs. Her look was almost enough to send me over the edge.

I sighed and stroked her hair. "Britney."

Maddie's smile disappeared. She closed her eyes, slithered up to my chest, and threw her arms around my neck.

"I love you, Ty. We'll get through this."

I kissed her forehead and pushed a tendril of hair away from her eyes, placing it around her ear. "I don't know what to do," I said. "I just want to stay in this bed with you forever."

"It's hard on me, too. I'm just glad you're here. We might not be able to stay in bed forever, but I'd settle for all day."

Maddie's arms were comforting. If only we'd come together sooner, but I assumed the timing wouldn't have allowed for it any other way. I wanted to hold out hope that I could save Britney, but my resolve was dwindling with each passing day—with each bout of insanity. Love had blinded me for too long. I had missed all the warning signs.

I wondered what had happened between Brit and Maddie to end their friendship.

Nineteen

I spent the next afternoon out at my parents' house researching mental illnesses. A few conditions may have explained Brit's behavior, including bipolar disorder. I learned that the symptoms varied from person-to-person, but bipolar I included those whose manic episodes could be severe and dangerous. Those suffering from the disorder were also more likely to engage in impulsive sexual behavior.

It described Brit in a nutshell. Yet the shaking incidents and communicating with the dead didn't seem to fit. But I wasn't sure. I wondered again if she was putting on a show. Maybe she was tired of our relationship and needed a convenient way out. It wasn't like her though. Somewhere inside, I knew she couldn't be responsible, at least not consciously responsible.

I was the fool who kept going back. And the danger was no longer lurking beneath the surface, but the eyes and snout of the monstrosity had been visible for weeks, threatening to tear its teeth into my flesh and drag me under the water. I wouldn't let that happen—it was time to take action.

My family once took a trip through West Virginia, and we stopped at the Trans-Alleghany Lunatic Asylum—billed as the top attraction in the state. The asylum operated as a mental health facility from the end of the Civil War until 1994. The building was actually the second-largest stone-cut building in the world behind the Kremlin in Moscow, but what stuck out to me were the low standards for involuntary admission. Many people were committed because of traits such as alcoholism, wasteful spending, and going through menopause.

Commitment thresholds changed over time, but Brit would still be committed—without a doubt. They would throw her into the "violent women's wing." I might even be committed for staying with her for so long. I'm not sure "undying love" would be a legitimate defense.

My conversation with GG bubbled up once more. His words probably rang true for most situations, but at a certain point, unabashed optimism becomes delusional insanity. I wasn't sure how much longer I could stay the course. For now, my gut feeling was still prodding me along. It would improve; it had to. I was committed.

August first triggered our anniversary month, and I found it hard to believe that we would celebrate our fifth anniversary in less than four weeks. I wondered if we would celebrate it while in the arms of our lovers, or maybe ES and GR would pay me a visit. I was still concerned about the messages, but nothing had happened yet. I feared they were stalking their prey.

While I was knee-deep in research, I heard my bedroom door move. I swung my head around, frozen.

SHE'S TOXIC

"Kourt, is that you?" I asked.

The door stopped moving, or maybe I'd imagined the noise.

I turned back to my computer, but sensed someone on the other side of the door. I didn't hear the floorboards creak, but I felt the energy punching through the air.

I looked back toward the door. "Kourt? This isn't funny. Say something." I searched for anything to use as a weapon. If nothing else, I'd use my chair—or the computer.

The door slammed shut. My heart exploded.

Before I could rise from my chair, the door swung open again. Brit walked into the room grinning. "You're not watching porn, are you? Pervert. I did something bad. Will you spank me?" She laughed like a lunatic.

Her voice made my skin crawl, it sounded like fingernails on a chalkboard. Questions still abounded in my mind regarding Mike's death. Yet part of me didn't believe he was dead. I felt so numb. I turned in my chair to keep her in front of me.

"What did you do, Brit?" I asked while turning off my computer—before she could see my research. I was careful not to turn my back to her. She had just flashed a knife at me the day before, but here I was, still trying to help her.

She threw herself on my bed and laid spread eagle, looking up at the ceiling. "What do you think? I told you what I would do, but you didn't listen. You kept pushing me."

I didn't have the energy to go through this again.

"You have no reason to be concerned. There's nothing going on between me and Maddie." I walked toward her. She smiled as she followed the fan with her eyes, counting each revolution.

She broke out of her trance and looked at me.

"Bullshit," she said. Hysterical laughter.

"Why are you doing this to me?"

"You're doing this to yourself." She smirked and moved to the edge of the bed so that she was next to me. "Boy, you need to learn how to lie." She slapped me across the face. My blood boiled. I was losing my patience. "Maddie won't be bothering us anymore though, thank God. Now we can get to what's really important. Me and you."

She leaned in to kiss me, but playtime was over. I pushed her back against the bed and jumped on top of her.

"Now we're getting somewhere. Come on, Ty; take out all that anger and frustration on me. I promise I can handle it."

I yelled into her face, "You are insane! You are a psychotic bitch! And what do you mean she won't be bothering us?"

"Ugh, you're still on that? I meant that I talked to her when I was at the store, and she promised that she's going to leave you alone," she rattled off while staring at the ceiling. She took a deep breath, then returned her penetrating gaze.

I stared back.

She smiled and laughed. Brit composed herself, looked at me, and said, "No, I'm just fucking with you. Maddie is dead."

"What do you mean she's dead?" I shook her shoulders; my hands might have unintentionally slipped around her neck.

"Get your hands off me!" she yelled. But it wasn't like anyone could hear her. We were out at my parents' house in the middle of nowhere. I could take her out to the cornfield and bury her alive.

Nobody would ever know.

SHE'S TOXIC

I raised my hands over my head and stepped back from the bed. "There's no way she's dead."

She stood next to me. "Oh, there you go, being a little bitch again. Yup, she's dead, just like your hot little friend Mike."

I threw her to the ground and restrained myself from kicking her in the face while she was vulnerable. She laughed. I wanted to bust her face open. I wanted to see blood coursing from her wounds. She brought out the worst in me.

"Get the hell out of here," I said.

She got up and danced out of the room, smiling and laughing. I somehow kept myself from doing anything to her. Not sure how, it was tempting.

I didn't believe Brit until I logged onto Facebook. I checked Maddie's wall; the messages were trickling in. The first post I read was from Kayla:

I can't believe this happened. We have been friends as long as I can remember. I don't know what I'll do without you. There are so many memories running through my head, I don't have any memories from high school without you): I love you so much and I'll miss you more than words can say. I know you're in a better place and I can't wait to see you again someday.

Britney was right about one thing: Maddie was dead.

Twenty

I was stunned. I spent at least ten minutes staring at Kayla's post until it became a blur. I read a few other posts, much of the same. Many of Maddie's friends had already changed their profile pictures to include Maddie or had even posted pictures of Maddie by herself.

Nobody knew what happened. It was rumored she was shot in the head. Someone said that the responding officer hypothesized that someone broke into Maddie's apartment and shot her while she was watching TV, spraying blood against the wall.

If the murder had happened several hours ago, it would have given Brit enough time to shoot Maddie and sneak into my house. She might have shot me too if I hadn't turned around. I didn't see a gun though, so I might have been safe.

It was difficult enough to cope with Maddie dying, but I also had to deal with the possibility of Brit being responsible—but no, it wasn't possible. I'd known Britney for five years. It was beyond her capability. I wasn't sure if I loved her anymore, but I felt some obligation help her regain her sanity.

SHE'S TOXIC

I thought of the messages from ES and GR, and the message I received while on my dirt road with Maddie. I wondered if the Colombian Lords were coming at me from another angle. Maybe they murdered Maddie to get to me. If that was their intent, then they had delivered a crushing blow.

Spending time with Maddie had reminded me of old times spent with Britney. I'd relished the opportunity to establish such a genuine connection with Maddie, but I felt guilty because of Brit. Brit had been a beautiful girl with a beautiful heart when I met her—and throughout our relationship. Her abrupt deterioration had blown my mind and was illogical. Others must have noticed her slide before Mike's death, but for whatever reason, I didn't.

And I still didn't know how or why Britney had changed so much. Maybe my being kicked off the football team had finally taken its toll on her. She might have wanted to support me when shit hit the fan, but in the end, it might have proven too much for her to handle.

I would continue to protect Brit for the time being. It didn't seem rational considering that she might have been responsible for the deaths of Mike and Maddie, but I had no proof, and she was all I had left.

If I spoke to the authorities, I wouldn't disclose that I'd had sex with Maddie. Disclosing our relationship would open the door for any inquisitive detective to rush to a conclusion, especially in a rural area where crime was uncommon. I didn't want to become a suspect. They'd quickly find motive. Detective Minden terrified me. I didn't want to face him.

I phoned Britney after reading the news on Facebook.

"Hi! You have reached Britney, please leave a message!"

I received a text message from an unknown number as soon as I got off the phone:

Guess u found out the whore is dead. Boooo fucking hoooo. It's better this way.

I shook my head. Unbelievable. I assumed the message was from Brit, but I couldn't be sure. I sent a text to both numbers, just to make sure she got it:

Go to hell you crazy bitch!

Maddie's wake was the Thursday afternoon following her death. I planned to ride to St. Luke's Catholic Church with Kourt as my chauffeur. She had renewed contact with me following the news of Maddie's death. She wanted to attend the wake together, so I relented. I had to remember that Kourt was just a year younger than Maddie, and they had developed a friendship during high school, primarily after I'd graduated.

After they had become friends, Kourt would sometimes tag along when Britney and I went out with a group. I remember being shocked the first time my sister brought a date along. I jumped at the opportunity for the role reversal and for a chance to be a commentator on her love life. Those were the days.

I drove out to my parents' house where Kourt was already outside, waiting next to her car. I hugged her, but her body felt lifeless in my arms. She wasn't doing well. She still hadn't snapped back from whatever had knocked her down the year before. We got into her car and took off for Gentry.

"How are you hanging in there, sister?"

SHE'S TOXIC

"I'm okay, I guess. I was closer to her in high school, but it's still a bit rough. How are you getting by? You two had been close lately." She wiped a tear from her cheek.

"I couldn't believe what happened." I paused, not wanting to say it, but went ahead anyway. "I'm worried about Britney more than anything. I think she might have been involved. She's getting worse every day. She's lost it, but I want to help her."

I hadn't told anyone that I thought Britney was involved in Maddie's death. I also hadn't told anyone about how Brit laughed after telling me the news. I followed the chain of suspicion in my mind and saw myself becoming a suspect. I couldn't let that happen. I was skirting a slippery slope.

"Why would Britney do anything like that? I'm almost certain Maddie killed herself. She hadn't been doing well; I'm sure you knew that."

She would do it because I had sex with Maddie. "No idea." I hated lying to my sister, but she would never forgive me for cheating on Brit. If word got out, people might suspect I'd silenced Maddie.

"She's seemed off for a few months now," I said. "And it's been much worse lately."

"But do you believe she could kill someone? That's intense, even if she's crazy."

"Yeah, you're telling me. I'm not sure what to do though. I loved her for so long, but I can't handle it anymore." It felt good to open up. Once again, if only I'd listened to Mike—or anyone.

We both fell silent as Kourt pulled into the church parking lot. I assumed she had run out of things to say. She parked her car, then took a deep breath before opening her door.

The church was located in downtown Gentry. St. Luke's was a Catholic church built over sixty years ago. In typical Catholic style, it had a large steeple—reaching toward God, towering above all other buildings. The interior was massive and ornately detailed. Large stained-glass windows lined the north and south walls. I counted at least thirty rows of pews on each side. The church could hold at least 600 average-sized people.

Most of the people who settled in the area were Catholic or Lutheran, similar to many places in Illinois. Two people will seldom interpret scripture or an event the same way. There's always room for interpretation, especially when emotion is involved. Likewise, there were several ways to interpret Maddie's death, or at least the cause.

I wanted to discount Brit as a suspect, but I couldn't. She had laughed. Why would anyone in their right mind laugh about such an atrocity? She had motive, but it seemed like a stretch. Although the authorities were investigating Maddie's death as a homicide, she could have killed herself. I had no way of knowing.

I had witnessed Maddie's mental deterioration firsthand. She was never the shining example of healthy self-esteem, but to commit suicide? She would have had to exhaust all other options, and I couldn't see it, even though she had asked me if anyone would miss her—it had seemed like hyperbole. I didn't want to believe that all the signs were evident. It was probably my fault for not saying anything.

But Brit knew that people would be so quick to jump to suicide as the cause.

Psycho bitch.

SHE'S TOXIC

Kourt clung to me as we entered the church, similar to the way Britney had hung onto me at Mike's funeral. Maddie's coffin was centered up front. It was a closed-casket, but a large picture of Maddie graced the front of the church. In the picture, she was wearing a black dress, looking every bit like the vivacious young woman she was—or had been. The flowers atop the coffin might have been light purple, but I had to look away after a second. I was suffocated by the knowledge that she was inside that cold block of steel. I attempted to swallow back the tears, but I failed.

The routine was getting old.

I recognized Maddie's parents standing nearby, with presumed family members to their right. To their left, a line of people circled around the right side of the pews, extending to the front doors of the church. There were also hundreds sitting down—many of them much too young to lose a close friend. The church was filled to the brim, reflective of Maddie's reach. She probably had friends in every town within an hour of Gentry.

Faces were red and tear-stained. Intermittent sobs filled the church, along with the occasional sneeze and "I'm so sorry for your loss." A somber country song played, it sounded like "If I Die Young" by The Band Perry.

Her wake was a blur, just like Mike's funeral. The priest had known Maddie her entire life, so he was able to recount several stories from her childhood up to the present—although Maddie liked to party, she had remained active in the church. Maddie's mom, grandpa, and two of Maddie's college friends gave eulogies. I expected Kayla to share a few words, but I didn't see her among the numerous mourners.

Britney was not in attendance. I hadn't seen her since she broke the news of Maddie's death. She'd claimed that she had to visit her grandma in Ohio for her eightieth birthday. I was the "selfish asshole" who was "in love with Maddie" because I preferred to stick around town to attend her wake. Brit even accused me of wanting to rape Maddie's corpse before she was buried.

Nope, I am not a necrophiliac.

I shouldn't have been so ecstatic to be alone for a few days. I relished the opportunity to collect my thoughts, and to decide if I was going to speak to Detective Minden.

Or I could run.

Twenty-One

Detective Minden resurfaced two days after Maddie's wake. He had contacted everyone with recent contact or extensive contact with Maddie. I would admit to confiding in Maddie about Mike, though I might fail to mention that the primary reason we spoke was because of our shared relationship with Britney.

Minden had left two, hand-written notes on my parents' front door, which seemed peculiar. I needed to respond to ensure that I wouldn't become a suspect. He had already somehow developed an affinity for me, and I suspected he would be dying to hear my voice again. Truth be told, I kind of missed the guy. I also needed an update on Mike's case.

I looked outside as Detective Minden approached my parents' house in his black Challenger. I paid more attention to his car this time—it was designed as an undercover car, but the additional antennae and berry lights against the back window gave it away. He pumped the gas and spun out as he entered the driveway. It made me wonder how fast he ever drove that thing. He didn't need to rely on the Autobahn—he could floor it wherever.

"Hey there, son, what's going on?" Detective Minden jumped out of the car. "It's been a while since we've had a little chat. How have you been? Sorry to hear about Maddie." He gave the sign of the cross. "Your friends are dropping like flies. How do you explain that?"

"Bad luck I guess."

"Yeah. Bad luck. *Right.*"

"Have you made any progress on Mike's case?"

"Well, I do have some good news regarding Mike, though I do realize that it can't be *good news* considering he's still dead. But Ty, we believe that his death was the result of nothing more than a routine car accident."

Unexpected response, but I was relieved—for Brit's sake.

"But you said you thought his death was the result of foul play; there must have been something that made you change your mind." I'd wondered why I hadn't heard from Minden in a while, but now it made sense. And I'd distanced myself from Gentry, for the most part. Notwithstanding, telling me before now would have been a decent thing to do.

"Ty, my boy, I can't disclose that information with you, as it's technically an active investigation. Suffice it to say that we missed something. I told you that Britney was the last person to see Mike alive. Well, we were misled. That's all I can tell you now, but you might be able to draw a conclusion based upon that information. You're a smart man."

"Unbelievable. I wish you could tell me more."

"What more can I say, Ty? I've already told you more than I should have. But now that we've cleared that up, do you have any

SHE'S TOXIC

information regarding Maddie's death? I haven't been able to crack this bad boy open. I mean, I have a few theories, but they're just that, they're theories—until I can get more information."

He cleared his throat. I was about to speak, but he continued, "Some people assume it was a suicide, but there's a problem with that. There's no gunshot residue. Plus, the angle of the gunshot doesn't quite coincide with a self-inflicted wound. You see, the bullet entered here, at this angle. There's no way she could have held her arm like *this* and pulled the trigger. And I apologize if I'm being too graphic, but hey, we're both men, right? Just speak up if you can't handle it and I'll temper it back a little." He paused. I wasn't sure if he expected a response or if he was preparing to launch into another mind-blowing monologue.

I responded, "Thanks, detective, but I'm not too sensitive. You can describe anything you need to. I want to help, but I'm afraid I don't have much information." My eyes fell to my feet. I hoped I'd held eye contact long enough to be believable.

"First of all, please call me Ron or Ronnie. I think we know each other well enough by now to move past the formalities. I want this to be as casual as possible for you." He clasped his hands together as he looked around the farm for a few seconds. He reestablished eye contact after two hard blinks, which wrinkled his entire face. A confident smile emerged. "Ty, I have these theories, and you would be surprised at how much useless information can help. It might seem useless to you, but to me, that information is like gold, bud. Like gold! I need to strike it rich."

He leaned forward and put his hand on my forearm, leaning into me like he was trying to keep someone from hearing our conversation, "Okay, now if I can just get a little information from you. Hey, it might not even seem relevant at first. But I might acquire another tidbit from the guy down the road. Hell, that might not be relevant either, even coupled with your tip. But if I get to the next guy, and he can give me info that ties it all together, then we got something."

He clapped. "Then we got gold, baby! Gold rush! Hallelujah—the spirit is within!" He rocked back on his heels and threw his hands up to the sky, appearing to have been reborn.

This guy was a trip. I needed to get rid of him.

It seemed like he wanted irrelevant information so I would give him just that. If he was going to put the pieces together, it would happen regardless.

"I talked to Maddie a few times before she died." *We had sex. My girlfriend is psychotic—she threatened me with a knife.* "We consoled each other after my friend Mike passed."

"Bravo, Ty, bravo! I knew you had it in ya!" I wasn't sure if he was being sincere or an arrogant asshole. Naturally, he continued before I even thought to respond. "See, that's what I'm talking about, my man, little pieces. They add up. They add up to something big. That's the gold rush I've been telling you about. It's coming. I can feel it. I can feel it deep down inside me." He gave a tooth-filled smile. He must have had a few extra teeth; something didn't look realistic.

Minden interrupted my thoughts. "Okay, so let me ask you this, and if you don't feel comfortable answering, that's fine, but why did you talk to Maddie instead of Britney? Why didn't you seek consolation from your girlfriend? It's those little pieces of

SHE'S TOXIC

information, Ty." He appeared more serious as his eyes narrowed. "They add up."

I tensed as I sensed that Minden already knew what had happened, that he had pieced together the motive for Britney, and possibly a motive for me. *Shit. Shit. Shit.* His confidence was unnerving—he never missed a beat, but maybe he was full of shit, trying to get me to slip.

"Is there anything else you'd like to tell me? We could drive back into town and maybe you could talk a little more this time." Minden was zeroing in for the kill. But he didn't have me yet. He was bluffing.

"It looks like you might have something on your mind, son. I know this because I read people; and no, that's not necessarily part of the job description, but that's what I do. It makes my job a little easier. In fact, it makes me a damn good detective. I'm trying to read you, Ty, and my gut is telling me that there's a hell of a lot more beneath the surface."

I looked him in the eyes, unwavering, for once. "If I think of anything else, I'll call you. Do you have a card? I lost the number you left me." I needed to get rid of this hometown hero who felt like he had accomplished something in this damn town.

"Nah, no card. You should know that by now. I don't do business that way. I like to build a more, how do you say, personal relationship with people. I can write my number down for you, son. That way you can have an autograph from the best *damn* detective in Gentry. It's the same *damn* town you grew up in. It's the same *damn* town you played football for." He shot me a wink. At least we operated on a similar wavelength.

His patronizing was getting old, but I told him that was fair enough. I found a receipt so he could give me a number that I'd never call again. I regretted waiting around the house to speak with him. I should have taken off and kept running. I could have driven to Vermont, and nobody would have ever known where I went. But I'd convinced myself that he had no clue. He wanted to try to scare me into submission. He was a small-town hero who was once on top of the world, trying to hold on to his power and sanity. He feigned having the case under control, but it was all in his mind, some bullshit delusion.

Minden fired up his car and shot off into the sunset, or more literally, in the opposite direction of the sunset. He waved back at me for two hundred yards before flooring it. He squealed his tires when he shot south at the intersection, leaving a small cloud of dust in his wake.

Back in Gentry, I drove to The Barnyard for a drink. I'd always enjoyed drinking, but I was now doing it with more regularity. Carly was working yet again—it was the third time I'd seen her working in the last month or two. I couldn't be certain how long it had been since my fight with Mike.

The bar wasn't busy; there might have been ten people scattered between the bar and the high-tops. The larger dining room was dark, already shut down for the night.

"Okay, Ty, this is three times now since," she paused to look at her phone—hand in the air, "June 20th!"

"Wow, that's impressive. How do you remember the date?" I asked as I cozied myself up to my familiar barstool.

SHE'S TOXIC

"Oh, don't feel too special." She laughed. "That was the last Saturday night I've worked. How's life been treating ya?" She grinned and lowered her voice. "How did it go with Alexa the other night?"

"We just caught up, nothing too crazy," I said. Carly raised her eyebrows. "I feel good, but shit's been crazy."

"I'm sorry, Ty. I heard about Maddie, poor girl."

It was shaping up to be the exact conversation I didn't want to have. I changed the topic and she eventually lost interest.

I spent the next several hours in a dramatic staring contest with my beer, drinking whenever I lost. I couldn't be sure how many I had—maybe four, maybe eleven.

I left the bar a few minutes after midnight and took a stroll downtown, inspecting the old buildings that I seldom gave a second look. I walked down an alley, and that's when it happened.

"Surprise, mother fucker!"

The back of my head went numb; I fell to the ground. I scrambled across the dirt, attempting to regain my bearings. My head was in a fog. I looked up and saw a man looking back at me rubbing his right forearm down to his elbow, back and forth. His forearm must have been his weapon of choice.

"Yeah, you like that, bitch?" The man who hit me laughed as three other men joined him. I thought I recognized one of the men, possibly from my research into the Colombian Lords. As they came closer—within striking distance, I closed my eyes, and prepared for the worst.

One man took a knee beside me. He pulled my face to his and whispered into my ear, "Esteban and Guillermo told you stay away from Britney. What part of that did you not understand?" He grabbed my chin. "Answer me!"

"I'm trying to help. Something's wrong with her," I squeaked. I now had names for both "ES" and "GR." My eyes shifted away from the man speaking to me. The guy I recognized was now hidden behind the crowd.

"Help her? The only thing that's wrong with her is you, so you're damn right it's your fault." He readied his right fist and brought it to my face, but stopped just before making contact. He guffawed as I exhaled. By the time I finished exhaling, he reared back again, but he didn't stop short this time. "Piece of shit. She's with Logan now. Let her go!"

He backed away, and two others replaced him above me. One man was wearing an Oakland A's jersey with green wristbands on each arm.

A kick to my ribs, followed by another kick to my back.

As I attempted to avoid another blow, I overheard a muffled voice in the background. "Don't kill him, just fuck him up. Make sure he gets the message."

Another kick. A punch to my face.

They had busted open the top of my head; the profuse blood flow obscured my vision. I struggled to protect myself, but my options were limited.

"Help! Help!" I tried to scream out, but they were blaring music. Cars were parked on each end of the alley, making it difficult for a passerby to see what was happening.

"Remember me?" One of the men stood over me, grinning. It was the guy I thought I recognized. I thought he had been the

SHE'S TOXIC

first to kick me, but I could barely see through the blood. "Yeah, that's right, you have to remember me."

I tried to concentrate through the fog that had developed as a result of having the shit beat out of me. It looked like Miguel, the guy who had warned me about Britney so long ago.

"Miguel?" I choked out, spitting blood from my busted lip.

"Yeah, mother fucker. That's right. Funny how things work out isn't it, pretty boy?" He laughed. "But you're not looking so pretty right now." He leaned down and grabbed the right side of my face for closer inspection. "Damn, that looks like it hurts." He turned to walk away.

I closed my eyes and tried to sink into the ground, but Miguel wasn't finished. "You're fucked up, man. I wouldn't do this if you didn't deserve it. I told you that Britney Boyer was crazy, way back then, but you couldn't let her go." He pulled his right arm back and brought it within inches of my face before bringing it down to his side.

"Rough him up a little more. But remember, not too much. We're not catching a case because of this little bitch." Miguel fell back toward the vehicles as the other three men approached me.

"You take it just like your sister," Esteban said, before punching me again, knocking me out cold.

Twenty-Two

I awoke in my bedroom at my parents' house. I heard someone shuffling around in Kourt's room; I hoped it was her and not Miguel or one of the other guys who had jumped me. I couldn't remember anything after they knocked me out, but I guess it was possible that they had dropped me off out here. It was that or I'd called someone to give me a ride.

I remembered what Esteban had said and wondered if Kourt could have hooked up with him. Considering her susceptible state, I wouldn't have put it past her. I hated to think that my sister might have been involved.

My thoughts turned to Miguel. He had dealt weed back in high school and was a hot head, but I couldn't believe he was involved with the Colombian Lords. He had been obsessed with Brit back then, so I wasn't even sure why he would want to help Logan.

Miguel was indeed a stumbling block in the infancy of my relationship with Brit. It had been especially bad during football season when I would see him every day. Whenever he walked by

SHE'S TOXIC

me, he would throw out quips such as *she crazy* or *better watch out, man*. I tried not to let him bother me, but he was a difficult guy to ignore. He had continued to send me random text messages and tried to send Britney texts until she blocked him.

He had toned it down after football season, likely due to having a steady girlfriend. After my graduation, I didn't hear from him until I came back to Gentry to attend prom with Britney. I remembered that night because of how dazzling Brit looked, but I also thought back to Miguel's continued warnings.

"I guess she hasn't scared you off yet. You're a stronger man than me," Miguel whispered into my ear while patting my back. He then tried to introduce me to his new girl, but I gave a simple nod, eager to get back to my girlfriend.

I made my way back through the crowd of high school kids to find Britney. She was still in high school—only a junior, but she wasn't any different from the college girls I ran into at CIU. Brit had matured significantly in the two years I'd known her, but she was still the same in many ways. Her smile, her eyes, and her voice had all continued to drive me crazy. I didn't think that would ever change.

"Darling."

"My prince." I took her outstretched hand and led her onto the dance floor.

Brit was radiant. She was wearing a tiny, strapless red dress that looked as if it were custom made for her. She complemented her dress by donning what I presumed to be her mother's jewelry. Diamonds adorned her neck and wrists. I wasn't sure if she had snuck them out or if her mom had allowed her to wear them.

I'd rented a Tom Ford tuxedo from a place in Springfield. Prom was important to Britney, so I didn't want to cut corners. I'd even wrangled up silver cufflinks to complete my ensemble—it was easy to spend a little money when I was on a full ride. I looked good on my own, but with Britney on my arm, I was unstoppable.

"You better not leave me when you become a big-shot NFL quarterback," she said.

I laughed. "No way, Brit. You have nothing to worry about." I kissed her lips.

She frowned. "But what about actresses and models? If you turn into a big star, they'll be all over—"

I stopped her with a finger to the lips. She trailed off mumbling; she closed her eyes and kissed my finger. When she opened her eyes, she still didn't look convinced.

"Britney, as long as you tell me you love me, I'll be right here. Even if you stop loving me for some reason, you can bet your life that I'll try to change your mind. I'll never let you go without a fight. What we have is special.

"There's something about you that hypnotizes me and doesn't let go. I felt it from the first moment I saw you. It's not just your beauty, but it's something much deeper. I love your beautiful soul. I guess it's kind of like that old Jesse McCartney song." I laughed.

She giggled while a few tears slid down her cheeks. She hugged me hard. "I love you so much, Tyler Matthew. How did I ever get so lucky?"

But that was then, and this was now. That part of my life was over, and I needed to accept that Britney wasn't the same. I would

SHE'S TOXIC

tell myself that I needed to get away from her, but once she returned from Ohio, it would be too easy to regress back to whatever I was trying to do with her. I wasn't sure if I was trying to love her, help her, or save her—probably a combination. I guess it would depend on if anyone else died.

I'd promised to stand by her side, but I had to take a different kind of stand. Something had to give, and I wasn't sure what I would do. I wondered if I would stand idly by as she poisoned both of us. Or maybe I would poison myself after believing she'd died—just like Romeo. Maybe I already had.

Even in this lifetime—the lifetime where I thought I'd secured her love—maybe we were still star-crossed lovers. Maybe tragedy had always been, and would forever be, an inescapable facet of our connection.

Twenty-Three

I had missed three calls from Detective Minden within twelve hours. He had called twice the night before around eight, and again at 6:15 in the morning. He had failed to leave a message after the first two calls, but left a *riveting* message after the third:

"Ty, my boy, we need to talk about our little situation. I think you know what I'm talking about. The river is flowing, my friend. And by 'river is flowing', I mean the gold rush is on! Let's schedule a time for a pow-wow. We can even sit around a fire if you like, smoke a little peace pipe. I'll give you reefer immunity. Ha Ha. It's up to you, son. Give me a call back, you have my number, but I'll leave it again..." He left his number at the end of the message, along with a hearty *"Talk to you soon, son."*

I didn't have the time or strength to be preoccupied with his shit. My head was pounding from the beating I'd taken, and all I wanted to do was convalesce in my bed. I hoped he would discuss arresting the guys who had jumped me, but I knew better. And If I heard him talk about the "gold rush" one more time...

Minden knew where I lived—if he wanted to talk, he'd come find me. *It's all a ruse*, I kept telling myself. The guy was a small-

SHE'S TOXIC

town, insecure loser on a power trip, masquerading as a big-time detective.

I heard the rev of an engine from at least a mile away, south of the turn for my parents' place. I turned and saw a vehicle heading north toward our road. I couldn't quite make out the color, but I knew it was Detective Minden coming to jostle me.

As the car made the turn, I could discern that it was Minden's black Challenger. I spied the extra antennae, but couldn't yet see the lights. As soon as I tried to make out their outline, the berries flashed. He floored the accelerator, blasting his car forward.

Less than a quarter-mile separated us—I wasn't sure how he would slow down enough to make the turn. As he approached, he drifted sideways into the driveway. I'd never seen anyone drift like that in person.

Minden hung out the window. "Check it out!"

What in the hell is with this guy?

I was frozen in my tracks. I'd wanted to take off once I realized he was coming down the road, but he would have caught me. He'd probably try to run me off the road or shoot out my tires. I stood immobilized as he hopped out of his car.

"Ty, my boy, why no call? Damn, you look like shit. What happened to your face? Oh well, not important right now. But rest assured, I will be looking into this." He spat his chewing tobacco and licked his lips. "Ty, I thought we were in this thing together. I thought we were going to strike gold together. Get rich to-ge-ther!" He clenched his right hand into a fist and pumped it into the sky to emphasize each syllable. I couldn't tell if he was furious or having an orgasm. He released a long sigh after he brought his arm back down, and he closed his eyes. *I guess he had an orgasm.* I wasn't going to ask.

"Well? Come on, this is a dialogue, not a monologue. This needs to be one man talking to another man. I'm beginning to feel a little crazy talking to myself over here." I snapped back to reality, or at least what had become my reality.

"I'm sorry. I just got your messages. I had my phone off and—"

"You're lying to me, Ty. I don't like it. Let's be friends here. We can be two friends scouring the Illinois prairie, panning for gold. Now there's a reason why you've been slippery, and I think I've pieced it all together."

It was all a show. He was just trying to get me to talk, but I wouldn't give him anything else.

I gained some courage and threw a wrench into his thought process. "Yeah, Maddie killed herself, right?" I looked as close to his eyes as I could—comfortably anyway.

Minden let out a boisterous laugh, "How stupid are you? Someone shot her in cold blood. POW! Blood everywhere. That girl didn't want to die. You should have known that. You two were humping, weren't you? Hell, I don't need you to answer that, your semen was all over her place—it was on every article of her clothing. God damn, boy. You two must have gone after it like rabbits."

He held up a hand as if requesting a high-five. I was too shocked to say or do anything.

"Good for you, man. I'm impressed. But who did it, huh? Who pulled the trigger? I have texts and calls between you and

SHE'S TOXIC

Britney just before Maddie's death. It was a conspiracy, right? Had to cap her. You felt guilty, had to prove to Britney that you loved her. Britney is a fine piece of ass in her own right. I knew it from the instant I laid eyes on her in that parking lot. Woo-whee! And you probably knew that Maddie was going to either kill herself or find someone else to screw sooner or later. She was quite the drunk little slut after all. Excuse my language. Or hell, maybe Britney did it herself, jealous of your trysts. That's the one missing link. But I'm close, Ty, I'm so damn close." As before, he zeroed in on me, eyes narrowing as he pulled closer, before whispering, "You're going down for this, one way or the other. I know what happened. I just have to prove it."

In one fell swoop, Minden made it obvious that he wasn't full of shit. Was he messing with me the entire time? It was all a goddamn game to him. I hadn't done anything though. He could theorize it was a conspiracy that I had somehow helped Britney execute, but he had nothing on me.

Nothing concrete.

If Britney was going down, then I guess it was better her than me. She had put me through some horrible shit. But yet, I despised this man, possibly even more than I feared Britney. Brit and I at least had a beautiful history together. This guy was just a pompous asshole.

"Gold rush." He winked before turning back to his car. "You'll be hearing from me soon. I might even have a shiny pair of handcuffs for you to try on next time." He smiled and laughed as he reversed into my yard. He revved the engine, sending dirt clods flying. "See ya later, Ty, my boy!"

I needed to go somewhere to think. I'd previously considered going back into the woods to mediate, but I needed my dirt road. I needed a place with positive memories—and with visibility.

I drove out to my spot.

I was glad that Brit was in Ohio, for at least another day. I thought back to the first night we came out here together, back when I was on top of the world—when we were on top of the world. But since that time, our lives had taken a dramatic turn.

I never once thought I'd bring anyone else to the same spot, even if we ended our relationship—it was sacred ground between us. But I had come out here with Maddie. Maddie and Brit used to be such great friends, and that aspect might have broken my heart more than anything else.

It was a quiet night, almost too quiet. Part of me wondered if it was the calm before the storm. Minden was closing in, and I wasn't sure what he might try to pin on me. And now I had to contend with Miguel, Logan, Esteban, and Guillermo. I prayed that Miguel was merely trying to put a scare into me following what had happened in high school. Yet they seemed intent on terrorizing my life because she was with Logan and I was interfering with *their property*. I still had the welts—and possible internal bleeding—to prove it.

I checked my phone and noticed a voicemail from yet another unknown number. I played the voicemail: *Ty, this is Britney. Please call me back at this number. We need to talk.*

Against my better judgment, I called her.

"Hey, it's Ty."

"Oh, hi. What are you doing?"

SHE'S TOXIC

"Just hanging out on my dirt road. How's Ohio?"

"You better be careful, be very careful. You are such a little bitch."

Click.

Twenty-Four

I returned to The Barnyard the next night to make sense of my life. I sat at the bar, beaten and alone, wondering how I could move past all that had happened in the last two months. I told myself I would only have two beers but drank a little whiskey instead, hopeful that it would do more to mask the pain radiating throughout my body.

Carly wasn't working, so I didn't feel as much pressure to talk to anyone. I sat at the end of the bar and was able to avoid any meaningful conversation. It was a Monday night, so the bar was dead to begin with.

I finally left the bar, smelling the whiskey strong on my breath. I stood outside and stared into space until I heard the roar of a familiar engine heading down Main Street from the west. I didn't even need to look as I knew it was Detective Minden. The man was adept at always knowing my location.

I wondered what kind of monologue he had prepared for me today. He would probably talk about the gold rush, flash some handcuffs, and practice his drifting. That much was certain. He

SHE'S TOXIC

would also find a way to fit in some condescending speech. I was tired of his pontificating.

His engine roared over the otherwise silent downtown. I braced myself. I wanted to run, but there was no escape. Besides, I had nothing to run from. It wasn't like he could arrest me for anything. I'd only done what was right, what anyone would have done under similar circumstances.

I stood only a few feet from the front door of The Barnyard, in eager anticipation. Minden drifted around the corner with AC/DC's "Highway to Hell" blaring through his speakers.

I couldn't help but shake my head; no point in trying to figure this guy out. *Cocky cock sucker.* I waited for some words of wisdom from my new best friend.

He jumped out of his car, all smiles. "Ty, my boy! I can't believe that you're still around this town. I figured you would have hopped on one of those buses that go down to Me-hi-co, crossed the border like that fella from *Shawshank*. I must say, I do admire the integrity. I appreciate that you're willing to stand up and take responsibility for what you've done. That says a lot about a man. You may have fucked up—may have been responsible for taking a life, but at least you're here to answer for it. I had you all wrong, Ty. Had you all wrong."

He walked toward me with a bottle of whiskey swinging in his hand. He was no longer concerned with hiding his alcohol in a thermos. "Want a drink? I'll try to be a decent guy about this. Hell, we struck it rich, Ty! Gold rush!"

I snapped out of my bewildered daze. Once the guy opened his mouth, he pulled me in. I couldn't pry myself away. "Nah, I'm not thirsty. And I haven't done anything illegal." I knew where I wanted to stick a handful of gold though.

He clapped his hands and pointed his right index finger at me. "That's a lie, Ty, and now I can prove it. You might sit there and try to tell me that you're a law abiding citizen, and you might attempt to explain any wrongdoing as some kind of necessity. But what you're failing to understand is that you're responsible.

"I *know* what happened between you and Maddie, and I *know* what happened between you and Britney. Once Britney said her piece, you had to remedy the situation in your own special way. I'll admit that I was running in circles like a dog with three legs for a while. I had trouble separating the truth from the bullshit, Ty. You fed me a lot of bullshit. Lies. I was disappointed at first, but I suppose I can't blame ya. Letting go of a woman like that? I couldn't do it either."

I finally had a chance to interject. "I swear. I don't know where you're getting your information from, but there wasn't a situation I had to remedy. I've never hurt anyone my entire life," I said, without hesitation—believing I still needed to cover Britney, even though it probably made me look guilty. I'd dug myself into a hole by loving her too much and by hanging onto our love too tight.

He sighed. "Ty, look at me." He pointed a finger to each of his eyes. "My sources are sound. I don't even need a witness because I have something much better. Now, I don't quite have your prints on the gun yet. We haven't been able to find the murder weapon, but I'm taking you in on another charge." He flashed his tooth-filled smile.

SHE'S TOXIC

"Another charge? You have nothing on me!"

A marked police cruiser parked next to Detective Minden. Detective Miller.

She stepped out of her car with a pallid expression. "Mr. Reynolds" was all she could muster.

"Well, well, well, it looks like I have back up. I promised that I'd bring out a shiny set of handcuffs, and I'm a man of my word. I told you that you're going down for this one way or the other, didn't I?" The left corner of his lips turned up in a smirk.

"There's no way you'll ever have my prints on the gun unless someone plants them! I know for damn sure I didn't kill anyone."

"Ah, but you did. Now let me slide these cuffs around your wrists, and we'll take a ride to the county jail. Consider it a free lift." He laughed as he pulled out his cuffs and started toward me.

"Ty, please, make this easy on yourself," Miller pleaded. They had the good cop, bad cop routine down.

I panicked. I was sweating through my shirt. I tried to turn and run, but Minden overtook me, pushing me into the ground. "Come on, Tyler. You're only making this more difficult on yourself. You know that you're guilty. It's time to repent, son. Repent and ye shall be set free!"

"This is crazy. You can't do this!" I squirmed, trying to escape his iron-clad grasp, which was a mistake. I heard the whoosh of a nightstick, and then the burning sensation of the contact against the back of my head.

Twenty-Five

When I finally came to, I had no idea of the time. I was lying on a cement floor in a holding cell—hungover as hell. I looked at the vertical bars on the door, the metal toilet, and the barely cushioned bed; I guess I'd decided the floor was more comfortable.

Detective Minden must have heard me stir. "Ty, why did you have to resist arrest? That wasn't intelligent, son. What am I supposed to do with you now?"

"I swear I'm innocent." I tried to rise to my feet, but my body was aching from the tackle and whack over the head. "I didn't resist arrest either. I was lying still."

"Now Ty, we all know that isn't true. You were squirming, trying to get away from me for some reason. Why would you ever want to leave me? You're having an increasingly difficult time distinguishing facts from lies, truth from fiction. It's becoming problematic for you. But I do have some good news. Well, good news for you, but sad news for me. You somehow posted bail." He motioned for a guard to open the door. "So get the hell out of my sight, son. I'm tired of looking at you."

SHE'S TOXIC

The cell door opened, and Detective Minden, assisted by two terrified-looking guards, escorted me down the hall and outside the Nash County Jail. I wondered who had bailed me out. There was a short list of people I knew who were still alive, and I couldn't imagine Miguel forking money over. My parents were still in Hawaii, so I figured it must have been Kourt.

I walked outside and had to shield my eyes from the sun—it was so damn bright. Kourt greeted me, though *greeted* might not have been the operative word.

"Would you please tell me why in the hell you did that?" She grabbed my wrist and swung me around so that I was facing her. Her strength surprised me, or maybe I was just weak.

"I'm not even sure why they arrested me," I said. "This crazy detective wants to arrest me for Maddie's death, but he said that he doesn't have enough evidence yet. Did they tell you why they arrested me?"

"They said you were disturbing the peace, that you became confrontational with a detective. Ty, I know you've been through a lot, but you can't— I'm sorry, I'm sorry."

"Yeah, I might have said some things to him, but it's because he keeps trying to pin Maddie's death on me."

"Maddie's death? Why would they try to pin Maddie's death on you?"

"No idea. The detective has something against me. I swear he's the one harassing me. I was defending my rights."

We walked across the street to her car, parked along the opposite curb. The morning air was refreshing in light of the recent heat, but the pollen in the air made me sneeze.

I needed an allergy pill.

Kourt rolled her eyes. "You owe me for this one, and you better not violate your bond. I had to borrow money from Mom and Dad's safe."

I wondered how much money she had to take. If Minden ever arrested me for Maddie's murder, Kourt wouldn't be able to scrounge up enough to post bond. I also wondered how often Kourt had *borrowed* money from my parents' safe.

"You didn't tell Mom and Dad about what happened, did you? And how in the hell did you get in the safe?" I asked as she pulled away from the curb.

"No, I didn't tell them. They won't be back for another week, and hopefully they won't notice it's gone." She sighed. "I never take *that* much."

"Yeah, I bet."

She glared at me. "They've spent so much more money on you. I don't think it's a big deal if I take a few twenties now and then. And you're welcome by the way."

I wasn't sure how they had spent *so much more money* on me. Our parents had bought each of us vehicles when we turned sixteen. Both vehicles cost close to $30,000. If anything, hers was more expensive. But I had more pressing concerns at this point.

"Thank you," I relented, but quickly added, "Who in the hell is Esteban?"

She nearly ran the car off the road.

"How do you know about him?" she asked.

"He beat my ass the other day when his gang jumped me. I thought you brought me back to the house."

SHE'S TOXIC

"I did, after you called. But I'm sorry. He was just a dumb mistake…"

I tried to process her words, but it wasn't too surprising. I just hoped she wasn't somehow involved. No way, she couldn't be. We sat in silence for a couple minutes. I noticed a tear fall down her face.

I didn't want to push her regarding Esteban, so I backtracked.

"Whatever. We don't have to talk about that right now." She looked relieved. "But do you believe me? The detective is harassing me, and it's been worse after Maddie's death."

She paused. "Honestly? I don't know what to believe about this life anymore. I used to have the perfect life—we both did, and then just like that, our lives changed. We're always taught that bad things happen to bad people, and we believe that we're somehow above experiencing a tragedy—because we're good people, but we learned that's all bullshit."

Kourt had talked to a psychiatrist when she struggled with depression (which was another reason why my parents spent more money on her). I hated to bring up that part of her past, but I needed to speak with someone who might have answers regarding Brit's condition. I was running out of options, and I feared that I would take the fall if I didn't act fast.

"I still think Britney killed Maddie. She needs help. I didn't want to say anything, but I don't know what else to do. I'm running out of ideas."

"Ty, come on. You don't honestly believe that, do you? I know that losing Maddie was hard on you—it was hard on me too. I think about her every day."

After her prior statement, I felt no need to cushion her feelings. She sounded too much like Mike. It was clear she didn't believe me, so I came right out and asked, "Who was the shrink you talked to down in Springfield?"

Kourt sighed and patted her steering wheel, staring straight ahead. "I'm sorry, Ty. I didn't mean to upset you. I'm worried, that's all. I spoke with Dr. Niles."

"I think I should talk to him. Maybe he'll be able to explain what's happened to Britney. I'm running out of options. I can't talk to Mike, I can't talk to Maddie, and you think I've lost my damn mind."

"Maybe you should talk to him. He might be able to help."

"I sure as hell hope so."

"I hope so, too."

We both fell silent during the ride out to our parents' house.

Twenty-Six

Doctor Niles scheduled my appointment late the same afternoon. As I approached Springfield, I hoped he would be able to help. I needed to convince Britney to speak with someone to get the help she needed, but we hadn't spoken in days—other than her threatening phone call when I was out on my dirt road.

I drove down either Fifth or Sixth Street in downtown Springfield—I couldn't remember which of the one-way streets went south. His office was located on the southern tip of town. I could have stayed on Interstate 55 a little longer, but I kind of wanted to see the historical buildings. *Land of Lincoln.*

I turned onto Toronto Road, looking for an office complex across from a strip mall. I saw a sign for a "PXΠ event" at The University of Illinois at Springfield. It was probably a fraternity toga party disguised as a humanitarian relief effort. I imagined they even had their own *Godfather*. It was a life I envied.

I found the strip mall and parked next to a blue BMW M6; I wondered how many car payments my sister's visits covered for him. The outside of the office complex was nice but modest.

MATT ABRAMS

I walked into the office of Dr. James Niles, which housed a conservative lobby. There were four chairs in a waiting area, and a large window separating the receptionist from the *crazy assholes*. I imagined some of the crazies who had walked through the doors. I had to remind myself that my sister had been a patient, but she wasn't insane—she just had problems coping, but nobody knew what had happened to her, other than she had suffered from a depressive episode.

"Hi, I'm Natalia. Can I help you?" A beautiful young woman called out from behind the counter. She caught me by surprise with her raw, natural beauty. She was young, blonde hair, with an Eastern European or Russian accent. I guess it made sense considering her name.

"I'm Tyler Reynolds. I'm here to see Dr. Niles—but it's not for me. I'm here to talk with him about someone else."

"Mis-ter Rey-nolds," she drew out my name as she looked at the appointment book. "Oh, yes, you're a few minutes early *which is perfectly okay*. If you'd like to take a seat, Dr. Niles will be with you in ten to fifteen minutes." I didn't appreciate the tone, but I reasoned that was how she spoke to the clientele. I also caught her taking an extended look at my busted face. I must have been quite the sight.

I plopped down in a cushioned chair and thumbed through a pile of magazines. The general theme was "don't do it, you're worth it." I sighed as I contemplated my reality. I couldn't believe how this could have happened. While in high school, I never imagined that I'd be waiting to see a psychiatrist. I had the perfect life. But hey, I was still alive, and that had to count for something.

SHE'S TOXIC

Dr. Niles's assistant emerged from beyond the void while I was deep in thought. He called me back and told me to take a seat in room #11—my high school football number. I saw only a few rooms, but I wondered if they changed the numbers around to give his clients a room that corresponded with a pleasant memory. That wouldn't be a bad touch.

Niles walked into the observation room and asked me to follow him to his office. He was an older man, probably in his mid-sixties. He had a full head of snow-white hair with a thick beard and mustache. His hair made his blue eyes appear abnormally bright. He had a gentle look.

"Mr. Reynolds, it's great to see you." He raised his eyebrows. "Did you get into a fight?"

"I'm okay," I answered while shaking his hand.

"Please, take a seat. Your notes indicate that you're worried about someone close to you. I'm not sure how much I'll be able to help, but I'll do what I can." He pulled out a notepad and clicked open a pen. "So who are you concerned about, Tyler?"

I sat in a chair across from him. "My girlfriend, Britney."

"Ah, I should have guessed. When a third party seeks my services, they usually want to speak about their spouse or child. What are your concerns regarding Britney?"

"I'm not sure how to begin, but I think she's lost it. She flies off the deep end at the smallest provocation—it's almost like she's possessed."

"When did all of this begin?"

"I'm not sure, but it's getting worse. If I had to pinpoint a time, I'd say she went downhill after my friend died."

"Sorry to hear about your friend's passing. That's unfortunate." Niles gave my forearm a couple pats.

"Thanks. It was sudden. I probably haven't been the same since then either. I don't know, sometimes I think I've been too critical of her because of what I've been through. But she's not the same, and like I said, she keeps getting worse."

"It's often difficult for the human mind to respond to unexpected, negative events. What has worsened regarding your girlfriend?" Niles asked as he scribbled a note before leaning back in his black leather chair.

"Everything. She's never been so irrational. I didn't know who else to talk to, but I'm trying to figure out what's wrong with her. I've tried doing my own research, but I haven't had much luck. I think she might have bipolar disorder."

Dr. Niles moved forward to make another note. "You said that she has been irrational; could you elaborate?"

"She's become violent, doctor. When we fight, her eyes glaze over and it seems like she's possessed. I know that sounds crazy, she might not be possessed, but maybe it's a split-personality."

"It's unlikely she's possessed. Religious-based pseudo-science of preceding centuries commonly diagnosed someone as *possessed* when, in reality, the victim suffered from one of a host of conditions such as manic-depression and schizophrenia. Now, it's quite possible she's suffering from some disruption of sound mental health. Sadly, mental illness is far from an uncommon occurrence. Were there ever any prior indications that her mental health was out of balance?"

"Out of balance?"

SHE'S TOXIC

"Yes. If you can think back, did anything happen before the death of your friend that might have indicated some psychological impediment?" His eyes zeroed in on me.

I shuffled around on the couch, trying to find a more comfortable position. "Well, her ex-boyfriend in high school told me she was crazy. He said I'd find out sooner or later. I'm not sure if he was actually ex or just obsessed."

"Back in high school, you say? How long ago was that?"

"It's been a few years."

"How many years exactly?"

"Met Britney five years ago when I was playing football. I was the quarterback and she was a cheerleader. I led our team to the state championship my senior season."

"Wow, that's quite an accomplishment. Congratulations. Did you play college football?"

"Yeah, I got a scholarship from Central Illinois University." It wasn't a subject I enjoyed talking about.

"Central Illinois has an exceptional team. Do you still play?"

"No. They took away my scholarship last season. I red-shirted my freshman year and was back-up as a sophomore. I loved playing football, but I had to take a break from school last fall." I closed my eyes and let out a rush of air.

"That's a shame. I guess college is different from high school. Things change, don't they, Tyler?" he asked.

"Yeah, they sure do." This guy was astonishing at stating the obvious. "Maybe that's when things went downhill. I don't think I spent much time with Brit last fall, but I have trouble remembering the details. Maybe that upset her."

"Okay, now we're getting somewhere. You said that she might have been upset, but did she ever give you any indication that her condition was more serious?"

"It's hard to say. I was lovesick at the time, so I might not have noticed. When I look back, I can remember that things weren't always perfect between us."

It was helpful to retrace the steps of our relationship. I was infatuated with Britney. I wondered how much I had overlooked with my rose-colored glasses, my blinders. She was perfect in my eyes. But no one can be *that* perfect.

"Okay, so now you say it wasn't always perfect between you," Dr. Niles said. "But what's happening now?"

"We've been fighting. We fought before, but this is different. Like I said, she is irrational—she always makes something out of nothing." I thought back to Britney striking me in the back of the head with my phone. I also remembered her threatening me with the knife, acting like she was slitting my throat.

He was now scrawling in his notebook. Without pausing, he asked, "Could you please provide an example of one of your fights? Did she do that to you?" He gestured to my face without looking up.

"No, that wasn't her, at least not directly," I said. I tried to recount the fights to the best of my knowledge, emphasizing the names she called me and each time she hit me. I also told him how she quickly recovered each time I told her I loved her.

"Well, Mr. Reynolds, there isn't much I can do to help her unless she comes in herself. I would be more than willing to continue speaking with you if you'd like."

SHE'S TOXIC

I rubbed my forehead. I was hitting a dead-end. "What should I do?"

"I can't tell you precisely what to do, but you need to be careful around her. These relationships are the epitome of precarious situations. Ms. Boyer has shown an inclination toward violence, which concerns me because the most trivial disagreement between you two could send her over the edge." Niles tapped his pen against his desk. "This could cause Britney to harm herself, harm you, or harm those she might perceive as *getting in the way* of your relationship."

I thought of Mike and Maddie.

"I think she's trying to frame me for Maddie's death. I also think she may have been involved with Mike's death, but that seems like a stretch."

"Do you believe that Britney perceived that Mike and Maddie were both obstructing your relationship?"

"I think Britney killed Maddie because I was having sex with Maddie. Mike and I also had a fight about Britney one night, and Detective Minden had originally told me that Britney was the last person to see Mike alive."

"Has the detective made any progress in either case?" Niles asked. He took down another note.

"Well, now he says that Mike's death was an accident, but I'm not so sure. She could have made it look that way. And Minden is still working on Maddie's case, but he thinks I'm responsible. I don't understand how or why. He kept saying that Britney was the primary suspect, but now he seems adamant on bringing me down. He even arrested me for disturbing the peace."

"Ty, I hate to interrupt our session, but I need to meet with another client. You are more than free to schedule another appointment if you'd like. In the interim, I must stress the importance of exercising extreme caution around Ms. Boyer."

SHE'S TOXIC

Twenty-Seven

Speaking with Doctor Niles did nothing to alleviate my concern. I now felt much worse than I had before my trip to Springfield. At least I felt vindicated—that Britney could responsible for not only Maddie's death, but also for Mike's. To my knowledge, Mike's investigation had been closed, but maybe Minden wanted to keep me uninformed, for whatever reason.

I drove back to Gentry and spent the evening at the grocery store. Some of the staples at my parents' were running out or growing old. I loaded up with eggs, bread, deli meat, cheddar cheese, Sun Chips, and Bud Light—all the essentials.

After walking outside, I trembled when I saw Minden's black Challenger parked next to my Jeep. The detective was stationed on the hood of his car, with his right leg bent over his left knee. He was laughing at something on his phone when I approached.

"Ty, my boy, you need to check out this video. Shit is hil-ar-i-ous! Damn, that's rich. Speaking of rich." *Not again.* 'I've struck more gold, Ty. This is getting too good. I didn't know you had your girlfriend committed. And outside of Nash County? That's smart, son. Now the way I look at it, it seems an awful lot like perjury, maybe some obstruction. I suppose it doesn't matter too much, you'll fry with this impending murder charge. But hey, if it doesn't work out, I'm glad we have you on something else."

"Committed?" I started, not sure how to proceed. "I don't know what you're talking about. I talked to a psychiatrist about Brit, but that was it."

I hadn't talked to Britney all day, but I thought she was still in Ohio. I would have been overjoyed if Niles had somehow taken action and had her committed, but he made it clear he couldn't do anything for her unless she came in. Maybe he concluded she was a danger to others and had her involuntarily committed.

"Yes, that's right: You don't know what in the hell you're talking about. I could have told you that much, son. You're messed up. You can't tell the truth. You haven't been able to tell the truth since I've met you. It's like you're living in your own universe, with no concept of reality. I'm glad you finally talked to a psychiatrist, I really am, but I'm afraid it's too late for you.

"Maybe you'll run into a sympathetic ear in prison: a kind fella who will let you cry on his shoulder late at night. I'm sure you'll find someone." He laughed. "Oh, Ty, they'll *love* a pretty boy like you in there."

"I need to leave, unless I'm under arrest for another crime. I haven't violated my bond."

He jumped up from the hood, onto the ground next to me, and leaned close to my ear. "You're finished, you're done. Run all you want, it won't matter. I'll track you down wherever you go." He ran in place and clapped. "You'll never get rid of me. I'm here to stay. Maddie's voice will speak again. You won't get away with what you did to her."

I ignored his scrutiny and hopped into my Jeep without saying another word. Someone knocked on my window and asked if I was okay. I gave her a slight nod before pulling away. She probably didn't realize that Minden was a detective—considering his get-up and eccentric behavior. I sped back out to my parents' house, hitting 107 on the blacktop.

Back at my parents' house, I thought back to my conversation earlier in the night with Minden. Despite his threats of locking me away for obstruction, it was some of the best news I'd heard in a long time. I wasn't convinced she had been committed, but I was holding out hope.

Her forced commitment might even strengthen my defense if Minden tried to pin Maddie's murder on me. If I could prove that Brit was insane, it would be more believable that she set me up. That would also explain why Minden was so pissed off. He knew that her commitment would shoot a gaping hole through any potential case against me.

I pulled out my phone to see if Britney had called. I remembered the first message I had received from her several years ago. Her adorable laugh and awkward first voice mail captivated me from the beginning. I was checking to see if she called, but I was hoping for a call from a normal girl. I thought of Maddie for a second, but she was gone, just like Mike. I looked at the flashing blue light on my phone. I thought it signaled a voicemail, but I couldn't keep the notifications straight anymore.

Yup, I had a voicemail. I listened to the message:

"*Ty, my boy, it's time for us to get together again—there have been some rapid developments in the last hour. Don't worry; this will all be over with soon enough. Hang tight and I'll see you soon. Gold rush! Woohoo!*"

Before I could react, another voicemail came through. The second was from a private number. I listened to the message:

"*You need to leave your house by six this evening to avoid being arrested. Meet me at The Barnyard by seven, and I will have further instructions. If you do not abide by my directive, you will meet a most unfortunate demise.*"

Okay, so Minden was coming to arrest me and someone else was toying with me. I assumed the second caller had blocked his number—probably Logan or Miguel. It was a male's voice, but it could have been a woman using a voice manipulator, just like Alexa had used in my dream. It seemed like something Brit might have done, but I wondered why.

I scrolled to Brit's name and called her. After two seconds I heard a tone followed by: *I'm sorry, but the number you have dialed has been disconnected...* I dialed again. *I'm sorry, but the number you have dialed has—*

"Bitch!" I threw my phone onto my bed. *Disconnected?*

If Britney had blocked me, her phone might have given me the same response as if the number had been disconnected. Or maybe she had actually disconnected her phone.

I checked the time on my alarm clock: 5:14 p.m. I wondered if the caller would be brave enough to be at The Barnyard. I feared Miguel was somehow involved. It was a public place, so maybe I could avoid being jumped again.

But I *knew* that Minden was on his way, so I needed to get out of my parents' house to avoid being arrested.

SHE'S TOXIC

I found a suitably clean pair of blue jeans and threw on a "Bulldogs Football" shirt—the same shirt I'd worn the night of my fight with Mike. I didn't fill it out anymore, as I was continuing to shed weight. Since losing my scholarship, I'd dropped over 20 pounds to a meager 180.

I hadn't realized the magnitude of the disaster in my room—my childhood room. It was in utter disarray. Weight loss and complete disorganization are apparently side effects of your girlfriend flying off the deep end, coupled with the deaths of your best friend and the girl you recently slept with.

After a quick look in the mirror, I grabbed my keys and shot out of my bedroom. It was five-thirty, still well before my six o'clock deadline for leaving the house. Not bad after taking five minutes to find jeans.

Before I made it to the bottom of the steps, a loud knock stopped me cold. My first thought was that Detective Minden had arrived ahead of schedule.

I tiptoed down the remaining steps and made a left into the living room. If Minden was at the house, he must have had his music lower than usual. *Yep, he was outside.* I spied his Challenger sitting in the driveway. I walked through the living room, then went down to the basement, planning to hide there until he left. Another knock, this time louder. I turned on the TV and laid down on the sectional.

After a minute, the knocking finally stopped. I waited.

The dining-room window screeched open, and a body fell hard against the floor directly above me. Before I could move, footfalls raced across the kitchen, to the staircase. *Shit.*

"Ty! Are you here?" Kourt called down the steps. *Whew*. I must have misidentified the cars. I may have been just a little paranoid.

"Yeah, down here."

Kourt bounded down the steps. "Why didn't you answer the door? I forgot my house key and couldn't get in. What are you doing down here?" Her tone was somewhere between angry and defeated, I wasn't sure which.

"I'm sorry. I thought Detective Minden was coming to harass me." I didn't mention the phone call I'd received. I wasn't sure she would believe me.

"Ty, seriously? I swear you're obsessed with this guy." She dropped her head. "Sorry, I shouldn't be upset, but I'm scared."

I rose to my feet and gave my sister a hug. She didn't look quite as ragged as she had been at Maddie's funeral, but something was still off about her—something much deeper.

"Are you excited about college?" I tried to show concern for her life, but she wasn't interested in my random pleasantry.

"Well, that's random. Ty, what's going on?" She paused. "I realize that losing Maddie wasn't easy. I'm sorry."

"Yeah, and I'm still dealing with Brit. I just got a weird phone call. I think she's messing with me. I tried to call her back, but she must have had her phone disconnected. And I think Minden is coming to arrest me for murdering Maddie."

Kourtney reached for the sectional and slumped down to take a seat. She looked at me, but didn't say anything.

"I know it sounds like a crazy conspiracy. I still have those gang members sending me messages—the guys who jumped me the other night. It sounds insane, but Britney is somehow behind all of this."

"Ty," she started and stopped. She closed her eyes.

"What?" I demanded, joining her on the couch.

"I didn't realize how bad it's been. I'm sorry. It's my fault. I've been distant, and like I said, I didn't want to believe it could be true. I feel like this is my fault. I thought it was better after we talked about Mike."

"Believe me, it's not you. It's Britney. She's a lunatic—she needs to be sent to that place we went to in West Virginia." I turned to leave. My sister wouldn't be able to help. She was too distraught to even think straight. "I'm sorry, but I need to go see who's waiting for me at The Barnyard. If Minden comes by the house, tell him you don't know where I am."

"Ty, wait. Let me drive you to town."

"Kourt, I'll be okay. Please don't let Minden find me. I'm sure he's going to arrest me tonight. I swear Brit's framing me for murdering Maddie, maybe even Mike. I swear."

"Okay, Ty. I'll tell him whatever you want me to tell him. Please, just be careful."

Kourt took out her phone and cried as I barreled up the stairs. I peered out from behind the curtains of each window to see if Minden was waiting outside; I didn't see him.

I ran out the front door and hopped in my Jeep. I took off east toward the intersection. Out of the corner of my eye, I saw Mrs. Stine flagging me down. It wasn't a good time for this, but I couldn't ignore a sweet old woman. I pulled into her drive and rolled down my window.

"Tyler, I'm so glad you came by."

"No problem." I tried to hide my rising anxiety. "What can I do for you?"

"I just wanted to make sure you're okay. It's been so long since you've stopped by to see me. I'd almost forgotten what you looked like." She smiled.

"I'm sorry, I've just been so busy lately dealing with—oh, it's not important. I'm sorry about that black car that keeps driving out here. You shouldn't have to put up with that much longer. But that might not be good for me."

She maintained her smile. "I haven't even noticed. I'm sure it will all work out for the best. We must all face our demons sooner or later. I'll let you get going. Please don't be a stranger. You should stop back in for a Cardinals game sometime."

Great. Detective Minden had probably stopped by to question her. He probably filled her in on all the details. I was surprised she even wanted to talk to me if she thought I was some deranged killer. I backed out of her drive and raced through the country, toward town.

A mile before I made it to Gentry, my phone went off.

Minden. I ignored the call, but the phone rang again. The process repeated three more times until I gave in.

"What in the hell do you want?"

"Woah, woah, woah. Ty, is that any way to speak to an officer of the law? I think not, son. Where are you headed off to anyway? I thought we would have our final pow-wow out at your parents' house this lovely evening."

"This is not professional. You have nothing on me."

SHE'S TOXIC

"Tyler, Tyler, Tyler. You can't run. Like I said, you're going down for this. Your prints are all over the murder weapon. You claim that Britney set you up, but son, your story doesn't jive. At the end of the day, you're responsible."

"Leave me alone!" I threw the phone against my window and punched the steering wheel, resulting in my horn going off.

"It's judgment day." I thought I must have broken my phone, but Minden's voice continued to fill my Jeep. "I hope you enjoy your last minutes of freedom. Bye-bye, Ty."

Twenty-Eight

I walked into The Barnyard, ten minutes before seven. I expected to see Brit sitting at the bar with an evil grin across her face. *Crazy bitch.* We'd fight for a while, but then I'd end up hate-fucking her in the parking lot. Maddie was gone and I needed a release.

I also expected Minden to be hiding somewhere, ready to pounce with a nightstick. I may have squirmed when he arrested me, but I knew his actions would qualify as police brutality.

A few random guys sat where I expected Brit to be. I ordered a drink from the bartender, a bald man in his thirties. It looked like a fresh shave to the scalp. *Bold move.*

"How are ya tonight, bud? I'm Jed, new here." He mentioned where he was from, some town in western Kentucky, so I guess he upgraded.

"I'm Ty. I'm meeting someone at seven, but I honestly don't know who."

"Blind date? Nice, bro." He handed me a Jack and Coke.

"Something like that." I made small talk, but my mind was focused on the phone call. My eyes were focused on the door.

SHE'S TOXIC

What I wouldn't give for Mike to enter.

I'd give anything to go back to that night. I wouldn't have acted like a bitch, we would have had a few more cold ones, and maybe he would have steered me away from that horrible girl sooner. The door swung open, interrupting my thoughts. I couldn't believe it: Britney walked in smiling.

No, she was just a girl who looked like Britney with her friends. It looked like they had already downed a few drinks. I turned back to my glass and polished it off.

"Another one, please."

It was quarter after seven. I feared the voicemail I'd received after Minden's call was lure and that Colombian Lords were waiting for me outside.

Well, I might as well get drunk. I could make things more exciting that way.

I put down three or four more drinks within the next hour, plus a shot or two of whiskey. I was about to order another drink when a strong hand came down on my right shoulder.

"It's my boy! Sorry I'm so late. Let's get this taken care of once and for all." I turned around. Minden smiled back at me.

I fainted and fell to the floor.

I blinked my eyes at a dark figure hovering above me. He held out a glass of water and a towel. "He's waking up. Holy shit, you took quite a fall! Are you okay, buddy?" It was Jed, the bartender. I was drunker than I thought.

I blinked again and raised my head from the floor. "Yeah, I'm fine. I thought I saw something." *Or someone.* I climbed to my feet and took a seat back in my stool. "I think I'm okay now—maybe just a little drunk."

"Whew, good to hear. I thought ya had a stroke and died or somethin. You were sittin here drinking, then out of nowhere, boom! Ya hit the daggum deck quicker than a louse on a mouse!" Jed laughed.

"Who walked in? Is he still here?" I had more significant concerns than trying to figure out what in the hell "a louse on a mouse" meant.

"'Who walked in?' Hell, a bunch of people have walked in. This place is busy if you haven't noticed." I looked around and saw many faces. Most were staring back at me. They whispered to each other. I saw a head or two shake in disapproval. They were judging me. They used to adore me. Most of them surely knew that I'd been arrested for *disturbing the peace*—it was a small town after all.

"Come to think of it, a fella asked about you, right after you fainted. I can't remember his name, but he's been in the shitter for a while, musta had some of that greasy wild game."

"Was it a detective?" I tried to sound like I wasn't guilty. *I wasn't guilty.*

"Hmm, not sure. He looked professional." His eyes narrowed. "Why did you ask if it was a detective? Are you running from Johnny Law?"

"No, not at all. They've just had questions—" I was stopped mid-sentence by Detective Minden busting through the front door, stride-for-stride with two other officers. A man emerged from the bathroom, another from the back door.

SHE'S TOXIC

Nowhere to run.

The bar fell silent as the man to the left of Minden yelled out, "There he is. Tyler Reynolds. He's the guy in the gray 'Bulldogs Football' shirt."

"Living in his past glory days," Minden added with a laugh. "Approach slowly."

The men each stepped toward me, closing the circle.

"I've been waiting all summer for this: Tyler Reynolds, you are under arrest for the murders of Michael Thomas and Madison Ross. You have the right to remain silent. Anything you say can and will be used against you in the court of law. You have the right to an attorney. If you cannot afford an attorney," Minden leaned close to my ear, "well, you're shit out of luck because the public defenders suck around here."

He laughed. "Nah, I'm just screwing around. I like to have fun with you, Ty." He stepped back and continued for everyone to hear, "If you cannot afford an attorney, one will be appointed for you." He continued reading my Miranda Rights. I closed my eyes. My life was over.

I turned my head to look over at Jed. His jaw was the floor. I tried to get up, but I was paralyzed, just like when Miguel jumped me. I tried again and found my feet. Before I could run, an officer shot his Taser into my lower back. I slumped to the ground in a heap, then I felt a sharp needle go into my back.

Twenty-Nine

When I regained consciousness, I was back in a cell—similar to the morning after Minden arrested me outside of The Barnyard, but this room seemed brighter. Even with my eyes closed, I could feel the radiant light against my eyelids. The bed was more comfortable than what I'd slept on at the county jail.

Was I in a hospital? Yeah, they probably took me to a hospital once they realized they had zero evidence against me. *At least I hoped they hadn't found anything.* I tried to open my eyes, but instead I rolled over and drifted back to sleep. I felt like I'd been drugged, or maybe I was just hungover.

"Tyler Reynolds!" a voice jarred me awake.

I stirred in my bed and finally managed to open my eyes. I took stock of my new surroundings. This was not a jail cell; the room was polished just enough to provide comfort—I even had a dresser. The walls were painted a pastel blue, similar to the color of my bedroom. Not a jail, but it also didn't feel like a typical hospital.

"Tyler Reynolds! Can you hear me?"

SHE'S TOXIC

"Yeah," I said, intermingled with a cough. "Yes." My throat was parched and my head was pounding. I wasn't sure how long I had been knocked out, but I hadn't slept long enough to expel the alcohol from my system.

"Please stay away from the door. We're coming in." The door swung open. Two men dressed in blue shirts and blue pants rolled a wheelchair into the room. I was relieved that I was in some kind of medical facility as evidenced by the men's scrubs.

"Could you please sit down in the wheelchair for us? Or will we have to do this the hard way?"

I wondered what they meant by 'the hard way' or why they would even ask such a question. "Yeah, no problem." I rolled my eyes and sat down in the wheelchair. They strapped me in—tight—and rolled me into the hallway. Fluorescent lights lined the ceiling above me. I saw rooms on each side of the hall, but the doors were all closed. "Where are we anyway? What happened at The Barnyard last night?"

"We're not at liberty to discuss that with you, Mr. Reynolds. We're taking you to see the doctor."

"As long as you aren't taking me to see Detective Minden." The men looked at each other with their eyebrows raised. *Good. They don't know who I'm talking about.*

They rolled me into a large office. One man left the other with me, telling him to be careful. My eyes scanned the wall for anything that would indicate my location.

I noticed several pictures of Chicago landmarks including Wrigley Field and Soldier Field. On the wall opposite, I saw a diploma, but I couldn't read the institution or name. I looked out the window but could see only trees, birds, and a few fair-weather cumulus clouds. I turned around just in time to see two men emerge through the door.

"What did I say, Ty, my boy? We've got you now."

My jaw dropped. I tried to escape, but couldn't break through the restraints.

I was trapped, again.

Detective Minden walked just ahead of Doctor Niles.

"Mr. Reynolds, I'm sorry we had to do it this way; you left us with no choice." Niles smiled, but looked like he might cry as he took a seat at his desk. Detective Minden stood next to him, smiling from ear-to-ear, as usual.

Good doctor, bad cop.

"It wasn't me, Britney set me up! Where am I?"

"Ty, you know that's not true. You're responsible," Minden shot back with his familiar response.

"Are you referring to Britney Boyer?" Niles asked.

"He's delusional, Doctor Niles, pay no heed to his bogus, bullshit stories," Minden said, while glaring at the doctor. Minden towered over the much smaller Niles. It looked like Minden wanted to beat him into oblivion.

"Yes, Britney Boyer. Where am I?" I demanded.

"Tyler, don't worry. You're someplace safe," Niles answered before Minden could say anything. "We are worried about you, and I hope we can make progress today. I know this will come as a shock, but there is someone behind this door who would like to speak with you. Actually, there are two people who are interested in speaking with you. I've concluded this is the best way to proceed, based on your present condition. I'm afraid you won't believe me, but Tyler, I've tried my best."

"It's going to shock me? Is it Britney? What's going on here?"

Minden shook his head and gave an angry chuckle. "You don't know, do you? It's definitely not Maddie, that's for sure—you sick bastard."

"Okay, get ready to bring him in," Niles said. "We'll leave you two alone." Niles and Minden left the room through the door behind the desk. The door closed for a few seconds before creaking open once more.

I looked in the doorway, fixated on and perplexed by the approaching figure. My eyes finally adjusted. I cried out, "What in the hell?"

"It's okay, buddy, it's me."

"Is this a fucking joke?" Both of my hands shook.

Mike was standing in front of me. He was as alive as ever, his face wrought with concern. Mike lifted his hand and gave a slight wave. "No, I swear to you, no joke."

Even though he was standing before me, I couldn't believe it. "But you're dead. I was at your funeral." My voice trembled as I tried to fight back the tears.

"I can assure you that I didn't die. Sorry about the fight between us. I wish I could have been here for you, but I've been in Wisconsin. Your sister called and told me how bad it's been. I came down as soon as I could."

"But you're—you're dead. I was there. I—I talked to your mom. Britney was with me…" I scratched my head, attempting to merge Mike's words with my memories.

"I'm alive as ever. My mom said she ran into you and Britney at my great uncle's funeral. She said you were a wreck. And I'm sorry I flew out to Milwaukee the night after we had that damn fight. It was bad timing, we never got a chance to patch things up. Like I said, I tried to call you, but I could never get a hold of you. I talked to Britney once or twice, briefly."

"Great uncle's funeral? No way. You were in the casket. I know you were. I saw you."

"Yeah, Corwin died—my grandpa Wallace's brother. My mom let me skip his funeral since I was busy getting the new restaurant going. Dad came back for the funeral, so I had to run things up there. That's where I've been all summer."

"There's no way…" I struggled to grasp what Mike was saying. *Or was he an imposter?* He had to be an imposter, had to be.

"You're okay, Ty. That's why we're all here, to help you. Kourt called Doctor Niles last night after you left your parents' house. They decided this was the best way. Nobody realized how bad it had become."

"There's no way this is happening. 'How bad it had become?' Do you mean that Britney went crazy and tried to kill me?"

Mike breathed deeply. "Britney isn't who you think she is."

"Yeah, I'm painfully aware of that by now. I never would have expected it either. I've known her for so long, but I guess you never truly know somebody, or what they're capable of."

SHE'S TOXIC

Mike stretched his arms outward as he tilted his head back and sighed. "Man, I was hoping I was wrong about all of that." He faced me. I could see tears forming in the corners of his eyes.

"You hoped you were wrong about what?"

"About Britney. You haven't known *Britney* since high school. That's what I was trying to tell you at The Barnyard. I should have been more direct."

"Sure, I have." I frantically recounted my memories. Yes, I met Britney during high school, at that football game. No doubt in my mind.

"I thought something wasn't right before, but I wanted to give you the benefit of the doubt. Do you not remember what happened to Britney, to Britney *Boyer*?"

"What kind of sideshow is this?" I yelled. "Get this guy out of here! Hello? Anyone there? Get this imposter out of here!"

"Ty, please listen; it's me. I'm your friend. I'm Mike. We've known each other our entire lives. I swear to God that I wouldn't trick you or lie to you. I'm here to help you, I swear."

"Bullshit. Get out of here. Minden put you up to this. This is some kind of elaborate set-up. You look like Mike, but you sure as hell aren't him."

The doors opened and the same two men in the blue scrubs escorted Mike out of the room. Their ruse hadn't worked. I wasn't going to buy their shit. It was all Minden, all part of his sick, twisted, delusional game.

"Bravo, Ty, bravo." Minden peeked inside the room before waltzing in.

I wanted to punch Minden in the face, but the restraints quickly subdued that fantasy. He brought his grinning face close to mine. I could smell Buffalo sauce on his breath.

"You won't get away with this," I said. "This isn't legal."

He whispered in my ear, "That's where you're wrong, Ty. Dead wrong. Have fun in here. You'll be in here for a long, long time to pay for what you did." He stepped back. "It's time to answer for your sins, Ty. I sure am enjoying this though. I love when I strike it rich. Gold rush!"

Niles reappeared and Minden vanished behind him. "Tyler, I'm sorry that didn't go well. But it must have been great to see Mike again, right?"

"That imposter wasn't Mike. I don't know what's going on between you and Minden. Whatever he told you is bullshit. He's turned everyone against me."

"Are you sure this *Minden* has turned your friends and family against you, or have you done that yourself?" Niles took off his glasses and breathed onto each lens before scrubbing them clean with his shirt.

"Are you in on this with him? Is this all some kind of damn conspiracy?"

Niles shook his head and sighed. "Someone else is here to see you, Ty. I hope that she will get through to you." He left the room and Kourt swooped in to take his place.

She almost knocked Niles down as she plowed through the doorway. Kourt galloped over to me, sobbing. "I'm so sorry, Ty. I tried. I tried so hard to help you. I didn't want to bring you back up here. Believe me. I can't take this. Oh my God, look at what they've done to you." She rubbed her hand along the restraints and shook her head. "I'm so sorry."

I looked at my sister, attempting to contemplate her words, but I was confounded. "You tried to help me? I have no idea where I am. Has *everyone* lost their damn minds?"

Kourt looked to the heavens, praying for guidance. "I love you more than anything, and I have to tell you what happened." She took my hands in hers. "I'm not sure if you're denying the past, if you blocked it out, or if it's somehow repressed. I'm not sure why you don't remember. I wanted to believe you were okay, but after we talked at Panera, it began to dawn on me—then after Maddie's funeral… I haven't known how to tell you. I tried a few times, but you shut me down. Those were the times we actually talked, without—"

"Without what? Are you in on this set-up? Kourt, you have to believe me; I didn't kill Maddie. I swear it was Britney!"

"Of course you didn't kill Maddie—she killed herself. She had a breakdown. She even wrote a note." Kourt wiped the tears from her face, but more quickly took their place. "I swear I tried to call you at least once a week, usually several times. Most of the time, you wouldn't answer. When we talked—whenever I'd mention Britney Boyer, you wouldn't listen."

"Okay, well I'm listening now." She had somehow managed to grab my attention. "Things keep getting worse and I need to know the truth, or at least what you think is going on. But do you believe me about Britney?"

"Britney is not who you think she is," she began, waiting for opposition. She reached for her back pocket, but hesitated and came back empty-handed.

"Well I've figured that out by now; she's insane. And somehow, she's convinced Minden that I'm responsible for something I didn't do. It's some kind of conspiracy against me."

"No, there's much more than that, please listen to me."

I listened.

"You met Britney Boyer five years ago, right? At your game?"

"Yup, that's right. It my first game as a junior and we were playing against Vandalia. I remember it like it was yesterday."

"Okay. You met Britney Boyer, right?"

"Yup, Britney Boyer. My crazy girlfriend."

She closed her eyes again and sniffled. I saw a tear fall from her eye. "Yep, Britney Boyer."

"Yep. Britney Boyer," I repeated, wondering where she was going with this.

"You remember meeting her, and I'm sure you remember the high points of your relationship, but you don't remember what happened to her, do you?" Kourt was crying, but focused.

"What do you mean? What happened? When?"

"A year ago. Last August—August of 2014."

"August? I'm sure I was getting ready for the football season." I remembered spending a regular summer with Brit, and I was also busy training—nothing out of the ordinary.

"Do you remember staying in Peoria for two months in the fall?" Her entire body was shaking.

"Two months? No way, maybe a night or two. I was in Reedville most the time."

"Believe me. You were in Peoria for two months. You remember taking the fall semester off from school, right?"

We both fell silent. My mind raced, trying to decipher her apparent riddle.

"I remember taking the fall semester off, but it was because I needed a break. I never stayed in Peoria for two months." My pleading seemed to bring her back to reality. She blinked hard, like she was trying to wake up after a long nap.

"But why did you need a break? Why would you decide you needed a break when you had your football scholarship? Why would you throw your future away without a good reason?"

"I'm not sure, but I didn't stay there for two months, there's no way. And I didn't throw anything away. Are you in on all of this too?"

"Yes, you stayed here." She shook her head and swallowed hard. "You were at The Lanphier Home for two months receiving treatment. You were *here* for two months. We had to have you committed after you—after she—" Kourt broke down. Whatever memory she had was too much to bear.

"The Lanphier Home? Committed? You better tell me right now what's going on. Did Minden talk to you too?"

"Who is Minden?" She was hysterical. "I'm sorry, but you need to read this." She sobbed and wiped the tears from her face while retrieving a rolled-up, battered manila envelope from her back pocket. "I've been carrying this around in my car lately. I wanted to tell you sooner, believe me. I just didn't want to believe—I didn't want to make you relive what happened."

I couldn't believe that Kourt was in on this elaborate game. She opened the envelope and pulled out a handful of old letters and newspaper clippings. I read a clipping she placed in front of my face and trembled. She showed me an excerpt from one letter, and then another. If I wasn't already restrained, I would have crashed to the ground.

"What? How in the—? There's no way this is true. Where did you get these? Who created these? Minden, where are you? Show yourself, you son of a bitch!"

"I swear it's true. You sent these letters while you were here."

She showed me the envelopes. The return address for each letter began with my name and concluded with Peoria, Illinois. The letters were all addressed to my sister, mom, and dad. The handwriting was mine, but was much sloppier than usual.

I read the words but couldn't comprehend what was laid out before me. My hands were trembling within their restraints.

My sister dropped everything at one point because her hands were likewise unsteady. I had my sister show me the materials multiple times before reality began to sink in.

My world had been shattered. The reality I thought I knew was turned on its head.

I locked eyes with Kourt. "How did this happen?"

She attempted to hug me around the restraints; she continued to cry. "I'm so sorry, Ty."

Thirty

The clippings revealed the date: August 28, 2014. It all came back to me. I wasn't sure how I could have ever forgotten. I was transported back to that fateful late summer day.

The bright orange sun hung high in the August sky—not a cloud in sight. I was on my way to pick up Britney to celebrate our fourth anniversary.

"Hey there, darling," I answered her call on the first ring.

"Hey! I can't wait for tonight. Is there anything I should or shouldn't wear?"

I had a way of orchestrating surprises for Britney. My plans generally went off without a hitch unless Brit overdressed for the occasion. Once, I'd planned to take her four-wheeler riding, but she'd showed up at my parents' house in a dress and heels. I'd tried to keep her guessing by claiming we were going somewhere extravagant. I didn't always think things through, but I'd like to think I was getting better.

I joked about the four-wheeling incident. "Heels will be okay tonight. They'd actually be a great idea tonight."

I heard her smile through the phone as she responded, "Yes, I love getting all cute for you."

"Oh, you're always cute, tiger. Can't wait to see you."

I informed her of how I'd spend my next few hours. I planned to get a snack, go workout, take a shower, and spend an excruciating five minutes getting ready.

"Aww, I'm such a lucky girl. You're going to spend five minutes getting ready? You usually get ready in one minute! This must be quite the surprise."

"Well, what can I say? You're a lucky lady. I'm going to look so damn good."

"I can't wait. Hey, I need to let you go though so I can finish getting ready. I love you and I can't wait to see you."

"Sounds good. Love you, too. Bye-bye."

I smiled. The night was going to be magical. I reached my hand into my pocket and pulled out the little black box I'd purchased earlier in the day at Zales. I'd caught myself pulling out the ring every five minutes to make sure it was still there. The ring was stunning, and probably ten times more than I could afford—even with a full ride.

The day progressed just as life progresses, and I was on my way to pick up Britney from her parents' house. I called to tell her that I was on my way, but reached her voicemail.

I left a message:

"Hey there, baby. I just wanted to let you know that I'm on my way. Hope you remember that heels will be okay tonight and I hope you're not wearing your camo. I'll be there in five minutes, so I guess I'll see you then."

SHE'S TOXIC

I continued my drive through Gentry. I drove past the high school where we met, past the football field where she cheered for me, and past other venues where we had shared memorable experiences. The town was replete with the lyrics of our song.

I heard sirens, which brought me back to reality. *Where the hell is that coming from?* I looked ahead and couldn't see anything. I looked back, but still couldn't see anything.

"Hmm. Oh, there it is," I said aloud. An ambulance came into view through my rearview mirror. I turned my Jeep to the side of the road and allowed it to pass. As soon as the ambulance passed, I heard more sirens and saw two police cruisers approaching. "Damn. I wonder what happened."

The vehicles disappeared into the distance, and I continued on my familiar trek to Britney's house without a second thought. I went over my proposal speech one more time:

"Britney, I know we're young, and that you just graduated from high school, but I love you more than words. I can't imagine living a single day without your loving embrace, without seeing your precious smile, and without looking into your eyes. Your eyes are the window to a beautiful soul. I would be honored to spend the rest of my life with you. Britney Marie Boyer, will you marry me?"

I'd rehearsed my proposal many times. Each time my eyes welled about the time I'd say, "I can't imagine living a single day without your loving embrace." I envisioned her expression when she realized what was happening. I knew she would say, "Yes," at least I hoped so.

"Shit. What's going on here?" I turned down Shelby Street and was met with yellow police tape and barricades. I was only two blocks from Brit's house.

An officer approached my Jeep. "Sorry, son, you'll have to turn around and head down Pike or Fayette if you're trying to get through."

"I just have two blocks to go. Can I get around?"

"Afraid not; there's been an accident at the next intersection." For the first time, a dark thought crossed my mind. Upon seeing the ambulance and police cars, it had not occurred to me that Britney may have been involved. Even when I'd turned down her road and was stopped by the officer, I'd never considered the possibility. But I was so close to her house.

Not Britney. Not my Britney.

Memories filled my mind. I remembered meeting Britney, our first kiss while eating frozen custard, my first ride in her Celica, her red prom dress.

I shifted my Jeep into park and threw open my door. I needed to get closer.

"Sir, I'll have to ask you to get back into your car and turn around. You cannot get out here," the officer pleaded.

"I'm sorry, but I need to know what happened." I ran past the officer, fearing the worst. As I continued down the block, the scene became visible. I could see a Ford truck and a small car, but couldn't tell if it was Britney's. My run turned into an all-out sprint as I raced toward the wreckage. Two ambulances were at the scene, as well as two police cars and a fire truck.

SHE'S TOXIC

Another officer began running toward me. "Sir, you cannot come any closer! Please stop!" Ben Tannehill, who was a former high school wrestler, met me about 100 feet from the accident. He cradled me and dropped me to the ground. A third officer arrived just as I was about to squirm free. He placed my hands in front of me and slipped them into loose handcuffs.

"These are for your protection, bud." The officer was one of my former classmates, Ryan Kaufman. We'd taken most classes together in junior high and high school.

I looked up and finally caught a good glimpse of the car. It was Britney's. The driver's side was smashed-in and the car was smoldering. The result of the charring made it difficult for me to identify the car from a distance, but now I had no doubt.

"Is she dead? Tell me! Is she dead?"

"Tyler, please have a seat on the curb." Ryan wiped a tear from his tanned face. He turned and said something to Ben. Both wore grave expressions.

"Tell me what happened!" I had no interest in sitting down. Full panic set in.

An ambulance took off in the other direction, siren blaring.

"Is she in there? Answer me!"

"Yes, Ty. She is," Ryan said. "She was seriously injured in an accident. I'm sorry."

"Why can't I see her? Is she going to be okay? I have to get to the hospital!" I turned to run, but the officers corralled me.

"We will take you, but—" Ryan hesitated.

"But what?"

"She's unconscious and she might have broken her neck. She couldn't move anything. I'm so sorry, Ty."

"Let me see her. I need to see her!"

"Come on, we can take you there if you want to hop in back." The ambulance was well into the distance so I agreed.

Ryan took the cuffs off of my wrists and led me into the back of the car. "Watch your head, bud. We will get you there, don't worry about that."

I realized that I'd just left a message on her voicemail. *Was she trying to reach for her phone when I called? Did I cause the accident? Could this have been my fault?*

Two hours after arriving at the hospital, I was in Britney's room, fixated on her face. Ignoring the world.

"Hey, baby." I somehow managed a smile as I spoke, but she remained unresponsive. The heart rate monitor showed signs of life, but aside from her heartbeat, she was gone. I took her hand in mine and broke down. "I love you, Brit."

No response.

I leaned over to hug her, placing my cheek against hers. She was still warm. *She's sleeping.* I could imagine her waking up, a smile crossing her face, and listening to her beautiful voice say, "Good morning, sunshine." I raised my head and looked back at her, praying I would see her piercing brown eyes gazing back into mine. *Just one more time, please. That's all I'm asking.*

Nothing.

I tried to wipe the tears from my face, but more continued to

SHE'S TOXIC

fall. I kissed Brit's cheek and then her lips. "Please wake up. We have such a long life ahead of us."

A doctor came into the room, followed by Britney's parents. Julie was a wreck. Trent looked like he was trying to hold it together but was failing.

"My poor angel," Trent said.

Doctor Shephard explained to us that Britney had suffered hemorrhaging in her brain due to blunt-force trauma, and the odds she would come out of her coma were not good. She had also suffered second-to-third-degree burns over much of her lower body. He said that they would monitor Britney over the weekend to determine if they would keep her on life support.

I waited by her side the entire night, but I must have dozed off at some point. When I woke up, Britney's mother was brushing her daughter's hair.

"How is she?" I asked. Julie looked as if she hadn't slept.

Julie closed her eyes, trying to fight back the tears. She took my hand and looked me in the eyes. "The doctor told us her body temperature has dropped, and she's experienced brain damage." She paused, tears now streaming down her face. "She'll never be the same, even if she comes back, so—I'm just going to brush my baby's hair..." She sobbed, throwing her hands over her face. The brush fell from her hands and clattered against the floor, but I barely even registered the sound.

I put my arm around Julie, allowing her to cry against my shoulder. I was still in shock. The chances of recovery were dire, but Britney was strong and our love was strong. I was still hanging onto hope. She'd be okay.

Doctor Shephard appeared in the doorway. "I'm sorry, but we have exhausted all options. She is not responding. I would like for you to consider what you would like to do at this point." Shephard made his quick speech, then left the room.

Julie continued to weep while Trent stood in the corner with his hands covering his face. They were beginning to accept the reality of their daughter's impending death. I didn't want to accept it. There had to be another way.

"There must be something we can do to help her. We have to bring her back—somehow," I stammered as my body shook. If I was standing, I would have fallen over.

"Ty, we have thought about this. We have to let her go. We have to ease her pain," Trent said.

"No, you can't! She'll be okay. She'll come back to us." Each word became softer, until I whispered, "She has to be okay."

Britney Marie Boyer was declared dead at 1:15 on September 1, 2014—a Monday afternoon.

Her parents held on for another day due to my insistence. I believed she would spring back into consciousness, and that she would be the same wonderful young woman from before the accident. I desperately wanted to believe she would come back to me, but my girl was gone.

Thirty-One

"Britney Boyer died a year ago. I'm so sorry, Ty. You've been dating a girl named Britney Connell," Kourt said in the present, just as I had finished retracing the events of that fateful day.

"Now come on, Ty, we all know this is bullshit," Minden said.

"How in the hell did he get back in here?" I asked.

"Kourt is putting *lies* in your head. Mike put *lies* in your head. Besides, you wouldn't be able to distinguish fact from fiction anyway. You know you're responsible for Maddie's death. You know you're responsible for Britney. And now, you must pay the price. You can't get away with what you've done."

"What's going on, Ty?" Kourt looked at me, terrified.

"I don't know, but it's not true. I didn't kill anyone."

"I didn't say you did. I believe you, Ty. I swear."

Minden slammed his fist down on the desk. "You believe him? How can you believe him? He ruined your life, too, you know? Ty ruined your life, Britney's life, Maddie's life, his parents' lives, and his own life. He needs to learn his lesson. He needs to sit in a cell for a long time. He can't be trusted in society. Gold rush, Ty. Gold rush! You see how it's all come full circle?" The detective pointed a damning finger at me.

Kourt stepped in front of Minden's gaze. "Ty, what is happening?" She grabbed me by the shoulders and looked into my eyes. "What are you talking about? *Who* are you talking to?"

"Yes, Ty, answer her. I'd sure as hell like to know." Minden laughed. I glared back at him.

"I'm sorry!" I yelled. "I was in love with Britney and I couldn't handle it when she died. I couldn't handle it! I was young and thought my world was over. I should have been stronger."

"There it is, Ty. That's what I've been waiting to hear." He threw his hands together. "I'm glad you have finally accepted responsibility."

"Ty, it's okay. I forgive you. You didn't even do anything wrong. We've talked about this all before. I love you so much." Kourt pulled me close to her. "It's okay. It's okay."

"I know you believe me. But it was Minden."

"Ty, there's nobody else in this room." Kourt looked scared and confused. She hugged me again.

I looked around, but Minden must have run out again. "He was just here. Damn, where is he? Kourt, what's happening?"

"Ty, I promise we'll get through this."

I was at a loss. It was difficult to process the current situation. *My* Britney, the girl I'd planned to spend my entire life with, was dead. She'd been dead for a year. I couldn't fathom how I could have blocked the entire chain of events from my conscious memory, and now I was locked up again.

SHE'S TOXIC

"How is this possible?" I asked Kourt.

"I don't know," she said. "At first, we all thought it was just a coincidence you found someone with the same name. I mean, it happens quite a bit. It didn't sink in for a long time that you—"

"Wow. I am insane."

"No, you're not crazy. You were hurting and we didn't recognize it, then we didn't want to believe the reality of your situation. I didn't realize just how bad it was until Julie Boyer called me. She said that you kept calling Britney's phone number and sending her messages. You were calling the wrong Britney. Her mom didn't have the heart to call you back. She finally disconnected Britney's number a few days ago. And then last night, before you left for The Barnyard, I called Doctor Niles."

I couldn't respond. Julie had read those horrible messages I'd tried to send to Britney. And that's why Britney Connell never answered and always called me from an unknown number.

"I feel so horrible that I didn't call Doctor Niles sooner. I just didn't want to believe it, but it kept getting worse." She placed a consoling hand on my arm.

"But what about Alexa? She said that Britney was the girl she lost out to—when we were at The Barnyard."

"Alexa might not have known about Britney's death. She's been out in Colorado and they weren't close. Or maybe—"

I didn't let her finish. I didn't want to hear it. "How could this happen?" I yelled out in disgust as I propelled my wheelchair against the wall, leaving a small indentation. It was too much, I wanted to run. I needed to escape my twisted reality.

"Ty, we all love you. We will find a way to work through all of this, believe me. I know it's a huge shock, but you're a strong man. Many people go through similar episodes when something so awful happens."

"I feel like I don't even know myself anymore. What about Ms. Crazy? I'm sure that's why I found someone crazy, because I'm insane. They say that 'like attracts like,' right?" I wanted to slam my fist against the wall, but the restraints negated that idea. "I guess it's only fitting: two crazy people hanging out together." *Or had I imagined—or embellished—my fights with Britney Connell?* Probably. Mike was alive, and I wasn't sure if Minden ever truly existed outside my head.

I remembered one of my run-ins with *Detective Minden*. He had mentioned that I'd had Britney committed. I didn't know what was true anymore. It made zero sense.

Niles came back in, flanked by two orderlies.

"It's coming back to him. I think he's remembering what happened to her," Kourtney said to Niles.

"Thank you, Miss Reynolds. Thank you for being here for your brother." Niles turned his attention back to me. "Tyler, I've been listening in on your conversation. I'm sorry you had to find out like this, but believe me, this was the best way to disclose your past. Even with Mike and your sister present, I still wasn't sure you would come around."

"Where is Britney? Britney Connell?" I asked.

"She's here, Tyler. And she's not well."

Thirty-Two

The Lanphier Home dominated ten acres on the southeast side of Peoria. It consisted of a large central office with four wings shooting outward, like spokes on a wheel. The grounds also included a fountain pond, a rudimentary community garden, and three red sheds.

Surrounding the premises was an old stone wall, succumbing to the advancing years. Repair would have been an impractical expense, as the outside wall was a lingering relic from when The Lanphier Home operated as a small prison. It had transitioned to a home for the mentally infirm in the 1990s.

Within the walls, The Lanphier Home was well maintained. In the common areas, the original stone floors had been covered with laminate, and the brick walls were lined with colorful murals depicting Illinois history, which consisted primarily of Native Americans, French fur traders, and Abraham Lincoln.

It was now one week after I'd found myself back in the mental health facility. I was enjoying my second tour at Lanphier—maybe not enjoying it, but at least my reality had become *reality*.

A few of the orderlies remembered me from my prior visit. One woman, Elise Waters, mid-forties, remembered mortifying specifics about my prior commitment. She had given me the play-by-play of what she remembered seeing and hearing during my first night.

She had said, "I remember you lying in your bed. You said, 'She's gone. She left me. Why did she leave me? Someone please tell me why.' It was a sad sight. And then another resident yelled across the hall, 'She's never coming back. She doesn't love you anymore. That's why she left you. Now shut your *(effing)* mouth!'

"Many nights went like that. You seldom slept. You would lay face-down on the floor, with your head tilted toward the side. You used your fingers to trace the letters B-R-I-T-N-E-Y on the wall next to you. I would walk from this wing to check on the others, and by the time I would come back—maybe an hour later, you were still doing the same thing. You hadn't moved an inch."

It was unsettling news, but I wasn't surprised. Once she recounted what she had heard, the fragmented memories began to materialize.

I was sleeping better—the medication probably helped with that. I would go to bed around ten, wake up like clockwork at six; Doctor Niles stressed the importance of establishing a routine. My days consisted of breakfast, lunch, and dinner with individual and group therapy sessions sprinkled between. I was left with plenty of time to think.

After a week, they let me have visitors. Kourt was my first.

"Hey brother." She tried to smile. "Any idea when you'll get out of here?"

SHE'S TOXIC

"Soon, I think. Niles said I would have already been released, but they want to observe me a little longer. I guess he needs to make sure I'm on a medication that works."

"It's always pills. They never treat the root cause." Her eyes flickered. "But if it helps, then I guess you better keep taking them. Do you remember being here last time?"

"I've heard a few stories that have triggered my memory, but I still don't remember much. Do you remember anything?"

She began, "The first time I came to visit last year, you were writing in a coiled notebook. You said, 'How? How did this happen? Why?' And you never looked away from your notebook. You had your arm bent over what you were writing to keep me from seeing anything. You said, 'We're supposed to be together. I loved her so much.'

"I cried, of course. I can still remember the mascara smeared across my face when I looked into the mirror afterward. I pleaded with you to come back to us, but you kept writing. I told you I loved you. I said, 'I hope that you can see past this. You have your entire life ahead of you. I realize you can't see it now, but you'll get past this. You'll find someone else. You have to. That is what Britney would want you to do. I'll always be here for you. We all will.'"

I looked at her. She was staring ahead, beyond me. I wondered if she had memorized her speech. My heart broke thinking about what my sister must have endured.

She continued, "I thought you had stopped writing when I explained that Britney would want you to move on, but it might have been wishful thinking or my imagination. I'd experienced my own doubts regarding my perception of reality. I'd ask myself, 'What if I'm imagining all of this?'"

She laughed. "I'm not laughing because it's funny. I'm sorry. It's just because, like I said after I picked you up from the jail, 'bad things happen to bad people'—not to people like us."

"What was I writing?" I asked.

"Huh? Sorry, I'm not thinking straight." She blinked.

"In my notebook—what was I writing?"

"I have it with me. Are you sure you want to see it?"

I nodded. She took a piece of paper from her back pocket, unfolded it, and placed it before me. I read an entire page of the same words repeated on each line:

Why? Why? Why? I love you Britney. I would rather die.
Why? Why? Why? I love you Britney. I would rather die.

Thirty-Three

A few hours after Kourt's visit, I was back in Dr. Niles's satellite office, located within the walls of Lanphier. I'd forgotten that Dr. Niles was not only my sister's psychiatrist, but he had also been my psychiatrist after my breakdown. "Forgotten" might not be the appropriate word, but I hoped he would be able to explain my condition a little more.

I inched to the edge of the plush leather couch. I did not want to lie down and kick back like a certified crazy person, but I knew that I had been in this room a year prior, except many of the details were beyond my accessible memory.

It was frustrating.

"I still don't know why I couldn't remember what happened to Britney *Boyer*." I stressed her last name—hoping it would help me remember the difference. At least I was now aware of the two distinct Britneys: Britney Boyer and Britney Connell.

The doctor removed his glasses and placed them on his desk. He leaned back in his seat, but kept his eyes trained on me. "You came in to see me several times after Britney Boyer's unfortunate accident. I tried to help you cope with her death, but then you spiraled ... out of control. We had made progress, or so I'd thought. But when you came in to speak about Britney Connell, it was clear that you weren't well. Once I discussed Britney Boyer's accident, you stormed out."

I shook my head. "You said that Britney would kill anyone who got in the way of our relationship."

"I did not say that. You began twisting everything I said. You might have believed that I told you that Britney would kill anyone who got in the way of your relationship, but I can assure you I said no such thing. Instead, I was attempting to reel you back into reality. I'd begun to explain what happened to Britney Boyer, and that's when you became argumentative, and then you ran out. You couldn't accept Britney Boyer's death."

"I don't remember that at all. Why is my memory so different from what actually happened?" My legs bounced rapidly against the floor. I wanted to punch something.

"Tyler, you're suffering from dissociative amnesia. Due to the inordinate trauma you suffered, your mind refused to remember Britney Boyer's accident and death."

"But why did I continue to believe I was dating her?" I flicked sweat from my forehead.

"You have been in a state of psychosis since the accident. Paranoia, delusions, and even hallucinations are common in those experiencing psychosis. These symptoms may even be tied to a more chronic mental disorder such as schizophrenia." He looked outside and quickly looked back at me. "I will need to further monitor you to make a proper diagnosis. A common onset age for schizophrenia is in the mid-twenties, so it's possible. Your genetics would be the primary contributing factor."

The words hit me hard. "I'm a schizo? But I don't hear voices or anything like that. Why didn't you tell me the truth?" I was surprised by my restraint. Maybe I was out of feelings. I'd just learned of Britney Boyer's death—again, I'd lived with the false belief that Mike had died, and I'd attended Maddie's wake. It was too much too soon.

"You exhibited many of the behavioral and mood symptoms, such as social isolation and withdrawal. You also suffered from the psychological effects of delusion and hallucinations." He wrote something in his notepad as he said, "How else would you explain your belief of your *Inner Demon—Ron E. Minden's* existence? Your clever subconscious developed a perfect anagram. Each name is composed of the same letters, but arranged in a different order."

Niles turned his notepad toward me. He had written-out the letters of the anagram. Unreal. I dropped my head, clasping my fingers together over the back of my neck.

"Tyler, your symptoms are consistent with cases of schizophrenia. It's often difficult to pinpoint why some people develop the disease. As I stated, it is heavily genetic, and its onset can be triggered by a traumatic event or by substance abuse."

He leaned back in his chair and said, "I tried to speak with you many times, but you always hung up the phone when I called, that or you wouldn't answer. I have been calling at least once per week for the last year. Kourt also tried so many times. She loves you, Tyler."

I struggled to hold my tears back. I was terrified. My life, my reality, had been manipulated by my own mind.

I looked back at Niles. "Why? How? How could I believe that Britney Connell was the same person as Britney Boyer? They kind of look alike, but how could I not see the difference? I see it now."

"Your belief that Britney Connell was Britney Boyer is not ordinary. Your enduring love for Britney Boyer became your persistent reality; your feelings were strong enough to circumvent any other possible perception. If the two women hadn't looked so similar, it might not have happened. But once you met someone with the same name who looked similar—it was an overload. You had tied so much emotion to Britney Boyer that you desperately tried to bring her back into your life, and in a way, you did."

"But I saw Britney Boyer. I know I did. There's no way—"

"Yes, your mind likely saw Britney Boyer. As I alluded to, your synoptic nerves sent the corresponding message to your brain. It was delusion, but it was your reality. Your delusion likely began when you first saw her face."

"A friend introduced me to Britney Connell at a party last winter. I kind of remember. Is it normal to remember?"

"Yes, dissociative amnesia can be reversed. You have already recovered many memories. The newspaper clippings and letters were enough of a trigger to allow some of your memories to return. But if you are schizophrenic, then that's another story. The disease can be treated, but there's always the possibility," he clicked his pen, "that you'll regress. The emotion, the love you harbored for Britney Boyer, was so strong."

"This might sound kind of crazy, but in some twisted way, my delusion allowed me to be with Britney Boyer more. With all that's happened—the negative stuff, I don't know how to explain it, but I don't feel the same about her."

"Yes. I believe it was some form of closure. Your perception of Britney Connell as Britney Boyer gave you permission to move on," Niles said.

"But if I loved Britney Boyer so much, why did I believe she was crazy? If I loved her so much that I couldn't let her go, then why was I so quick to believe she was insane? Why was I so quick to believe what Mike said?"

"I believe your delusion, including your paranoia, intensified after your fight with Mike because you thought you were going to lose Britney again. You hung on so tight to her memory and how your life used to be. Anything that threatened the status quo threatened your sanity."

It made sense. I held on to Britney too tight, even when I was with her. I idealized her before, during, and after our relationship. We weren't always perfect together, but I refused to remember that. I romanticized her. After she died, I put her on the highest pedestal. Mourning her death was human, to remember all the good times we shared, but it turned into an obsession.

"What about the Colombian Lords? Were they all part of my delusion?"

"I believe they were—at least to some extent. You were wounded, but those wounds could have come from anywhere. They could have even been ... self-inflicted."

"But it felt so real."

"I'm sure it did. Ty, I believe this might help you in your mental progression. As I've previously informed you, Britney Connell is here, and she is not well. Would you like to see her?"

My visit with Britney was arranged, but I didn't know if I could handle seeing a stranger, because that's what Britney Connell was to me. Although I would have liked to believe that I was gaining a grasp on reality, I still had to stress the last name.

I entered the doors to the waiting area with trepidation. Dr. Niles accompanied me to the visiting area where I would speak with her. As I walked through the facility, I feared the orderlies were eying me, debating whether to shoot me with a tranquilizer and throw me into a straitjacket.

Walk with purpose. Walk with confidence.

"Candace, would you please direct Mr. Reynolds to where he can wait for Ms. Connell?" Niles asked. "Andrew will be in to retrieve Mr. Reynolds in a few minutes."

Candace raised an eyebrow but remained silent. She pointed to a row of green chairs aligned against the back wall. I wondered how much Britney's parents had pleaded with Candace each time they came in to visit their daughter. I was sure her parents blamed me for everything that had happened. I feared her commitment was my fault.

"Thanks," I said as I took a seat. I had no idea what to expect. I caught myself hoping she was legitimately insane, so that there would be some truth to my recent experience. But I suspected that I'd pushed her over the edge—cracked her sanity.

An orderly came into the room from the door to my right and

SHE'S TOXIC

motioned me to follow. "Follow me, Mr. Reynolds." I looked for places to run if I needed to escape. I wanted to escape, to create a new reality.

I walked through the door and followed Andrew down the hallway. There were a few offices to my right and left.

Niles met us by the door. "Have a seat in here. She'll be down in a few minutes. You'll be directed back to my office once you two have completed your session."

I took a seat as Andrew nodded to Niles and closed the door behind him. Fear set in as I wondered how Britney would react to my presence. I pictured her lunging at me with a phone clutched in her fist, or hiding a knife behind her back, waiting for the right opportunity to plunge it into my jugular.

The room was bare except for a long metal table and metal chairs. I discovered the chairs were bolted to the ground when I attempted to rock back in my seat—the chairs must have been secured for a reason. I could imagine someone picking up a chair and trying to throw it at someone—maybe *I* had tried.

I heard a sliding door open on the far wall. *Oh boy, this is it.* I peered across the room, but didn't see movement. It was difficult to shake the thought of Britney charging at me with a weapon. The longer I waited, the more my thoughts drifted toward the negative.

She walked into the room from the dark corridor. *That can't be Britney, can it?* The woman's hair was a tattered, tangled mess. It looked like it hadn't been washed for weeks. She was wearing baby blue hospital pants with a pastel yellow short-sleeve shirt. She took two hesitant steps forward, then looked up.

"Britney?" I choked out. "Hi."

Britney tried to smile as she sat down. "You did this to me. Why did you do this to me?" Two tears rolled down her cheeks. She was heavily medicated—a shell of the woman I used to know, though I wasn't sure how much I ever knew *her*.

"I'm sorry for whatever I did to you." I was at a complete loss. "I was messed up."

"You will never know what you did to me." Britney managed a smile, wiping a tear from her cheek. "I'm okay now. I'm at peace. I want to thank you from the bottom of my heart."

I wasn't sure what to think. I assumed they had her chock-full of anti-depressants. Nonetheless, her statement perplexed me.

"Wait, why do you want to thank me? You want to thank me for doing *this* to you?"

"You wouldn't understand." She smiled from ear-to-ear, her face still red from crying. I wanted to believe that she was legitimately whacko, but I feared it was just the drugs. I held out hope regardless.

"I just wanted to stop by and apologize for anything I might have done to you. I feel horrible about the way things ended. You're a sweet girl and I know you meant well."

"Thank you. I appreciate your apology, but it's unnecessary. I must bid you farewell. This is my home now."

"No way, I need to get you out of here, then we can try to make things right. I promise I can treat you so much better."

"What? Do you think we can be together again?"

"Well that's kind of what I was hoping for." I felt so bad for what I'd done to her; all I wanted to do was hold her close. I wasn't sure how Dr. Niles thought this would help me, her, or both of us.

"Why do you think I would want to be with you? It can't happen." She kept smiling.

"Why the hell not?" I was shot back by her acerbic response. I should have taken a deep breath before responding.

"I've met someone."

"Met someone? Are you talking about Logan? He's a damn gang member." So maybe the Colombian Lords were real.

"I know what you're thinking, but he's good to me. I met him because of you." She smiled as she placed a hand on my forearm before looking me in the eye. "I'm in love. That's why I want to thank you, Ty. You helped me find true love. He was there for me when nobody else was."

My eyes fell to the ground. *How had it come to this?* I put my right hand on the table to hold myself. I leaned across the table and whispered, "I miss you. I need you."

Britney turned to face me, leaning forward so that her forehead was pressed against mine. She placed a hand on my cheek, then slapped me softly. "We could have been together. We were together." She pecked my lips. "I'm sorry, but it's too late now."

"It's never too late. If it was great once it can be great again."

I'm not sure I even believed my words. It was never great between us because it wasn't real. It was all a delusion, but I was striving for normalcy. I needed to remind myself that Britney Connell was not Britney Boyer; she was not my girlfriend of five years. Somehow, I needed to hammer that fact—the reality—into my mind. I shook my head, trying to let everything sink in.

"Ty, they're going to get you. They're all going to get you. You are going to die, you little bitch!" She fell back laughing until she cried. Two orderlies came in and pulled her away.

I emerged from the visiting room on a mission. I walked back into the waiting room and demanded to be taken to see Dr. Niles.

"You have to help her! She has lost her mind!" I yelled in the hallway. I thought of the warning Brit had given me, or at least the warning I thought she had given me. I knew the Colombian Lords weren't real.

But I don't know for sure. They might be.

"Mr. Reynolds, we need you to calm down," Dr. Niles charged out of his office. "Please, follow me so we can discuss this further."

I followed Niles—flanked once more by two orderlies, into his office. I assumed they were there for protection, like two bodyguards to protect him from me.

"Okay, Tyler. Let's discuss Britney Connell," he said as we entered his office.

"There isn't much to talk about. Someone needs to help her. This has been a huge mistake, and she doesn't deserve to be in here. If she acted out, it was because of me. It's not her fault!" I slammed my hand against the office side of the door. The guards looked at me, then back to Niles, but he waved them away and took a seat.

"It's true that Ms. Connell showed no signs of mental illness before you met her, other than one depressive episode in high school, but she is sick. I've met with Ms. Connell on numerous occasions, and you can rest assured that she needs to be in here—

SHE'S TOXIC

not only for her safety, but for the safety of those around her. She has not yet shown any signs of improvement."

"That's because she's so drugged up. She's not like this!" I paced the room. Niles remained sitting at his desk, unfazed.

"Ty, I'm sorry, but how could you know Ms. Connell's usual psychology? You feel guilty because she's here, but I can assure you, she needs additional treatment. I'm going to order you back to your room. We can do this the easy way or the hard way."

I threw my hands in the air and allowed the orderlies to take my arms. I wanted to say more but it was pointless. I needed to be released if I wanted to help Britney—to remedy the tragedy of having her committed. She had snapped because she couldn't handle my delusion.

My grandpa came to visit me the next morning. I surmised—based on the letters from Kourt—that he visited me several times during my prior stint. We were seated across from each other in the same room where I'd spoken to Britney.

"How much longer are they going to keep you here like some kind of animal?" he asked. He looked as good as a man his age could be expected to look. He still had hair on the top of his head, albeit wispy and gray—he usually colored it. His cinnamon eyes sat a little farther back than they used to, and he had all the natural lines and wrinkles of an eighty-year-old.

I cracked a smile. "Not long. I guess I respond well to the new medication. I'm here for observation more than anything. Please don't tell my parents I've been in here. I want them to enjoy the rest of their trip."

"I won't say a word… I'm so sorry, Tyler. I know this is my fault. What happened to Sam and your Uncle Patrick—and Josh, and what's happened to you…" He was breaking down. I'd never seen this side of my grandpa. He had always been so positive. "I'm sorry that I wasn't stronger, but I've always done the best I could. I hope that someday you will be able to forgive me." Tears were building in his eyes, but not yet falling.

My grandpa had never opened up like this—at least not to me. I was floored by his revelation and didn't know what to say.

"But this isn't your fault," I said. "I put myself in here because I couldn't get over Britney's death and then I wasn't—"

"But why did all of that happen, Tyler? I made a few mistakes when I was young, and I'm afraid they've come back to haunt our family. I'll explain what happened when the time is right, but I know it won't change our cumulative fate. I pray that you can find it in your heart to forgive me." I'd always thought my grandpa was mentally sound, but he wasn't making much sense. I struggled to comprehend how an action in his past could be responsible for my present hell.

"Sure, of course. But there's no reason I'd ever need to forgive you. You've always been the best grandpa I could ever ask for. I love you, GG."

A tear fell down his face. "Thank you, Tyler. I've done the best I could in my older, wiser years. But I fear the damage has already been done."

Thirty-Four

Summer was transitioning to autumn, but I figured summer would fight with all its might before relinquishing its stranglehold over the Midwest. Like most others, I enjoyed the crisp fall nights; they reminded me of playing football, which always brought back pleasant memories. I wanted to do all I could to feel normal. I was clinically insane, but *other than that*, my life was back on track. The perfect life with the white picket fence continued to elude me, but it was an improvement.

It had now been eight days since I'd spoken with Britney Connell, and I'd just been released from Lanphier. Once I was medicated, I was fine. I was now taking 2 mg of a new anti-schizophrenic and major depressive drug called *Rexulti*. Niles had started me on 1 mg, but he had adjusted the dosage upward based on the severity of my condition. He had told me I could expect to gain a little weight and could have suicidal thoughts—something to look forward to.

Niles had bounced between Springfield and The Lanphier Home during the last week to monitor my progress, and to ensure the medication was working. I passed the release test with flying colors. Unfortunately, the same could not be said for Britney; she continued to struggle. It was as if the script of my past life had been flipped onto Britney Connell.

And I was responsible.

My grandpa's words stayed with me. He must have endured a traumatic experience when he was young, and he continued to blame himself for anything negative that happened to our family. He was always so strong—I could have never expected his admission. I'd assured him of my forgiveness and that I would treat others with respect, but questions continued to prod me.

At least I was free. After learning the devastating news about Britney Boyer, there was only one place I wanted to be.

I drove to Brit's grave.

Niles was right; it was easier to accept Brit's death after everything I'd been through regarding Britney Connell and Maddie (other than my minor hiccup while visiting Britney Connell). But that's not to say it was easy to face her grave. There's a difference between acceptance and ambivalence.

I began to hyperventilate as I turned into St. Luke's Cemetery, the same cemetery where Maddie had been buried. I eased onto the rock driveway; the tears flowed. I'd already put a dent in the box of Kleenexes I'd brought with me.

Kourt told me where Brit was buried, so I had no trouble finding her marker. I could see the top of the tombstone from forty yards away. I drove two, maybe three miles per hour; I stopped a few times to delay the process. I didn't want to see her stone. She was underground, now less than fifty feet away.

I tried to look the opposite direction as I neared. I blew my nose once more, took a deep breath, and climbed out of my Jeep. It was a beautiful day, making the visit easier. It was like she had sent me the weather to help me through the difficult process. I struggled to keep my head up as I walked toward her stone.

Britney Marie Boyer
Loving Daughter and Girlfriend
December 13, 1995 – September 1, 2014

Memories flooded back, overwhelming my senses. Our effortless banter from day one; her unmistakable scent that permeated my belongings for four years; her smooth skin, flushed red each time our bodies came together; the taste of her body; the softness of her lips; her tender caress.

I couldn't handle it. I needed to get out of there before losing my mind again—but not before properly telling her goodbye. I took a knee beside her grave, placing a large bouquet of purple chrysanthemums next to the gravestone. I touched her stone with my fingertips, tracing the edge.

"Britney, baby. BB. I didn't want to believe that you were gone. The worst part is imagining the pain you went through and not being there for you. I know I shouldn't regret anything. I keep trying to tell myself that there's nothing I could have done. But I miss you. I love you."

It was brief, but that was probably for the best. I needed to move on. I didn't want to regress. I was terrified, not knowing what could send me back over the edge.

I got up to leave, but my legs were cement. If I was going to get out of there, I needed to walk away without looking back. I finally put one foot in front of the other, but I had to take one long look back. As long as I could look back without being stuck in the past, I'd probably be okay.

I got into my Jeep and drove out to my parents. I attempted to decode my life during the drive, but I knew that was going to be a lifelong mission.

My parents were due home any time—their trip would end up running the full six weeks. I couldn't believe all that had happened in the time since they left. And to my knowledge, they were still unaware of my recent commitment. I had tried to keep anyone from burdening them with the news.

My mom and dad's discussion a few weeks before they left now made more sense. My mom's persistence had struck me as annoying then, but she knew the truth—or at least had a healthy suspicion. But she either didn't want to believe my delusion or didn't know how to bring it up. Then again, she might have tried, but I probably shut her down or likewise dismissed her as insane.

I wanted to leave the house before they made it back. I wasn't ready to face them because my initial mental break had been so hard on them. I remembered their looks of fear mixed with shame, wondering how their *perfect son* could have fallen to the low of living in a mental institution.

I felt guilty for everything my parents had to endure. Not only did I go from being the town's golden boy to a resident of The Lanphier Home, but I'd also caused the mental breakdown of Britney Connell, and Maddie committed suicide while dating me.

SHE'S TOXIC

I wished that I could have been stronger for my parents' sake. They had to endure the scorn and ridicule form the community—from the parents of the "normal" kids. I would never wish the same calamity on anyone else, but I wished that others could understand that it could happen to anyone. Nobody is immune from an accident that could immediately and drastically transform the lives of everyone around them.

I returned to my apartment and took a seat on my couch. It was the same apartment where Britney had flashed a knife at me. Well, it was where I was *certain* she had flashed the knife at me. There had to be degrees of truth, but I couldn't be sure. I wanted to ask Britney, but I wasn't sure if she would talk to me again, or if she was even lucid.

I needed to take my medication. I didn't want to take my medication, but I knew I had to.

I thought back to the threatening text messages I'd received from the Colombian Lords. *The messages.* I checked my phone, and they were still there—those familiar warnings glaring back at me. Their continued presence gave me some comfort; at least I'd accurately perceived their reality.

"Hmm," I said aloud, "maybe I need to show these messages to someone else."

Shit, crazy people talk to themselves.

I also wanted to check for any new messages on Maddie's wall. I missed her. For a second I wondered who I was actually having sex with while I was with Maddie.

No, it was Maddie, definitely Maddie.

I was finding it difficult to discern fact from fiction, just as Minden had told me.

Minden doesn't exist.

I needed to see if anyone else could see the messages I had received from Logan's associates. I needed to know if I was still in danger. I went through a checklist:

Britney Boyer: dead.

Maddie: dead.

Kourt: I'd hurt her too much already. She'd cry if I asked her to verify reality.

Doctor Niles: I was afraid he would lock me up.

Britney Connell: Lovely combo of insane and doped out.

Mike: Maybe the only person who would believe me.

I called Mike. He answered on the first ring, before it had even concluded.

"Hey bud, how are you doing?" he said. "I'm glad you called."

"I'm good, I think. What are you doing for dinner tonight?"

"I can't say I have plans. I'm down for whatever." I wondered where he would draw the line, or if he would ever draw the line when it came to our friendship.

"How about we grill out over here? I have something I need help with—some messages on my phone I want you to look at."

"Sounds good."

"And I hate to ask since I'm the one inviting you over, but do you have any food or beer? I don't have much of anything at my apartment."

"No problem. I have a package of brats, and I'll see what else I can whip up. No worries. Be there in forty," he said.

SHE'S TOXIC

I imagined that he had to walk on eggshells around the crazy guy. I couldn't blame him—I'd done the same thing with Britney Connell for a couple months.

Mike arrived at my apartment; his speakers blared an old Garth Brooks song, "Ain't Goin' Down ('Til the Sun Comes Up)." It was the first time I'd seen him since we spoke at Lanphier. I'd kicked him out and claimed that he was part of an elaborate hoax at my expense. I wasn't sure he'd even want to see me.

"I want to apologize for what I said to you at Lanphier and for what I said that night at The Barnyard," I said as soon as he exited his truck. "I also want to apologize for any other time I ignored your calls or yelled at you when you tried to help."

"You have no reason to be sorry," he said as he removed a large red cooler from his truck bed. "I can't even imagine what you've been through. How are you feeling now?"

We walked around the back of the law office to a community patio. There was a slab of concrete and a small fire pit surrounded by whickered patio furniture.

"I think I'm fine. I've always thought I was okay, and that's what scares me. Niles has me on medication that's supposed to keep me from slipping back to my delusional state," I said.

"That's good. You'll get through this. I'm here to help you in any way I can, you know that, right?" Mike asked as he tried to get the grill going.

"Yeah, I know. I'm sorry I didn't listen to you and didn't hear you out before. Sorry I said those things to you when you were trying to help." I wondered if things might have been different if I would have somehow been able to heed Mike's earlier warnings regarding my situation. Maybe I wouldn't have gone off the deep end. I might not have driven Britney Connell over the edge.

Mike backed away from the grill. "You don't have to be sorry about anything. I should have been smarter about what I said. I can't blame you for getting pissed off at me that night. It was just so hard to talk about. I didn't know what to say. I didn't know what you believed, and I honestly didn't think it was possible that you didn't know the difference between them—at least I didn't want to think so. I thought I must have been hearing you wrong."

It wouldn't have mattered what he had said that night. He had been direct in saying, "She's not the same girl," but I'd taken it the wrong way. I'd been in an irrational, psychotic state of mind.

At this point, I may have felt worse for Mike. He was one of the few people who had attempted to set me straight. I didn't listen. Maybe I couldn't have listened. Kourt and Niles had also tried to help me, but I'd shut them out. I'd been paranoid. I'd believed they were against me, but my family and friends had always remained in my corner.

I considered how exposed I'd felt when my life came crashing down around me. I wondered about those who had looked on while I believed I was dating my deceased ex-girlfriend. They might not have even considered it a big deal. It's not like I openly advertised that I thought she was the same girl. They may have just been like, *Oh hey, Tyler is dating another Britney. Yeah, it's creepy, but whatever!* They might have sung a different tune if they knew the true extent of my delusion. I hoped the majority of people never would.

SHE'S TOXIC

"It scares me to think that maybe I'm still imagining things."

He drank his beer and scratched his chin. "That should say something, though, that you're aware of all that." Mike paused. "While I was in Wisconsin, I spent each night wondering what was going on. I tried to call you, but—"

"Yeah, I know, I didn't answer the phone or answered and yelled at you, and then I forgot it even happened, or didn't form the memories to begin with. And to top things off, I somehow thought you were dead, so I never thought about calling you." I shook my head. "How in the hell does this happen?"

Mike appeared calm on the surface. I wondered just how uneasy he felt around me. I knew how I would have responded: *Because you're psychotic.* But Mike held steady. "I don't know. The only thing you can do is try to make the best of this situation. That's all anyone can do when tragedy strikes. There's no point in dwelling on the past because it will only make you feel worse. You're still alive, and you still have a great family and friends around you. I'll always be here for you."

"I appreciate it, Mike. If I happen to regress again, I want you to know that you're the best friend a guy could have, and I mean that. I want to have a normal time tonight, as normal as I can be anyway." I wondered if we'd had the same conversation after my previous release.

"I can help with that." Mike rummaged through his cooler. "I've got burgers, brats, and plenty of Bud Light."

"Doc said I can have a couple beers, but not too many. I guess they don't mix well with the medication." I went ahead and popped one open. "Thanks for bringing the goods; I kind of lost track of how little I had." I took a long drink. I tried not to think about the swirling shit storm that was my life.

I craved normalcy, so I delayed discussing the texts. It was refreshing to have a good time without questioning my sanity. *Or Britney Connell's sanity. Or Britney Boyer's death.*

I'd almost forgotten about the threatening messages, but Mike brought them up. "So what did you want me to look at? Some messages?" He seemed somewhat reluctant to ask. I'm sure he also enjoyed drinking a beer like we used to, back when we were two normal guys, back before my life spiraled out of control.

"Yeah, give me a minute." I retreated around the corner. I stumbled up my stairs, wondering if the medication had already amplified the effects of my beer. I found my phone and opened the messages—*yup, still there*—and went back outside.

"Right here," I said. "Check these messages out. Tell me what you think."

I peeked over Mike's shoulder to see if they would disappear before my eyes. I wasn't sure how that worked.

"Okay, let's see here, there are messages from someone named *ES* and *GR*. I can't say I know anyone by those names. Let's see, the *Colombian Lords*? Damn."

I'd hoped the messages weren't real. I was somewhat relieved that I'd correctly perceived reality, but I was also blasted off my feet by a wave of fear, more akin to a tsunami of terror.

"Shit" was about all I could muster.

"We need to do something about this. This is bad news. Have you talked to the cops? Kaufman might be able to help."

"I didn't want to believe it was real, but I wasn't sure; that's why I showed you. They're gang members who jumped me a while back, but Doctor Niles thought my wounds may have been self-inflicted. I still don't know if any of this is real…"

I fell to my knees, cradling my head in my forearms. I began to cry. I didn't care anymore; I was shameless.

"I can guarantee that this is reality. Believe me."

It may have been reality, but reality can be a bitch. Even though I was medicated, I still didn't trust the world around me; I didn't want to believe that my life had come to this. I suppose ignorance is bliss. Ignorance was bliss during the early months of my delusional relationship with Britney Connell.

"What are you going to do?" Mike took a knee next to me. "I'm here if you need help. I don't know what we're up against though. Have you thought about leaving her alone? It might not be a bad idea. Does she even want to see you?"

"It probably doesn't even matter what I do anymore," I said.

Part of me wanted to run, but I knew that running away would be similar to my failure to move on after Britney Boyer's death. At some point, I needed to face reality.

I continued, "They wanted me to stay away from her—and I have, but Britney said I need to be careful. She's still locked away so maybe they're pissed off. Plus, Miguel is still bitter because I *took* Britney Boyer from him back in high school. That guy is messed up."

"Miguel Taveres? He's in on this?" Mike restrained a laugh of disbelief. "Unbelievable. I mean, I believe you, but I can't believe that he's involved in this. I thought for sure he was getting his life back on track. What do you think they'll do?"

"They're capable of anything."

I could sense that Mike was becoming less enamored with the idea of sticking with me through thick and thin. But instead he put an arm around my shoulder, took a deep breath through his nose, and exhaled.

"Hey, we're brothers. If we have to kick their ass, then that's what we'll do. I'm with you on this. I left you before, and it eats at me every damn day. I won't let that happen again. I'd rather die than leave you hanging. Let's do this."

SHE'S TOXIC

Thirty-Five

Despite my fear, I owed it to Britney Connell to help her. She had deteriorated because of my insanity. It was my fault. And somewhere inside her, I still saw Britney Boyer. I also saw Maddie. And I saw myself.

Between Mike leaving and my falling asleep, I pieced together the night I'd met Britney Connell. I couldn't believe how insane I must have sounded to Mike. It was during Christmas Break, and I remembered being in his truck on our way to a party and telling him, "I think she's the one." I was talking about Britney Boyer, but she had died four months prior. Mike probably didn't know what I was talking about. He had changed the subject by laughing nervously and asking for another Bud Light.

We ran into Maddie and Kayla at the Casey's General Store on the edge of town. I asked them how they were doing with a shit-eating grin across my face. They were still struggling with Britney's death, but I was unaware of reality. I must have already blocked her death out to some extent. I couldn't remember my exact thought process.

Maddie asked how I was doing, and I replied, "Couldn't be better."

Kayla was dismissive, saying, "Unbelievable," at one point. Maddie was more sympathetic. She simply said that I was stronger than them and wished me well.

The party was already in full swing when we arrived. At some point in the night, Chris Parker introduced me to Britney.

"Ty, I would like to introduce you to someone awesome. This is my cousin Britney."

"Hey there, BB," I said.

"BB?" she replied.

"Well, of course, my beloved Britney." I smiled.

"It's like you two already know each other," Chris said.

"Oh, stop." Brit rolled her eyes at her cousin.

"I would hope so." I laughed.

Unbelievable. Doctor Niles was correct in suggesting that I saw *Britney Boyer* from the precise moment I met Britney Connell. I'd completely blocked out the accident and Britney Boyer's death from my conscious memory—a result of my dissociative amnesia. I picked up with dating Britney Connell like nothing had happened to Britney Boyer.

I reminded myself that Britney Connell was still locked away at Lanphier. Her poor parents. I wasn't sure if I'd ever met them. I'd seen her mom in her doorway but never up close. Now it made sense why she'd acted so differently toward me.

I learned that Britney Connell's parents had always lived in Reedville, and that Britney Boyer's family had moved away from

SHE'S TOXIC

Gentry following her accident; they couldn't live with the constant reminders of their daughter. So it was easy for me, because of my psychosis, to believe that Britney Boyer had simply moved to Reedville following her graduation.

Two days later, on a Saturday afternoon, I drove to Walnut Street to speak with the Connells. I didn't want to, but I felt like I owed them that much. They had *lost* their daughter because of me. I practiced the conversation on the drive over, but the reality of the conversation would be brutal.

Britney's mother came to the front door after my fifth knock. I wasn't sure if she could see me standing on the porch or if she saw my Jeep in the drive. Maybe my heartbeat blew my cover. I saw her unlock the deadbolt and turn her eyes to me. A startled frown crossed her face.

"Ty?"

"Mrs. Connell, I wanted to come by to explain," I said. She turned to yell for her husband.

"What is it, honey?" Mr. Connell asked from deep within the house.

"I just wanted to say I'm sorry—" I trailed off as I realized she had taken two small steps away from me.

Mrs. Connell looked back at me, then hesitated. She turned back to the house, finally replying to her husband, "Jake, Ty is here. Ty Reynolds."

I sighed and braced myself for a showdown. The pain in Mrs. Connell's eyes was palpable. I was sure she had aged five years in the past few months; her eyes were bloodshot, she had sagging, dark bags under her eyes, and her voice carried a profound strain. I could imagine her spending countless nights wondering what had happened to her precious daughter.

Jake Connell hurried around the corner—looking straight ahead, resembling a bull running through the streets of Paloma. I nearly fell backward when our eyes met; my legs shifted ninety degrees—I needed to be ready to sprint if he continued his charge. He could have pummeled me into oblivion, and I wouldn't have blamed him.

About as quickly as he turned the corner, he halted his charge and dropped his arm around his wife's shoulders. "It's okay, Rachel. Tyler, what are you doing here?"

"Mr. Connell, I just wanted to try to explain. I'm so sorry for what happened." My eyes diverted from his. Rachel struggled to hold back her tears. Her eyes closed for a few seconds as she dug deeper into her husband's embrace. She was seeking protection from me—protection from the havoc I had wreaked on their family.

"Nothing was wrong with her until she met you. Our attorney has scheduled a hearing for next week, maybe you can help then. But I'm afraid this isn't the time or the place. Rachel is so worked up. I'd prefer if you left," Jake said. Rachel sobbed as if on cue.

"Yes, this is my fault. If I could change things I would, but I can't. Believe me, I want to help."

"Why? Why did you do this to her? She loved you so much, but you ruined her life. She doesn't deserve this," Rachel said.

"I'm sorry. I didn't know what I was doing. I thought—" It was impossible to explain. Even if I told my story, it wouldn't be enough. "Forget it. I just want you to know I'm sorry, and I never meant for this to happen." I turned to leave.

I realized I wasn't the only victim, and neither was Britney. I thought about her parents and her friends. I tried not to blame myself, but if only I'd been stronger—none of this would have happened. My insanity pushed Britney Connell, and that's why she broke.

I needed to find a way to testify at her hearing, despite what she had put me through—or what I'd put myself through.

Thirty-Six

The Connells had retained an attorney from Chicago who hired an outside psychiatrist, Dr. Cynthia Meseke, to testify that Britney had experienced a momentary mental breakdown, and that she was no longer a danger to the public or to herself. The attorney, Kyle Young, dug into the history of what had happened between us, and he convinced her parents of my importance to her case.

Her hearing was held the morning of September first, exactly one year after Britney Boyer's death. I was terrified. For the first time, a large number of people would be privy to the specifics of my mental health.

I would be exposed, naked, and magnified.

I had spent countless hours regretting everything I'd put the poor girl through. But she snapped at some point, similar to what happened to me after the stress of Britney Boyer's death. I wasn't convinced that they should let her out based on the conversation I had with her at Lanphier. But I still felt guilty, and I hoped that if I helped her, she would call off whatever damage Logan's men planned to inflict.

SHE'S TOXIC

I wasn't sure if I cared what happened to me anymore—at least Britney would be free.

I arrived at the Reed County Courthouse two hours early to go over my story with Britney's attorney. There were still holes, but he simply told me to "be honest."

It was a decent courthouse for a small county. They had a marble floor in the foyer. It became a cheap ceramic tile deeper into the building, but at least they tried to class the place up.

Nash County wasn't as worried about image.

I still couldn't believe I'd spent a night in the Nash County Jail after being arrested for disturbing the peace. I realized I must have been yelling into the night rather than yelling at Minden. I was sure some bystander had alerted the authorities to a drunk lunatic outside the bar—and that's why Detective Miller arrested me. It all made sense.

I trudged up the stairs and opened the door to the small courtroom. I felt the judge eying me from her "pulpit" as soon as I walked in. Brit was sitting at one of the two tables near the front. She looked better than the last time I saw her, but that wasn't saying much.

I tried to keep my head down as I walked around the rows of benches placed behind the two tables. I took a seat in the gallery on the far side of the courtroom.

After several witnesses and two hours of testimony, the time finally came for me to testify. I slunk into the witness chair. I looked back at Britney's family, my mom, my sister, and several of Britney's (presumed) friends. Mike was also sitting in the back of the courtroom for support.

"Mr. Reynolds, could you please explain your current mental condition to this court?" Attorney Young asked.

"I guess I'm doing well. My doctor is treating me for symptoms of schizophrenia, but he said that I'm doing better now. He has me on medication."

The dynamic in the courtroom shifted. Eyes narrowed on me. I could sense Britney's parents had become more critical.

"Your doctor previously testified that you have suffered from dissociative amnesia, and he testified to your long-term psychotic state with paranoid delusions." All eyes were now on me. They studied my appearance, as if they could discern my mental health merely by looking at me. But it's impossible to know if someone is suffering from a mental illness by looking at them.

The attorney continued, "But how would you personally describe your condition?"

This wasn't necessarily an adversarial proceeding, but my blood boiled each time he asked the question. I felt guilty.

"It was a way of coping. I thought Britney was insane, but it was in my mind."

"And what were you coping with?"

"I dated a girl name Britney Boyer in high school. We were together four years before she died—in a car accident. I basically lost it afterwards. I spent two months at The Lanphier Home in Peoria. I thought I was okay, but somewhere along the way my wires got crossed, or stayed crossed. I wasn't taking my medication because I didn't think I needed it."

"Mr. Reynolds, I can imagine this is difficult for you. I want to express my sympathy. No one should ever have to endure that magnitude of loss. Could you walk us through what happened after Britney Boyer died?"

"I became withdrawn. I didn't do anything. I didn't eat, I couldn't sleep, and I lost interest in school. I missed football practices and was kicked off the team. I couldn't live without her. I vaguely remember my mom and sister taking me to Springfield to speak with Dr. Niles."

"Thank you. Again, I realize this is difficult, and I appreciate that you're willing to do this for Ms. Connell. Did you meet my client after your release from The Lanphier Home?"

Before I could respond, the door to the courtroom opened and three men entered. All three were dressed in blue jeans with green T-shirts. I was sure they were members of the Colombian Lords, there to intimidate me. I attempted to burrow deeper into my chair, but I had nowhere to go. I couldn't hide from the truth, from the Colombian Lords, or from my demons any longer. The men took their seats, opposite Detective Minden. Minden gave the men a welcoming nod.

Wait, there's no Detective Minden.

The Judge interrupted my thoughts by asking the attorney to repeat his question.

"Did you meet my client after your release?"

"Yes, I met Britney Connell at a party."

"And what did you believe at that time?"

"It was like Britney Boyer never died. I don't know how—well, I guess it was because of my dissociative amnesia, but I had blocked out Britney Boyer's death in my mind."

"And then what happened between you and my client?"

"I thought she was crazy. I must have imagined her trying to hurt me, and I thought she tried to kill herself."

Attorney Young guided me through each event, eliciting an emotional response from everyone in the courtroom. Brit sat with her head down, occasionally looking at me with sympathetic or damning eyes, I wasn't sure which. Jake held his wife—she wept during most of my testimony. Kourt's eyes were red, and I saw a few tears escape down her cheeks.

I wished I'd been stronger, that I could have taken Britney Boyer's death in stride. Everyone loses someone close to them at some point in their lives, but for some reason, I wasn't equipped to handle her death.

I wondered how I could ever discern reality from delusion. When someone is dreaming, they usually believe their dreams are "real," except for the rare phenomenon of lucid dreaming. The sole barometer for determining reality is how our thoughts and actions are perceived and received by others.

After a few more clarifying questions, I was dismissed from the stand. I gave Mike an optimistic glance before sitting.

Kourt snuggled into my side and whispered, "Good job."

Judge Ericson thanked the attorney and issued her ruling. "Based on the evidence presented here today, including testimony from Tyler Reynolds, Dr. Niles, Britney Connell, Dr. Meseke, and Rachel Connell, I hereby order that the involuntary commitment of Britney Connell be rescinded and that she be released from The Lanphier Home instanter. Ms. Connell, that means you can go home today."

Britney finally smiled. I breathed a huge sigh of relief.

SHE'S TOXIC

Judge Ericson continued, "This was indeed an unfortunate case. Everyone here has undoubtedly been affected by these dire circumstances. Tyler and Britney, you both went through an incredibly trying time. I'm sure your close family and friends did as well. I'm hopeful that each of you will move forward with a renewed, optimistic outlook on life."

I locked eyes with Jake and Rachel Connell as I stood. I couldn't tell if they were angry, sad, or jubilated. I wanted to sneak past them, but Jake lurched his way between me and the door.

He reached out his hand for mine. "I'm so sorry about your girlfriend." His voice was sincere. I shook his hand.

"I never meant for any of this to happen to your daughter," I said. "If only I could go back and change what—"

Rachel cut me off. "We know, Tyler. We didn't know before, but now we do."

Jake joined in. "We were upset when we found out what happened to our Britney, but that's when we believed it was some kind of elaborate set-up; we thought you put her in there on purpose." He looked like he felt guilty—guilty for believing his daughter was crazy or guilty for believing that I consciously set her up, probably a combination.

I wanted to apologize to Britney, but she was taken back to a restroom to change out of her institutional attire. The Lanphier Home personnel had brought her clothes to the proceeding; so thankfully, she wouldn't have to return to that place.

As I exited the courtroom, I noticed a few girls huddled around a bench—all around Britney's age. I wasn't sure if I'd ever met any of her actual friends. They eyed me with sympathetic disdain; it's not the most pleasant look that a guy can receive from a woman. I assumed they were her friends, maybe cousins.

One girl wearing white slacks with a frilly yellow blouse spoke first. "I'm Mary, Britney's friend."

My assumption was confirmed. The other two girls also introduced themselves at Britney's friends—Joanna and Nicole.

I quickly apologized for what I'd put them through.

"She would call and explain all the things you were doing, but we didn't think anyone could be like that. No offense." Joanna blushed. Each girl spoke with trepidation, like they were waiting for me to lash out and pin them against the wall.

I assured them I would give anything to change what happened. They expressed sympathy for my loss, adding that they weren't sure how they would react if they faced a similar situation. Most people would have no idea.

"We're still worried about her," Mary said before I could pull myself away. "She's in deep with Logan. I think he's in a gang."

"Yeah, they've been threatening me lately. I didn't want to believe it was real," I said.

Joanna piped up. "Yes, it's definitely real. We're afraid to say anything because we don't know what they'll do."

"He has her brainwashed," Nicole added.

"I'll make things right," I said before turning away.

I wasn't sure my words had any effect, but I meant what I said. Britney was released from The Lanphier Home, so that gave me some solace, but I remained fearful of the threats against my life, not only for my sake, but also for Britney's well-being.

Thirty-Seven

Britney Connell agreed to speak with me three days following her release. I ordered a chocolate shake while I waited for her to arrive at Kent's Diner in Reedville. Kent's was an old hamburger-and-fries stand that had managed to stay afloat through the years, and was now more popular than ever due to a changing market.

I was nervous but took a few drinks of my shake.

And then she walked in.

Scenes flashed through my mind. I saw Britney pulling out a knife; I felt her pummeling me with my phone. *Reality* or not, they were my memories—memories as real as any other.

I was surprised when she greeted me with a smile.

"Hey, Ty, it's nice to see in you in the real world again." She seemed sincere, but maybe she was hiding a shiv inside her shoe.

"I'm glad they let you out, and I apologize."

She took a seat next to me at the counter—it extended along the window to the left of the entryway. The sun would have blinded us a few minutes earlier, but a puffy white cloud now acted as a partition.

"You don't need to apologize. Thank you for testifying at my hearing." Britney smiled as she placed her hand on mine. "The drugs they gave me messed me up for a while—the drugs from Lanphier *and* from Logan."

"You're welcome. But it was my fault. I'm still confused about the specifics between us. Is there any way you could help me remember?" I asked.

She hesitated. "I can try. It was kind of scary a couple times. I remember the first time you flew off the deep end—whoops, sorry, I didn't mean it like—" I nodded that it was okay. "Well, I was out with my friends, and you became convinced I wasn't answering my phone and that I was ignoring you. You said I was sucking someone's dick all night. I wasn't doing anything like that, but it was like you were possessed." She waved her arms as she spoke, her dark brown hair bounced around her face. It was like seeing her for the first time.

"Damn. I thought you were acting like you were sucking a dick and wishing that mine was bigger." She stifled a laugh, but I couldn't blame her. "Yeah, I know. It's comical. What about that time you beat me over the head with your phone?"

"You jumped all over me. I kept trying to return your phone, but you kept yelling at me to stop beating you with it. I kept saying that I wasn't. I offered to give it back, and then I finally threw it onto the couch. I tried to run upstairs, but you tackled me to the ground…"

"If I was acting so crazy, why didn't you ever do anything about it?" I asked. Britney had been the closest person to me while my life was deteriorating. Mike and Kourt had each tried to

SHE'S TOXIC

help me, but I had shot down their concerns. I'd also deliberately avoided most human contact over the summer.

"I really liked you, at first anyway. You loved me so much. You treated me like you'd known me forever. I was a little thrown off, but you were so sincere, and I'd never had a guy treat me like that before." She flashed a sad smile and touched my arm. "Whenever I was about to leave, you would beg me to stay. You kept saying how much you loved me. So then I would say I loved you, too. You were struggling, but I hoped you would improve. I wanted to be there for you."

I ran my hand through my hair to the back of my head and scratched my neck. "That's exactly what I was trying to do the entire time. Even when I thought you were bat-shit crazy, I hoped you would improve."

A young waitress came over to ask if Britney wanted anything. The waitress probably had the typical life of a cute high school girl. I could imagine her going to parties, dressing up for homecoming week, and hanging out with her boyfriend. I suppose I had a normal life before Britney Boyer died. Maybe I still could.

Britney ordered a chocolate shake—at least we shared the same taste in milkshakes.

"I'll always be sorry that you had to live in a mental institution because of me," I said after the waitress walked away.

"I'm sorry, too. But I lost it a little, and I cheated on you with Logan. He had me on drugs and made me do a lot of things I didn't want to, but he was there when nobody else believed me—my parents didn't even believe me." She looked down, both hurt and ashamed.

"I can't blame you for being with him, especially considering the circumstances. There's something else that's been bothering me: Did you laugh when you told me that Maddie died?" I knew by now that Maddie's death was a suicide, but I still needed to know if I'd imagined Brit laughing about it.

"That was the last time I saw you before I was committed to Lanphier. You must have seen that Maddie died while you were on your computer. You turned around and shook me, asking me why I killed her, and then you threw me out of your room. That was the final blow. You called my mom and told her everything that happened, or at least how you perceived it. Because I'd been depressed before and tried to cut myself back in high school, they believed most of what you said. I don't know if they'll ever forgive themselves. But it didn't help that I probably was cracking by that point—and I was doped out. Like, I didn't know what day it was. It was bad. I can't blame them."

"Wow. I feel like an ass." I could have said more, but it was succinct and true. I decided to cut to the chase and ask about my predominant concern. "What about Logan's involvement with the Colombian Lords? Are they going to leave you alone now? Are they going to leave me alone?"

She looked confused for a second. "Oh yeah." She laughed, but I wasn't sure how it was remotely funny. "No, that was all bullshit. They were mainly a few guys from that town you beat in the state championship. Once Logan found out who you were, he wanted to mess with you. I didn't realize they planned on jumping you—that was my fault."

At least I didn't have a marked head.

SHE'S TOXIC

"Whew. That's a relief. And no, it wasn't your fault. In a crazy way, I guess I might have had it coming." My voice rose at the end; guilt swept into my consciousness once more.

Miguel had tried to convince me that Britney Boyer was crazy back in high school. All of those memories strengthened my belief that Britney Connell had lost it. But then there he was, involved with the threats and the beating I'd received. After all this time, he was still bitter about Britney Boyer. I may have had it coming from someone, but not from him.

I realized that hanging on to Britney Connell in a romantic sense would have trapped me in a disastrous cycle of regret. I'd never be able to look at her without remembering what I did to her or what happened to Britney Boyer. Dating her wasn't even an option. What I'd said to Britney at Lanphier was nothing more than my desperate longing for normalcy, coupled with regret. Because of my suspect mental state, I needed more time to ensure that I accurately perceived reality before I dated someone new.

After Brit left, I received two notifications in rapid succession. Somehow, I already knew who the messages were from. Despite Brit's insistence that I shouldn't be worried about the Colombian Lords, I knew it was them. I looked at my phone and sure enough, two new text messages from Esteban and Guillermo. Both messages were the same:

We warned you.

Thirty-Eight

Dr. Niles called to schedule an appointment. He was surprised when I answered; he explained how I'd ignored most of his past calls. It was haunting to be reminded of how much of my past remained beyond my memory. Niles wanted to ensure that I was still on track, now three weeks following my release. I was still taking my medicine despite the temptation to wean myself off.

Niles wanted to speak with me, but I also wanted additional information regarding my condition and his diagnosis on how I might progress. Reality could elude me at any moment, and I feared I would not be able to discern the difference.

I arrived at his office and spoke briefly with Natalia, who was again working the reception desk. She addressed me in a more humanistic tone this time. Maybe she had been filled in regarding the news, but at this point I realized she was still leagues above me—funny how things work. One day I could attract most girls in school—and within earshot of Gentry, but after my mental break, they weren't exactly beating down my door.

"Tyler, welcome back." Dr. Niles came out to the waiting area to greet me himself. "I'll try to answer your questions. I'm sure you have plenty, he said as we walked back to his office."

"Doc, I feel good," I said as I took a seat opposite Doctor Niles. "But I'm not sure how long it will last or what I should expect. I still question reality. I know this sounds crazy, but I'm not sure if anything in this life is real."

"I'm optimistic. You're medicated. Your brain scans look fine. I haven't heard you say anything out of the ordinary regarding your perception versus reality. I would like to tell you that your life will be clear sailing from here on out, but I can't guarantee anything. It's still possible that you're schizophrenic." He paused, looking at the lingering uncertainty in my eyes. "Ty, you have come so far in the last month. Mike coming back into town, your relationship with Maddie, your stint at Lanphier, and then the release of Britney Connell; all the events helped you recover."

I was hopeful, yet confused by one thing. I wondered how in the hell my relationship with Maddie helped anything. It seemed like her death made things worse for me.

He must have read my mind. "All of these events gave you closure in some way. Maddie was important. Because she was such a great friend of Britney Boyer, you were able to relive many of the emotions that you experienced with Britney. When Maddie died, you were sad, but you faced it and you'll get over it. In so doing, I believe it's helped you finally come to terms with Britney Boyer's death—a transmutation of grieving, in a sense."

"I guess I understand. But why did it take all of that? What if I hadn't fooled around with—talked to Maddie when I did? Would I have declined?"

"That I can't answer with any real certainty. It's impossible to know. Some of us freeze to death during winter, but others ski. Some people bounce back from a loved one's death, remembering the good times, but others never recover. You froze to death during winter, but now you're learning to ski. You're still taking your medication, correct?"

"Yeah, I'm taking it. I'm not sure I need it though."

"I want to stress the importance of continuing to take your medication. There's a reason you've improved, and that reason is your medication. Maybe someday you will be able to do without it, but that day is not today. It's too soon. Please, Tyler, you need to promise me that you will continue to take your medication. Can you do that?"

"Okay. I'll keep taking it," I said with some reluctance. "But what am I supposed to do about the Colombian Lords? I'm pretty sure they're real."

"Yes, they are a part of your reality. I didn't want to believe their existence based upon your previous delusion, but I saw them standing outside the courthouse when I left. Have you spoken with the authorities?"

I was sprawled out on the couch (now like a certified crazy person). I stared at the ceiling for a few seconds, closed my eyes, and looked back at Niles. "Nope, I haven't. Britney said they were just some guys messing around with me, but then they sent me more texts. I'm afraid that the cops won't believe me. I had a bad experience with Detective Minden, who I realize isn't even real, but I'm just worried they won't try to help me. I'm afraid they would only make things worse for me, just like—"

SHE'S TOXIC

Dr. Niles took a deep breath and removed his glasses. "Tyler, I know you're worried about what's real and what isn't. You're struggling to comprehend if their threats are legitimate or if they aren't. You said you knew one of your attackers from high school, so what Britney Connell conveyed could very well be the truth. It isn't too difficult to acquire green clothing and accessories." He put his glasses back atop his head. I wasn't sure if he was annoyed or concerned, maybe a combination.

"I'm sorry, Tyler, and I hate to do this, but that's all the time we have today. I've already delayed my next appointment to speak with you. Tyler, I'd like you to continue to be a success story, and believe me, we will continue to be in touch. Please schedule an appointment with Natalia on your way out."

I scheduled my appointment and took off for Decatur. I needed to put my life back together, piece by piece, one day at a time. My number-one priority, aside from maintaining my sanity, was to get through college (and possibly play football again). It was too late to enroll for fall classes, but I was going to speak to a counselor about registering for the spring semester.

I stopped at the Denny's along the interstate in Decatur. On my way to the bathroom, I nearly ran over someone I hadn't seen in months—Kayla Morrison.

I wasn't sure how she'd receive me.

"Ty!" She lunged forward and gave me a huge hug, knocking me backward. She engulfed me in a mess of auburn hair. "It's great to see you!" Her blue eyes sparkled.

I released her embrace. "Hey! What are you doing down in Decatur?" I asked.

"I decided to move back after Maddie died. I'll be going to school at CIU next semester."

"Wow, that's crazy. That's where I'm going. I wasn't sure how you would react..." I laughed softly.

"Well, I thought you were an asshole when you started dating the other Britney. Britney Connell? But I had no idea, Ty. I can't even imagine." She brushed her hair away from her face. Her red fingernail polish caught my eye for an extended second. "I'm so sorry. I've been so far away, and I had no idea what happened to you after Brit died."

"Thanks. I think I've accepted it now. I can't even imagine what you're going through, losing two of your best friends."

"Yeah it's been rough," she said. I'd stated the obvious. "I didn't think I'd get over Britney, but Maddie helped me so much. And now Maddie—" She turned her wrist, bending her fingers back so she could examine her fingernails. "If only I could have been there for Maddie. We hadn't talked for several months—it wasn't the same between us after I went away to Minnesota for school. The last time we hung out was when we saw you during Christmas break—at Casey's." She sounded like she had just admitted to gunning down a toddler. And I'd forgotten Kayla had moved to Minnesota. I didn't have the heart to tell her that I'd been seeing Maddie before her death.

Kayla continued, "You talked to her shortly before she died, didn't you?"

"Yeah, we hung out and talked a few times. She was a wreck, drinking and smoking every time I saw her. I tried to console her." It was the truth.

SHE'S TOXIC

"I hope you helped her. Maybe you reminded her too much of Britney." She raised her eyebrows. "But you also remind me of Brit, and that doesn't make me feel like killing myself. It actually makes me remember her in a good way. I remember how happy Brit was when she met you." She smiled and laughed at the memory. A solitary tear rolled down her cheek. "Gosh, she was so in love with you. That night she met you—she couldn't stop talking about you. I thought I was going to have to…"

"Yeah, I remember that night. I could never forget it. That's what I kept remembering throughout this entire fiasco. I remembered meeting her and hearing that adorable laugh."

"She was one-in-a-million, that's for sure. And Maddie was Maddie." Another muffled laugh. "I loved them both so much. I guess it's impossible to know what Maddie was thinking. I'm sure you helped her cope in some way. And I'm also sure you two hooked up. You were all over each other in the pictures I saw on Maddie's phone. But that's cool and I get it. Can't blame either of you for that."

I'd forgotten about Maddie's phone. I wondered how many people had seen the messages and pictures we sent each other. *Oh my God.* I made a mental note to have someone destroy my phone or at least delete any revealing messages and pictures when I die.

Hearing Kayla recount Britney's love for me made me break down a little. It had been a long time since I'd heard someone speak like that about *BB*—about her love for me.

I'd considered the possibility that I could have complicated matters for Maddie. Maybe Maddie felt guilty toward Britney by being with me romantically, like she was dishonoring her legacy or something. But maybe I kept her from doing what she would have done sooner. It wasn't like I forced her to do anything or like there was some dramatic separation of sanity between us. I couldn't blame myself. "It's a damn shame about Maddie. She was such a sweet girl. All we can do now is remember the good times." It was cliché, but true. "I loved Britney so much. It still doesn't seem real. It's always nice to hear stories about her."

Kayla smiled. "For Sure. I'm glad you were there for Maddie. Thanks for the chat, but I better get going. I have to go speak with an admissions counselor at the school and I'm already late. Please don't be a stranger. We need to be here for each other."

I hugged Kayla before she left. She was a strong woman to endure the deaths of two of her closest friends. I wasn't sure how she managed, but she kept going. I also needed to gather the pieces, put my life back together, and keep going.

Thirty-Nine

It was a cool, early September night. I was heading out to my dirt road to drink two or three casual beers—not enough to impede my meds. I needed to reflect upon the preceding months. And I now had ample time for reflection, as I couldn't enroll in school until spring. I'd even thought about waiting until next fall.

I still had memories shrouded in obscurity. Dr. Niles told me that I was remembering more than he ever thought I would, but there were still major gaps. My first stint at Lanphier was a blur. I struggled to remember the dark months between Britney Boyer's death and meeting Britney Connell.

If it wasn't a full moon, it was close, maybe a waxing gibbous. The bountiful light from the moon made it difficult to see as many stars as would otherwise be visible on a clear night. I popped the top of a cold beer and leaned back in my seat.

A pair of headlights became visible from the east. I hoped they would turn north or south at the intersection. I could usually sit for hours without anyone interrupting my tranquility. I heard a rumble to the west and turned to see another set of headlights heading my direction. It was probably the most traffic the road had seen since the farmers were planting corn and beans in the spring. Unsettling. My phone buzzed.

Messages from Esteban and Guillermo: *Don't even try to run. We got you.*

I panicked. I could drive down the field road a half-mile, but the road ended at the woods next to the creek. If I made it that far, maybe I could drive my Jeep deeper into the woods than their vehicles could travel—before they would get bogged down.

I shot off down the dirt road, kicking up dust in my wake. The vehicles from the east and west continued on their heading. I had my lights off, but I knew they could see me, illuminated by the ample moonlight. Corn lined each side of the road, so I couldn't take off laterally.

I had another message, and then another within seconds: *Why are you running? You're denying your destiny. You are going to die tonight.*

They knew Britney had been released; Logan had his men in the court room. But maybe she had tried to get away from him now that she was regaining her sanity. For once I responded to their messages: *Why are you still chasing me? Britney is out! I'm not trying to get with her. She's all yours. Please, leave me alone!*

They responded within seconds: *What's done is done. There's nothing you can do to save yourself. Sit still bitch.*

I threw my phone against the passenger side window and floored it, even though I was rapidly approaching the tree line. I let off the gas when a pair of headlights blinded me. There were at least two vehicles parked ahead of me, at the end of the field road. I brought my Jeep to a stop not more than 100 feet from the vehicles. I saw two men approaching me on either side. I was trapped. I prayed that this somehow wasn't real; maybe I was still at The Lanphier Home, somehow imagining all of this.

I looked in my rearview mirror and saw the two vehicles approaching. They were closing in. I had to abandon my Jeep and take off on foot if I had any hope of survival. I swung open my door and ran for the cornfield, but I made it only a few steps before a hand reached up, grabbed my leg, and spun me to the ground. From the ground I could see several other men spring into action around me. They were all dressed in green—lying in wait, circling their prey, ready to strike.

Like a bullet through a still night.

Britney had told me it was all bullshit. I figured Miguel was trying to get back at me after *what I'd put him through* during high school. Hell, I couldn't help it that Britney chose me over him—that was so long ago.

A man approached.

"So we meet again, Ty." Miguel beamed. "What did we tell you? I'll answer that. We told you to stay the fuck away from Britney. My buddy Esteban told you, and so did Guillermo." The two stepped forward.

"But you didn't stay away. And now you'll have to pay."

I was dumbfounded, wondering why Brit would have told me I was in the clear. And then the little devil appeared. Britney walked up to me with one of the men. He might have been a couple inches over six feet, muscular, brown hair to his shoulders. It had to be Logan. He had his arm slung around her shoulder.

"Hey, it's my man!" He marched in my direction.

Britney stared at me the entire time. She had a slight smirk on her face. Her eyes burned a hole through mine.

He spoke again. "I should thank you for bringing Britney in my life, but you fucked her up. I can't thank you for that. You deserve to suffer for what you put this poor girl through. She's a perfect angel." He kissed her lips and guided her behind him. "Now run along, baby. You don't need to see this."

She pouted as she walked away. "But I want to see it." She looked back and laughed. "Serves you right, Ty." She skipped away, looking back once more to gauge my reaction. I thought I sensed hesitation.

"How rude of me," the man continued. "I know all about you, and you might know me, but we haven't been introduced. My name is Logan. There's only one thing you need to know about me. I'm not a forgiving man. I'm not nearly as forgiving as Miguel, who let you crawl out of that alley. Or were you able to crawl? I know they kicked your ass, which I was grateful for, but it's time you paid for your sins."

Britney had set me up. I'd let my guard down. I wasn't sure how I could have believed her, considering Guillermo and Esteban had sent me additional messages. For some reason, I thought they were just trying to scare me at that point. I'd feared that I was reading too deeply into the situation, trying to imagine something that wasn't there, trying to imagine a reality much worse than what was before me.

But this was so much worse than anything I could have ever imagined. There were at least eight men present, maybe ten. One man brandished a shotgun; another pulled a .45 from a holster on his waist. Esteban swung a baseball bat; Miguel waved a hatchet. The blade of the hatchet reflected the headlights from a car parked alongside the clearing.

"How, oh how, are we going to teach you a lesson?" Logan spread out his arms, showcasing his men and all their weapons. "We could give you a quick death *or* we could drag it out a little bit. You would enjoy the quick death. It wouldn't be the best outcome for you, but it would be a hell of a lot better than what Miguel would do—he won't be so forgiving tonight."

Miguel approached me with his hatchet. He said, "I would cut off all your toes, Ty. I would make you eat them." He feigned slicing off a toe and popping it into my mouth. "You'd probably like it, you sick fuck." The guys cheered and laughed. "Then I'd move to your fingers. I'd cut them off, one by one, until they were all gone. I'd have to stop the bleeding to keep you with us, so you could feel every second of pain." He showed me a branding iron. "It would close the wounds. It would hurt like a bitch, but at least you wouldn't bleed out and die before we're done."

I attempted to yell for help, but nothing came out. I'm not sure it would have mattered. I was in the middle of nowhere, nearly a mile from the nearest house. Nobody could hear my pleas, nobody could save me.

"Miguel!" Logan said. "Are you ready to slice this piece of shit up?"

"I don't know, man." Miguel looked around at his crowd. "What do you all think? Huh? What do you want to see happen to this pathetic excuse of a bitch man? Do you know what this *man* did? He cried and cried because his girlfriend died. He's a weak man. He had to go to the loony bin because he was so weak. Then when he came out, he met this sweet angel here, and then he pulled her down with him. He fucked up her life—he abused her physically and mentally. Life for a life, right? Right!"

"Slice him up!" someone yelled.

"I want to spit on this mother fucker." Esteban was wearing ripped up jeans with a white tank. He had black hair and sleeve tattoos. He looked over to Logan, seeking approval. Logan was distant, so Esteban looked over to Miguel, who gave a slight nod.

"Fuck that, crack his ribs! Kick him in the fucking ribs!" Guillermo yelled.

Esteban spat on my face; Guillermo kicked me.

I attempted to roll away from the blow, but it was too late. The strike landed in the same place I'd been kicked during the previous attack. I winced at the pain and closed my eyes, praying they would get it over with and put me out of my misery. I also prayed that this was all some twisted part of my imagination, or part of my psychotic delusion. It couldn't be real.

"Take my bat, hit him across the face!" Esteban said before tossing the bat in Miguel's direction. Miguel dropped his hatchet and caught the bat with his right hand.

"You know, this guy might have a point," Miguel said. "Why slice you up right away when we can give you a few good bruises first?" Miguel gave himself some space and twirled the bat before bringing it back into a batting stance. He showed off a practice swing. "Oh yeah, that's the cut right there. I need to make sure I keep my weight back, wait for it, and POW! Over the fence!" Cheers erupted once more.

SHE'S TOXIC

Miguel took three steps forward, now within striking distance of my face. I knew that if he swung with the same force as his practice swing, I would be dead. Miguel twirled the bat within inches of my face before pulling back into his stance. "Ready, Ty? It's time for lights out!" He made two half-swings before shifting his weight back and drawing in a deep breath. He shifted his weight forward. I closed my eyes, bracing for impact.

In that brief second before contact, I thought of the roller coaster of my life—the dramatic highs and lows. I saw Britney Boyer's face. I also saw Kourt, my parents, Maddie, and Mike; they were all smiling. Somehow, even in the perilous moment, I also smiled.

But then, even with my eyes closed, I could sense that someone had flashed a bright light.

"Drop your weapons!" A voice fired out from behind me. The cheers from the gallery came to a halt as a few men ran for cover. I heard a rustling in the trees and looked up to see several police officers swarm the area. "Drop your weapons now!" the voice bellowed once more, aided by a bullhorn.

I heard a few guns click off their safety.

The men relented, all except for Miguel. "What are you going to do? Huh? What are you going to fucking do? Kill all of us? You can't kill all of us!" he yelled. He threw his bat to the ground and pulled a 9mm from the back of his jeans.

"This is your final warning. Drop your weapon!"

"Who wants it first?" He pointed the gun at the officer with the bullhorn. "Yeah, how about this pig right here? Time for a barbecue."

I heard two gun shots. Miguel went down in a heap, dropped upon raising his gun.

"Miguel!" Logan yelled; he had taken a few steps back at the sound of the gunfire. Two of the men inched forward, but were quickly neutralized by the officers.

The officers sprang to action, surrounding the men with their weapons down. *Get on the ground! Hands behind your back!* I watched Guillermo and Esteban fall to their knees. The officers gathered the plethora of weapons and began the process of cuffing the gang members.

It was all a blur.

My impending death had somehow transformed to a rescue mission. I wasn't sure what accounted for the change in events.

Several police cars and two ambulances blazed down the field road. Stunned, I climbed to my feet. Detective Miller materialized from nowhere and escorted me to an ambulance as the officers took the men into custody. She might have said something, but I was still in a daze.

I looked over to see Miguel taken away on a stretcher, his blood soaked through his shirt. Even though he wanted to kill me, I cringed at the sight of seeing his dead body before me. I saw a man who had been obsessed with Britney Boyer in high school. She broke his heart and he couldn't move on with his life. I wondered if he would have taken the same path if he would have moved on. I guess sometimes that's easier said than done.

Matters of the heart are seldom logical.

Detective Miller questioned me regarding the incident. She made it brief and left me to sit alone. I continued to watch the developing scene. I watched the cops force the Colombian Lords into their police cruisers. I looked over at the stretcher holding Miguel's body, but he wasn't there.

No way.

"There he is!" Miguel's voice came from behind me.

I turned around to see Miguel strolling toward me, unscathed, unimpeded. I was speechless. He had just been shot.

At least that's what I thought I saw.

Forty

Miguel continued his charge.

"No. That's impossible. How in the hell?" I muttered as I attempted to scramble to my feet, but I was again paralyzed by fear. Miguel closed in. I couldn't see any officers in the vicinity.

I finally called out, "Help! Please, someone, help me!"

Miguel raised his hands as he closed in on me. I gulped as I climbed to my feet. I turned to run, but Miguel caught me from behind and slapped his hand down on my shoulder. There was no escape this time.

"Hey, hey, relax. It's okay. I'm not going to hurt you, Ty." He raised his arms in a *surrender* motion before dropping them back to my shoulders. "I'm one of the good guys. Do you understand? I'm not with them."

"But you were just shot!" It was happening all over again. I was falling back into a dizzying spiral of insanity. I was about to faint until Miguel placed his hand on my back—pushing my consciousness back into the present.

"Yeah, they got me good." He chuckled as he threw a vest at me. "I was wearing a bulletproof vest, but that still hurt."

"I saw blood, you were bleeding!" I *knew* I'd seen blood.

"Nah, the vest releases a blood-like substance when it's struck. It helps throw people off. They'll never know I survived."

"I still don't understand why you were with them. You were there when they—"

"I was undercover, Ty. I'm an undercover police officer." A large smile flashed across his face. I was struggling to comprehend what had happened, and I wondered how the hell Miguel had become a police officer.

"But I got my ass kicked while you were there—in that alley. Why didn't you stop it?"

"I went undercover to bring down several members of the Colombian Lords who had come down from Chicago. I'm sorry you had to get your ass kicked, but it was all part of the process. I had to get more on them. We were trying to bust Logan on felony drug charges. We got enough to put him away for that, but I figured I'd stick around and get him on attempted murder. And believe me—Logan wanted to kill you."

"Unbelievable." My attention turned to Britney Connell. "Did Britney set me up?"

He sighed. "She told you that their threats weren't credible. She wanted them to teach you a lesson, but she didn't know they wanted to kill you. They tricked her, too—and I might have helped persuade her not to forgive you so easily."

"What? What if Logan would have killed me before the police officers swarmed? And how did you know where I would be?"

"I was communicating with the other officers the entire time. Britney knew where you went to unwind on the dirt road. We didn't know where you would try to go, so they scattered officers along the road. If all else failed, I would have bought time until we could have had enough men in place to neutralize the threat. Trust me, Ty. We weren't going to let anything happen to you."

It was a relief to hear that Britney hadn't known the details of their plan. But I wasn't sure I could have blamed her if she had. I'd thought she was sincere when she thanked me for helping her get out, but I'd wondered if she had been a little too forgiving. I'd let down my guard just enough to be set up. I could believe that she was unaware of their ultimate plan. I didn't think she was capable of anything so callous. Before I could give it much thought, Britney appeared behind me, in handcuffs.

"Ty." She kicked at the ground. "Sorry. I had no idea what they planned on doing. I just, I just wanted them to rough you up again, but that was before… And once I knew what they were doing, I wanted to speak up, but I was afraid they would kill me, too. So I went along with it."

That explained her hesitation. I understood. I was ultimately responsible for everything that had happened. I was also responsible for her arrest.

"Brit, hey, I can't blame you. Are they going to let you out?"

"They said it's for my protection right now." She nodded toward the occupied cop cars, now leaving. "I was so messed up. I was still messed up when they planned this. I swear I wanted to stop them, but I was scared."

I wanted to trust her, but I maintained a lingering, healthy suspicion. Miguel reappeared next to Britney. "Do you have any questions, Ty? I'm sorry I couldn't help you sooner. I feel terrible for you—first with Britney Boyer and now with these guys. Man, I can't even imagine."

He directed Britney Connell away and sat down next to me. "I thought I loved Britney Boyer," he said. "I may have been obsessed with her or whatever you want to call it. I was young and didn't know what love was. I said some things back then because I wanted to be with her. I knew you had her, so I tried to get in the way. Never apologized for that, but I'm sorry. I can't imagine what you went through after her accident. She was something special, and I'm not sure I'll ever completely forget her."

Yes, Britney Boyer was something special.

"I appreciate it, man. And I can't blame you. She affected me the same way. I'm sorry it didn't work out between you two. Maybe she wouldn't have died if you were dating her instead."

"No, don't say that. But I'm more than okay now. Like I said, I was young; I've moved on. I'm dating an amazing woman and I don't think too much about Britney anymore. I fell hard for her back then, and did things I wasn't proud of, but that was then. It's unfortunate she's gone."

"I'm just glad everything worked out for you."

"Thank you, Ty. I appreciate it." Miguel smiled.

"So you became a police officer? That's amazing, I didn't think you had it in you. No offense, but you were one of the last people I could have ever imagined saving my life in an undercover sting." Brutal honesty. I could have seen Miguel as the target of a bust.

"Yeah, yeah." He laughed. "That made it easy for people down here to believe I was dealing drugs for a gang. I got my life together after high school. To be honest, I owe a lot of that to you." He gave my upper back a hearty slap.

"Me?"

"Yeah, you were always so level headed and successful. You were the star quarterback, you dated *Britney Boyer*, you had a great family life, and you were a hell of a role model when I needed a kick in the ass. I guess I wanted to emulate you."

"But what about after I went crazy?" I stared at the ground ahead of me. I kept trying to tell myself that admitting it was the most difficult part. I didn't want to acknowledge that I'd sailed off the deep end.

"Hey, man, it could happen to anyone. It's unfortunate, but I never thought less of you. All that matters now is what you do moving forward."

"I doubt it could have happened to *anyone*, but I appreciate it. I can't express how thankful I am that you were here for me today. I owe you."

"Nah, we're even now. Who knows where I'd be without your influence. And that's that, okay? I need to run, though. I have a lot of paperwork because of you." He chuckled and shook my hand. Miguel joined Detective Miller in stride. He looked back and smiled over his shoulder. I was relieved I didn't see Minden walking alongside the pair.

Niles's words came flooding back—how he said that all my recent experiences allowed me to move on from Britney Boyer's death. I thought of my relationship with Maddie, helping Britney Connell, and the manifestation of my inner demon—Detective Ron E. Minden.

SHE'S TOXIC

I wondered how Miguel fit into the equation.

I realized we were one and the same. I was Miguel and Miguel was me, though not literally, not like Minden. I was unable to move on after Britney's death, and I'd pulled others down with me. Miguel was obsessed with Britney, but he was able to rebound and improve the quality of his life. I had become his imperfect reflection. Miguel was my positive, Minden was my negative. My positive was real, but my negative was imagined.

It gave me hope.

Britney Connell was released the next day. The Nash County State's Attorney was going to bring charges against a dozen gang members who had infiltrated her rural county, so hanging onto her charge against Britney wasn't necessary. She was far from a danger to the public, or so I hoped. She had set me up, but she hadn't been in her right frame of mind.

I empathized.

Forty-One

On September twelfth, less than three months after my fight with Mike, Kourt stood with me outside our parents' house, next to her Camaro. I had a brief flashback to our lunch at Panera. It was back when I was lost, with a tenuous grasp on reality. She had tiptoed around me then, unaware of what might set me off. She had hit rock bottom herself after I'd snapped a year before.

I couldn't imagine the torment and ridicule she was forced to endure. *Yeah, that's Ty Reynolds's sister. Did you hear about him? He went crazy!* I wouldn't go to school either if I had to endure similar sneers at her expense. But she was improving; she had reduced her drinking since I'd returned to her life.

"So this Miguel guy was undercover? I think I remember him, but I can't believe he's a police officer. I can't even imagine what that was like. It sounds like a movie."

"Yup, Miguel is an undercover police officer; who would have thought? They all think he died," I said.

Kourt was wide eyed. "Wow, that's so intense. Damn. What if another one of the guys would have shot you first?"

I didn't want to think about that possibility. I imagined it was a risk they were willing to take, but Miguel had assured me I was never in any danger.

"I hope the cops would have swarmed in before that could have happened. But I don't know what some of the other guys might have done." We had an awkward exchange. I'm sure we were both thinking about Esteban.

It wasn't the time.

I wondered what life would have been like if Britney Boyer would have survived. We would have gotten married, had three kids, and lived happily ever after—*riding off into the sunset*. No mental break or near death run-in with a bloodthirsty gang—and Maddie would still be alive.

Niles might have been right. Memories of Maddie softened the blow of losing Britney Boyer. Some people get so caught up in past relationships that they can never move on. They spend their entire lives trying to compare each future partner to *the one that got away*. Happiness eludes them. I knew my situation was different, as Britney had died, but it was the same principle.

Even when I continued to believe that Britney Connell was Britney Boyer, I was ready to let her go after I got together with Maddie. Then I lost Maddie. But I rebounded. I took Maddie's death in as much stride as a person could. Yes, Niles was right. It was just a shame that Maddie wasn't able to see the light of a brighter future.

I couldn't get lost in thinking about what might have been. Reality was all I had, and I was grateful I'd regained some sanity. But I knew all I ever perceived was *my reality* in a tragic sense.

"What's your next step?" Kourt asked, breaking the silence.

I needed to get away. I had to escape the memories that had held me back for so long. A fresh start would enable me to meet new people without fearing their judgment.

Kourt and Mike promised they would routinely check in with me. Dr. Niles also planned to contact me once a week to follow up. My grandpa said he'd also stay in contact; he was becoming increasingly worried about my cousins.

"I need to get away, try to find myself." I gauged her reaction. I hadn't yet informed Kourt that I'd be leaving her, even though I planned to leave within the hour. "I could take an extended vacation, maybe head out to Colorado for a few months. I've always wanted to do that."

She was taken aback, but composed herself. "You mean you're not taking me with you? What the hell, brother?" She hip-checked me, making me lose my balance. It had been some time since I'd received a hip-check from my sister. It reminded me of the first night I met Britney Boyer.

I laughed and returned the favor, but she looked sad.

I reassured her. "I'll sweep back through the area every now and then. Or, you could even meet up with me somewhere; how does Florida sound?"

Her eyes lit up at the suggestion of a coastal reunion. It wasn't my idea of a great time, but I would spend a few days on a beach with my sister.

My parents stepped outside as I finished telling Kourtney bye.

"Answer your phone when I call," Kourt said. "Love you, brother." She gave me a long hug and then waved to my parents as she ducked into her car and took off.

SHE'S TOXIC

"There he goes, just as mysteriously as he came," my dad said. I stretched out my hand, but he opted for a bear hug. "Take care of yourself. I love you, son."

My mom hugged me with more force than I thought she could muster. "Make sure you pick up your medication. Call if you need anything and don't be afraid to come back. You'll always have a bed here." She wiped the tears from her face. "My baby. I love you, Tyler Matthew."

I was blessed to have such a solid support system, but it was time to leave.

"I love you both, but I better get on the road." I smiled.

They stood in the driveway hugging each other as I prepared for departure. I gave my Jeep one last check to make sure I wasn't forgetting anything. I had my tent, clothes, computer, and a few random tokens, among which was BB's high school ring. I hung it from my rearview mirror in remembrance. I needed to let her go, but an innocent tribute couldn't hurt.

My Jeep had weathered the storm along with me. I had picked up Britney—Britney Boyer and Britney Connell—in this Jeep; it had also been used to drop me off at The Lanphier Home. And now here I was, ready to use it as a vessel of self-discovery.

My Jeep was my constant.

Once on the open road, the last thing on my mind was stopping. I wanted to drive as long as possible, to leave my past behind, and to reestablish a certain frame of concrete sanity. I wanted to leave Logan and his crew behind, to leave Minden behind. I wanted to remember Britney in a healthy, positive light. And I honestly wanted to give my family and friends a break.

Mike called when I was somewhere between Hannibal and Kansas City. He beat himself up over not being there for me, even though I'd escaped with my life. I had to keep reminding him that it was a sting operation and I was never in any danger. I reasoned that I'd felt the same way when Britney Boyer died. *If only I could have been there.* The big difference was that I was still alive, but Britney was dead.

If only Britney had survived.

The time finally came when I had to stop for gas. I pulled off Interstate 70 at a tollway oasis just west of Lawrence, Kansas.

I eased into the Lucky Pump, next to a red Mazda that closely resembled Maddie's car. *Well maybe that's a good sign.* A striking brunette stepped out of the car wearing Kansas University cheerleading gear. *Rock Chalk, Jayhawk.*

I walked around the back of my Jeep and we locked eyes.

She smiled as she approached the pump.

"Hey there, I like your car," I said.

"Awww, thanks. I *love* your Jeep!"

"I'm Ty."

"I'm Britney."

"Of course you are."

Acknowledgments

Thank you to my entire family for your unshakable love and support, especially my parents, Kent and Beth Riedle, and my grandparents, Alvin and Patricia Riedle and George and Amy Meseke. I wouldn't be where I am today without my family. If only "Riedle" were easier to spell and pronounce!

Thank you to Dane Torbeck, for your edit and for answering my many questions. Thanks to Jacob Riedle, for the first reading and your continued enthusiasm. Thanks to Sarah Benson, Michael Castelaz, Mary Knoche, Dave Knoche, Yana Nayshtut, Michael James Moriarity IV, Jason Opfer, Tessa Opfer, Angela Moriarity, Kiyah and David, Travis Williams, everyone at Bread Company (Panera) in Edwardsville, and the entire Kentucky Lake gang (not the Colombian Lords) of 2015—Kentucky was a turning point in the process. Thank you to everyone who provided encouragement along the way. Every show of interest and support meant so much to me. I couldn't have done this by myself.

Thank you to my graphic designer, Parker Gibson, for the sensational cover. Thanks to both Jessica Kraemer and Caroline Smailes for your edits. And thanks to Riverfront Publishing for making my dream a reality.

…At least I hope this is my reality.

Author Bio

Matt Abrams grew up on a farm south of Vandalia, Illinois. He is an adventurer and former attorney who enjoys traveling, storm chasing, and mountain climbing. He holds a Bachelor's Degree in History from the University of Illinois and a Juris Doctorate from the University of Kansas. He lives in Edwardsville, Illinois.

She's Toxic is his first novel.
She Knows will be published in early spring 2017.

Made in the USA
Lexington, KY
28 September 2016